Ed Adams
Chases a Dream

by

Art Myers

This is a work of fiction. Any reference to historical
events, real people, or real places are used fictitiously.
Otherwise, characters, places, and events are products of
author's imagination.

2020

ISBN 978-1-7357208-0-7

Cover design by Janet L Blankenship

Contact Art Myers: artmyersbooks@gmail.com

For those who are my friends.

Other Books* by Art Myers

MY STORY
How A Young Boy From California
Ended Up An Old Man In Florida

ADREW'S PIANO

A NEW LIFE FOR ROBERT JOHNSON

10,000 YEARS – Before Present

*To my readers: The above books have been written, are
in book format and planned to be published in 2021.

Ed Adams
Chases a Dream

Chapter 1

The fourth day of June 1994 dawned in a spectacular fashion in Palm Desert, California as it had dawned the day before and the day before that. It was a Saturday and Ed Adams was just completing a 2 mile run along the trails leaving the Art Smith Trail Head off Highway 74 just west of the Big Horn Golf Club. The sun was now fully up and the air temperature was starting it's inexorable climb towards the days comfortable springtime high. It had been a good winter and the wildflowers were displaying themselves in profusion and in vivid contrast to the desert's harsh sand and rocks.

With hands placed on the driver's side roof of his 1959 Porsche Coupe he stretched for several minutes, collected his thoughts and slowed his breathing. It had been a good run up to above Grape Vine Creek, doing a favorite loop that required concentration and athletic skill. He slid his 6 foot 2 inch frame into the drivers seat, started his vintage old friend and headed back into town. As he approached Mesa View Drive he saw a small Garage Sale sign pointing to the right and he made the turn that would soon change his life.

Following the small red arrows he turned left and through an open gate onto Monterra Circle South. As he rounded the first curve a car in front of him slowed and then continued on. Ed could see an elderly woman sitting on a folding aluminum chair in front of what looked like an empty garage. He started to continue on as the car in front of him had done when the lady stood and waved him into the driveway. Surprised, he did her bidding.

"You made it, just the way Little Willy said you would," was her greeting.

She was a small, weathered woman looking fragile and old. But her eyes were bright blue and conveyed a mischievous look that couldn't be ignored.

"The clubs are in the corner over there," pointing into the seemingly empty and darkened garage. "Bring them out here and we will see if we can make a deal." She laughed at this as Ed had a puzzled look on his face, unsure of how he should react, and stood almost frozen.

"Don't just stand there. Get the bag and let's get this taken care of so I can close up and get my life going again."

Ed did as requested and found a big staff bag stuffed with more than twenty clubs. He hefted the bag, let out a grunt at it's weight, and managed to get it out to the waiting seller. "What have you got in this thing? Who are you? Who is Little Willy?" Ed babbled in confusion.

"Pull up that other chair, have a seat and all will be explained. If you do the smart thing and make me an offer I can't refuse it will change your life. If you don't, you will regret it the rest of your life." This time there was no laughter in her voice. She was dead serious. Ed did as he was told.

"These are clubs my late husband made over the years. Some are twenty years old and some only ten. He died the day after he was satisfied with that 7 iron. The one with the blue tape on the sole. Take it out and hold it for a few minutes. Take a swing but don't you take a divot in my lawn." This time she spoke quickly and had a smile on her face.

Ed picked the club with the blue tape out and placed his hands on the grip. He was a 6 handicap golfer and had a good feel for a golf club. He knew immediately that this was a good one. It looked a bit odd and didn't have a good presence but it felt just right. Stepping over to the lawn area he took a few warm up swings and was surprised that the tempo of his swing was slightly different than usual. He then set the club to address and took a full swing. A smile formed on his face. He knew, positively knew, that had a ball been there the flight would have been perfect. He could almost see it and actually thought he could feel the contact of a cleanly struck ball.

"Well my boy, come over here and let's talk about what just happened." Her eyes were dancing. "Have a seat next to me and let me see you up close. We need to come to an agreement." She was excited and didn't try to hide it from Ed. She knew, and she knew Ed knew, that there was something special about that 7 iron. She also knew there was something very special about every club in the bag.

Ed positioned his chair to face her. He looked directly into her eyes and again asked, "Who are you and who was your husband?"

"That makes no difference. I am the wife of the man that made these clubs. That is all you need to know. He was a man who lived in a wheel chair most of his life and made golf clubs. He never sold any and every club he made is in that bag. None have ever struck a golf ball. Your swing of the 7 iron just now was the first time any of

3

these clubs has ever been swung. You are a good enough golfer to know what you just experienced. What's your offer?"

Ed sat still. He could neither speak or move. He knew he had to have these clubs and he had no money or any way to get what he would need to buy them. He couldn't speak.

"How much cash do you have in hand right now?" was her question asked as calmly as if asking for a dollar or two.

"About fifty, maybe a few dollars more," Ed stuttered out ashamed of what he thought would surely be rejected as insulting.

"That sounds about right with conditions attached. First is that you can never sell even one of these clubs. Never until your death can you part with any of them. And second, when you win any monies using these clubs you must contribute twenty percent to charity. That is it. Take it or leave it." Her voice sent a chill through Ed's body that made him physically shake.

He didn't hesitate. "You have a deal," and reached for his wallet. It was in the car and before he could speak she said "Go get your wallet and show me the money."

Five minutes later Ed loaded the clubs into the passenger seat which he had tilted back. He turned to say another thank you and goodbye and watched as the garage door closed. The house looked deserted as if no one had lived there in years. He hesitated then walked over and picked up the small arrow sign, as he had promised her, and drove back the way he had come in picking up the rest of her small signs.

Turning right and heading back towards downtown

Ed Adams Chases a Dream

Palm Desert he turned onto El Paseo and drove past the now closed art gallery he had managed until two weeks ago. It was then left down San Pablo Avenue toward Fred Waring Drive and to his small second floor apartment. Climbing up the stairs, shouldering the heavy bag, he entered his sparsely furnished domicile. He stood the bag in the center of the room, pulled up a chair and sat motionless staring at it for an hour afraid to move, to touch any of the clubs, or even the bag. He finally stood up, circled the bag twice, and headed for the kitchenette. A peanut butter and jam sandwich with a diet Pepsi was lunch.

Chapter 2

Ed Adams was two months short of his thirtieth birthday and was at this moment as lonely as he had ever been. He was an only child of parents who had no other family. His father had been disowned by his devout Catholic parents when he chose to marry a Vietnamese woman who was an orphan, atheist and with little knowledge of English or American customs. The fact that she was the most intelligent woman Ed's father had ever known, beautiful and a truly kind spirit made no difference. Even the arrival of Ed five years later, with his mother having achieved her Doctorate degree in international studies, his father's parents would never reconcile. The only sign Ed's father ever received that there was some regret was his father bequeathing him his 1959 Porsche Coupe which was now parked in Ed's parking spot in the garage below the apartments. It was there because his parents were both killed in a tragic and horrific automobile accident ten years ago.

Ed was between the fall and winter quarters of his junior year at Stanford when it happened. He was on a golf scholarship and was the teams number three player at the time but all that ended with his parents deaths. As he sat in his apartment staring at the clubs in the big staff bag the tears started again. He desperately needed his mother and father to be here. His life since they died had been a blur of efforts to find some meaning in life. Some experiences had been good but most provided no help. A girlfriend or two, friends that came and went, jobs that seemed okay at the beginning but then became unimportant and were lost or left. Golf was his only escape and as the years past he found that it alone could give him peace.

A year ago the glamorous Patricia Collins came to Palm Desert and opened the Patricia Collins Art Gallery on El Paseo. Her success was immediate as she had managed to quickly collect a stable of good artists. Ed had gone to the gala opening and him being tall, handsome and by himself was immediately taken in by Patricia. It was not sex she was after as that was of no importance to Patricia Collins. What was important was for her to find a gallery manager as management bored her. Ed had the looks and a manner that most found not only attractive but honest. Patricia cared little about this either but she needed someone to run the gallery as only the idea of owning a art gallery was important to her. The deal was struck and Ed Adams had a new career, and he was good at it. That is until Patricia Collins stopped paying her bills and the artist for their sales. Two weeks ago the gallery closed and various government and private lawyers were nosing about seeking her whereabouts but at present she seemed to have disappeared.

All this passed through Ed's mind as he looked at the big bag in the middle of his apartment living area. He finally made it out of the chair and took the few steps to reach out and pull one of the clubs out of the bag. It was then it all started for real. As odd looking the club head was, not numbered or identified, the club felt good when he gripped it. Just like the 7 iron he swung a few hours ago. He leaned it against the wall and picked another.

The line up of golf clubs along the wall was impressive. Twenty seven of the strangest combination you could imagine. A standard set of the allowable 14 was such a familiar sight that Ed's new set looked out of place in both numbers and appearance. There was no putter but that made perfect sense. As Ben Hogan was fond of saying, "Putting is a different game." The putter only had one purpose and that was to strike and roll the ball to the hole. It was indeed direction and distance but the ball stayed on the surface so only two dimensions were in play. And for most times the surface was uniform and consistent. Choose the line and make the stroke on that line to the right distance.

Ed selected 3 clubs that appeared to have almost the same loft, one of which still had the blue tape on the head. They were similar in shaft length and grip but not exactly. Each club head was different enough to be obvious. "Why have 3 clubs so alike? I will know why tomorrow morning," Ed asked himself and answered his own question, speaking out loud in the small room.

As evening came and it got dark Ed put a TV dinner in the microwave and after the bell sounded got his meal and moved to his Lazy Boy recliner chair. The television provided a distraction and he ate without tasting the food. He then headed to bed but sleep did not come as his thoughts continued wander between the clubs leaning against the wall, the big bag standing now empty in the middle of the room, and a small, frail lady with the dancing blue eyes that had made his day.

He got up and turned on all the lights in the apartment. Going to the clubs he hefted each one, placing his hands with his customary grip and addressing an imaginary ball on the floor. Each club had a different feel but each felt comfortable in his hands. He thought which ever he chose he could make the shot he wanted and it would go to the exact spot he was aiming for. There were no doubts. None. He had never thought this before and wasn't sure he should be thinking that way now.

Still wide awake Ed decided he should make an inspection of the bag. The staff bag was huge relative to his carry bag and it seemed this one was even bigger than most. He lifted it and realized it wasn't empty. Unzipping the lower front pocket he found 3 dozen Titleist Professional balls, loose but brand new and gleaming white. His favorite right now but too expensive to use except on special occasions. The next pocket had a handful of tees, several nice ball markers that looked like real silver quarters. Another pocket had a half dozen golf gloves still in packets and exactly his size. He stood back and as he looked about the room he had a feeling of apprehension descend on him.

It was then to the side pockets. The first had a bag cover for rain and was fit to the bag. The other side pocket contained a new rain suit, jacket and pants. He pulled them out and checked for size. He knew already what their size would be and sure enough it was his exact fit.

"Good Jesus, what is going on here?" was said out loud.

It was then he was sure he was involved in more than just chance. In the pocket for valuables was a Rolex watch, the band fitted to his wrist. This was too much and tomorrow it would be time for a visit to that little lady that waved him into her driveway and practically gave him this treasure. Ed knew that when something is too good to be true it usually is just that.

But before he would go to see his benefactor, to find out what was going on, he would hit some balls and see what happens when one of these clubs contacts a ball for the first time.

He went to his bed and climbed in between the covers and fell asleep. He dreamed of hitting golf balls, one after another, hour after hour. Every one perfectly struck. On target, the right distance to the right place. Ball after ball, each perfect.

Chapter 3

Ed Adams woke up tired. Hitting that many range balls was tiring but as his senses returned he remembered it had all been in his dreams. Opening his eyes slowly he looked around the room and spotted the staff bag in the middle, then the row of clubs leaning against the opposite wall. The events of yesterday came into focus and he slid out of bed and took the few steps over to the row of clubs. He picked the 7 iron with the blue tape and automatically laid his hands on the grip. Nothing had changed. The feeling that his next swing would be perfect and the ball flight would be just like the ones in his dream.

He quickly downed a glass of orange juice and bowl of cereal. Then a fast trip to the bathroom, shaved, face washed and teeth brushed he dressed in his uniform of shorts and golf shirt. Sandals on and golf socks in hand he finally noticed it was 6:30 am.

"OK you dumb ass, now what are you going to do?" speaking out loud again and starting to think he was losing it. "Calm down. You got two hours to kill."

Ed decided an early morning walk the length of El Paseo would do so he locked up his apartment and headed there. Early morning in Palm Desert is the best time of the day. The sky is almost always clear and the temperature with a little bit of chill. As he walked by the closed shops,

11

galleries and book stores, only the few restaurants serving breakfast were open. They were busy and would stay so until after 10;00 am leaving just enough time to prepare for the lunch crowd. Again, with a few hours break they would be ready for dinner customers. "Never be in the restaurant business," thought Ed.

He passed by the closed Patricia Collins Gallery and looked into the empty space. A month ago it had been filled with some of the best art on El Paseo and was doing what should have been a very successful business. Ed was glad he had a written contract that his position as manager was limited to store hours management only. Patricia Collins was to control all aspects of the gallery, from artist represented to all financial matters. He was only to see gallery hours be complied with and sales people performed. Everyone was on commission and they would be paid as soon as payment was received and cleared. He would handle no money other than credit cards and cash purchases, deposits to be made daily unless over the weekend. There was a small safe for the weekend sales. The gallery was open every day except Monday, 10:00 am to 9:00 pm. He was in charge of staffing, hours, hiring and firing only with her approval.

When Patrica Collins disappeared owing everyone that had done business with her his contract freed him from all liability. She owed him over $10,000 and he was certain he would never see any of it. The artists were the worst hit. Their claims came in over $100,000 and for many it was career threatening. It had started with a grand opening, catered wine and cheese, live music and well advertised and attended. Unfortunately that was last June and by early July the high season was over. Ed had run the gallery alone over the summer with shortened hours. In October business picked up and it looked like a very successful winter season could be expected. The first signs of some difficulties in payments to those owed became apparent by the end of March. By the end of April Ed was sure that Patricia Collins was a world class liar and she was lying to everyone. Money talks and by the middle of May Ed was the only one available, had no information to convey and had lost contact with the now missing Ms Collins. He locked up the gallery on June 1st after all the artists had removed their unsold works and he left the art world for good.

Back in his apartment he knew today things were going to be better, or at least different, and he prepped his carry bag with the three 7-irons for the first test of these strange clubs. His own set were Lynx Parralax, 2 thru pitching wedge, Callaway Big Bertha driver, Wilson Staff 5 wood, a custom no name sand wedge, and a ancient Wilson Winsum putter. He removed the 2, 3, 4 and 5 irons and slid in the three 7-irons. Shouldering the bag and carrying his golf shoes he headed for the College of the Desert Golf Center, just a block and a half away.

Ben was there. It seemed he must live there as every time Ed showed up, which was at least three times a week, Ben was at the desk with a smile.

"Big basket today?" was the greeting.

"Yep," was the answer and the wire basket was handed over. You filled your own from the bin just outside the door to the range.

"Going to try some new clubs. Funny looking," was Ben's comment having spotted the 7-irons in Ed's bag.

"Yep. Got them at a garage sale yesterday and have a promise they will change my life. Don't you tell anyone you saw me with them," Ed tried to say with humor.

"I tell you what Ed, there is a good patch of turf just past the end of the range tees and the maintenance box. Go use it but don't make a mess or I will get in trouble. Hasn't been used in a week and the turf is in good shape. Just mowed yesterday," Ben said with a secretive tone to his voice.

"Thanks Ben. I appreciate having good grass and a little privacy. This may turn out to be a joke on me," Ed was quick to respond.

Ed went to the bin and tried to find a hundred good balls to fill the basket. That done he sat on the bench, put on his golf shoes and then headed to the special place at the far end of the range. What he didn't see, or hear, was Ben picking up the phone, punching a speed dial number and saying "He is here with three clubs," and then hanging up the phone.

Chapter 4

Ed found the section of turf Ben had sent him to and it was perfect. Just like the fairways the pros play on. He stood his carry bag up on it's flip legs and went through the familiar motions. Pulling his new glove on his left hand he stretched it tight and then fastened the Velcro strap. He had tried to play without a glove, like his current favorite pro Fred Couples, but it seemed his fingers had fragile cuticles and the glove protected them. He also liked the glove's feel.

He did some minor stretches and then pulled out his Lynx 7-iron, swung a dozen swings and then another six just skimming the top of the grass. At the far edge of the good section of turf he spilled out about twenty balls, pulled one over and took his stance. He then backed off circled to behind the ball and sighted a target at about 160 yards. Returning to the ball he again took his stance, grounded his club, took one more look at his target and swung.

Ed had a good swing. His father had been a good golfer, as was his mother. They gave him not only lessons on swing mechanics but on how the game should be respected and played. His father had given him a child's club and Ben Hogan's "Five Lessons" on his fourth birthday. His "Five Lessons" was still in his book collection and he would often read it again whenever his swing deserted him.

The contact was perfect, the ball launched at the right angle and landed within 10 feet of the target. He repeated with nine more shots and had eight balls within one putt range if it had been the flag on a green. He wiped off the 7-iron and placed it back in the bag. It was now time and Ed could hardly work up the courage to pull the first of his new clubs out of the bag. He was concentrating so hard on this club selection he didn't notice the big black man seated in the ball retriever tractor fifty yards beyond carefully watching him.

"Okay, my little old lady friend, here goes. The first struck ball by your late husband's life pursuit. May it be a good swing." Ed said this out loud as he pulled the 7-iron with the blue tape still hanging off it's sole from his bag. He pulled the tape off and examined the club some more. It could have been a Wilson Staff iron at one time but the sole was rounded slightly and the face had a different groove pattern. It was a bit heavier and if looked at carefully the face may have had a slight convex shape. The toe was flared up. It was a golf club without a doubt but didn't look like anything Ed had ever seen before.

He pulled a ball over and set up on a new strip of turf and went through his routine, took one last look at his target and swung. He could feel his swing slow just enough to notice and his downswing was just countering that being just a bit faster. The contact was so good he could feel the ball compress and when he looked up to see the trajectory he saw a ball flight he had never seen before. It was straight and true, landed and stopped 15 yards directly behind his target. He stood still for several minutes to enjoy the moment.

For the next hour Ed hit 90 balls dividing them equally between the three clubs. The second 7-iron had a built in draw and flew the ball 10 yards farther while the third had a built in fade and the ball fell dead in it's ball mark 10 yards shorter. Ed found he could adjust his swing speed at will to adjust for distance and control draw and fade with just slight changes in alignment. By the time he hit the last ball he was thinking he had within his grasp clubs he could control beyond his wildest dreams.

While he concentrated on his shot making he didn't see the big black man continue to watch his every move. About half way through Ed's practice the big man opened his flip mobile phone and punched a speed dial. If you could read his lips you would have known he only said, "He can hit those clubs so damn sweet it makes tears come to your eyes," and then close up the phone not waiting for an answer.

Ed had put the three clubs in his bag, shouldered it, and started to return to the range office when he took another look at his target area. There were no other golfers hitting balls so he walked out and looked where he had been aiming. The 100 balls were grouped together within 10 foot circles. Four distinct groupings with the only balls outside one of these was from his first group using his Lynx 7-iron and the few hit for extra or less distance. The circles formed a line that directly pointed to from where he had been hitting.

It was while standing among these ball groupings that he realized he could control his ball flight to a degree he never thought possible. What was he going to do if the other clubs performed this way was seeping into his

17

consciousness. It frightened him to think at the level he could play at if that was the case. He didn't realize it yet, but others were already making plans for what to do with his newly acquired talent.

He heard the ball retriever tractor start up and saw it begin it's routine heading across the range away from him and then turn for the return run coming closer. The second run was closer yet and Ed hadn't seemed to be able to move. It came back for the next leg and this time would be just beyond his group of balls. The big black man stopped about 20 yards short and sauntered over looking a the groups.

"That's some good golf my boy. Some good golf-ing. Yes sir," was said with a giant smile. He shuffled back to the tractor and continued the sweep and on the return run swept up Ed's offerings.

As Ed approached the office a group of college kids had arrived and were excitedly filling baskets. At least a full bus load of them and the range was going to be a mad house for the next hour or two. Ben was busy but gave him a wave and smile as he went through the office. It then dawned on Ed it was Sunday and the range was usually closed on Sundays. It should have been closed today and the big black tractor driver should have had the day off. As Ed walked by the bronze lady golfer sculpture, with the putter under her arm, he stopped and asked her "Do you know what is going on?"

She didn't answer or even look his way.

Chapter 5

Ed was back in his apartment in a few minutes and set his bag in the corner. He took out the three clubs and leaned them together on the wall. Next would be the three drivers and the three fairway metals. He emptied his bag and loaded it with the six clubs. He wouldn't even try to hide what he was about to do. If anyone was watching they could watch. If asked what he was doing he would make up some answer about an old friend who left them for him in his will.

He put the Rolex in his pocket, headed to the garage and to his Porsche. Every time he saw it a combination of emotions overwhelmed him. First he loved the little car. Second was that his grandfather, whom he hardly knew because of the estrangement with his father, always took him for a ride when they were together and told him the exact same story. "This is a fine little car and was the first and only new car I have ever owned. It is for me like the first women you love and if you are lucky the first one is enough." He then willed it to Ed's father, which had been a surprise, who kept it in the garage and drove it sparingly. He had it restored to like new and maintained it that way. It became Ed's with the tragic early death of his father and Ed shared his grandfather's love of the little Porsche and wanted no other.

As he approached Mesa View Drive he slowed and made the left turn. He was nervous about how to handle the conversation now that he knew how special the clubs were and how it seemed this all had been planned out for him ahead of time. He turned into the entrance and then on to Monterra Circle South. At the first curve he started looking for the house the old lady was sitting in front of just about this time the day before. For what ever reason nothing looked that familiar to Ed so he pulled over to the curb, parked the car, and got out.

There were only three houses on the first curve that fit his memory and the one in the middle looked to be the best candidate. It didn't look occupied but Ed went to the front door and rang the bell. He could hear the chime but there was no answer. A second try with the same result. As he walked back toward the street he looked closely at the lawn and sure enough there was the sign of a neatly clipped, very shallow divot just where it should be. No doubt this was the right place.

He tried the next house hoping to find out who was their neighbor. A rather attractive women of about twice Ed's age answered the bell dressed in a rather poorly fitting bath robe. She smiled and asked, "What can I do for you young man. Better yet what can you do for me?"

Ed, who thought of himself as good in conversations in almost any situation, was caught of guard. After a couple of false starts he managed to ask about the neighbors next door, pointing to the house he had just come from. The woman adjusted her robe to expose a bit more of her ample breasts and answered, "Nothing! No one has lived there since I have been here. Five years now. Would you like to come in for some coffee and a croissant?" Another big smile.

Ed, some what awkwardly, excused himself and as he turned the women said, with a teasing lilt in her speech, "Try the house across the street two doors down. They knew the couple and I think they were friends. Good luck in your new life." He could hear her laughter as she closed the door.

Crossing the street Ed approached the house he had just been directed to and the door opened as he stepped on the porch. "We have been expecting you to come by. Come in as I think we know what you want to find out. We want to know about what happened yesterday morning across the street, too."

Ed met Harold and Carolyn Finegold, ages 89 and 86, respectively, 20 year residents in their home here and he quickly learned the couple across the street that he was interested in were Morris and Maureen Cornith and were both now deceased.

"Please come in and have coffee and a croissant," was next. This brought a smile to Ed's face and he accepted the invitation.

"They moved into their house the same week we moved in here. Morris was already wheel chair bound and they had their home modified for him to have access. Once that was done a large moving van arrived and the garage was turned into his shop. It was some kind of shop." Harold paused to take a few needed breaths and Carolyn took over.

"We became good friends. Maureen was a doll and cared for Morris without complaint. They seemed to be so compatible that his disability was hardly noticeable when we were entertained in their home. And so interesting, my

Lord they were fun to talk to. Right Harold!" and it was Carolyn's turn to take a break. The conversation continued this way and the coffee and croissants appeared and were consumed.

Ed thought that these people were of his grandparents generation but were such fun and full of happiness that he wondered if his grandparents had a relationship anything like Harold and Carolyn enjoyed. He did learn what he needed to know. Morris had been an employee of IBM in the early days of computer development until 1974 when he retired. He kept his contacts and did some consulting on the newest computers being designed. He also was granted time on their main frame super computers. It was in this format that he developed his golf clubs. Every step in their designs was coordinated with massive computer studies. Neither Harold, Carolyn or Maureen understood what Morris did in his hours in the garage but there was a lot of metal work being done, then various complex measurements accomplished and hours of computing time used. Eventually, when each club was considered by Morris to be done, he set it aside and started in on the next one.

Harold ventured, "I didn't have any idea of what Morris was doing. He never talked about it and he never let anyone touch one of his golf clubs. They just sat there leaning against the back wall. Once he finished one it was as if he had no more interest in it. It was the challenge of design and creation that he spent his time and what he enjoyed. He seemed content. He was a genius. The only one I ever met and knew."

"Don't take what Harold says to mean they didn't treat us as friends and equals. I miss them so much," and

Carolyn started to cry. Harold stepped over and gave her a hug, which helped. "It has been seven years he passed away. Maureen moved to La Jolla to live with her sister, Harriet, who was also widowed. She died less than six months later. That was who was there yesterday morning, her sister."

Harold then continued, "Nobody has lived in the house since Maureen moved in with Harriet over in La Jolla. Doesn't make sense but I think it has something to do with Morris's old IBM friend, Hank Morgan. He, I mean Hank, was into real estate here and I think he bought the house. Not even sure about that, however."

The conversation continued for a little longer and Ed knew he should make his leave. But first he took out the Rolex and told them it was in the bag and he didn't know what he should do with it. Carolyn looked at it and said, "That was the watch IBM gave to Morris when he retired. He never wore it. If it was in the bag it was meant to be for you so take good care of it."

Ed started to protest and Carolyn shook her head no. "You have been chosen to bring Morris's golf clubs to life. It has to be Maureen's sister and some of the older golfers here who have a sense of golf that transcends commercialism. That this needs to be done in Morris's memory. I think they have been looking for just the right person to do it and have found you. It may be a blessing, or a curse, but we hope it is the former. Will you keep us informed at how it goes? We would like to see Morris's golf clubs in action."

Ed departed their house knowing he now had new grandparents to visit and confide in. No way would he let these people down.

Chapter 6

Ed was back in his apartment and it was just past noon. The coffee and croissants took care of any need for lunch and he suddenly felt lonely. Looking around his small room the only thing he valued were the golf clubs. In the garage was his Porsche. Add to that a few books and there was nothing else he owned he truly cared about. He pulled out one of the drivers and gripped it gently and swung it back and forth slowly in a waggle motion. It felt ready to contact a ball but he would wait until tomorrow to give it a test. It felt good in his hands and after a few more waggles he put it back in the bag.

"Tomorrow my friend we will bond. My God, my friend is a golf club," he spoke his thought out loud and the gloom of being lonely settled in even more strongly. He left the apartment and not even thinking about where he was going ended up at the College Golf Center. The driving range was now closed but there were half a dozen golfers hitting their own shag balls about and some putting on the rather rough practice green.

The Jude Poynter Golf Museum was open so Ed headed there. He visited occasionally and always found something that he hadn't seen before. It seemed that no one was there so he looked in the first display case that had a nice collection of early golf balls. He heard the click of a ball being struck as in a putt and the soft metal clink as it hit and entered one of those plate like cups used to practice putting indoors. Then another click followed by the clink indicating the second ball had found it's mark. Walking around one of the high cabinets was a sight he would remember the rest of his life.

She was standing side-wise to him leaning in perfect posture addressing a golf ball with an old hickory shafted putter, looking at her target 15 feet away. Ed was wearing sneakers and had made no sound stepping around the cabinet and he held his breath. She was tall, slender and dressed in conservative golf shorts and shirt. From her sandals to the blonde pony tail laying over her right shoulder she was the most beautiful woman Ed had ever seen. Athletic but feminine. He just stared and dared not breath. She took one more look at her target, then the ball and with a flawless stroke rolled the ball smoothly over the carpet and into the cup having just enough pace to make over the little metal tab. Clink. Three balls in the cup. Her head came up and sensing someone there she turned to face him and smiled.

Ed would say later, many times, in that moment, he fell in love for the first and only time. He knew instantly that this would be the woman he would want with him from that moment on. But first he had to say something. Almost choking he blurted out, "Nice putt." She smiled again. He needed help and she provided it effortlessly.

"I didn't hear you come in. Not many do. Too bad as this is a really nice museum if you love golf. Have you been here before?" she spoke with a confident and clear voice.

25

It was Ed's turn to smile and just hearing her voice calmed him. "I practice here three times a week, sometimes more. When I have some extra time, or need a lift, I like to browse the museum and I usually find something here I haven't seen before that makes my day better. Like seeing someone with a Bobby Jones Calamity Jane putter sink a perfect putt."

"Well you haven't seen me before. Do I lift your spirits?" was said with laughter that was infectious and Ed's smile got even bigger. He couldn't speak or think. Again she saved him.

"Here, you give it a try," she said as she walked over to retrieve the three balls. Bending down to pick them up was such that Ed almost passed out. She handed him the putter, dropped the balls on the carpet and gave him another smile. He gripped the old leather handle and felt a familiar sensation. He wouldn't tell her until much latter that his father had a Calamity Jane just like this one, and it could have been this one as he had given it to a friend who knew Jude Poynter. Ed had made many putts with it, or one just like it, and was sure he could make good putts now. He took his stance, made one look at the target, set himself and stroked. Clink, then another clink and then one more.

"I think I have met my match. I think I may even get to like you. How about a Diet Pepsi and doughnut?" She smiled again and Ed smiled back.

Introductions were made. Julia Renquest sounded very nice to Ed as any name would have been just fine. She was pursuing her masters degree in ancient history at UCLA. She didn't think there would be any future in that field but enjoyed the subject matter. She had a golf scholarship, was second on the team with a 4 handicap and one more year of eligibility.

She then asked Ed what he was doing. He tried to smile and then could only offer the lame theme that he was between jobs and his last had been as an art gallery manager. She then ask him which one and replied, "Oh my," when he told her the Patricia Collins Art Gallery.

There was a lull in the conversation. They were sitting at one of the small tables outside and Ed was again saved by the approach of the big black man that operated the range's ball retriever machine. He strode up to the table, seeming to be even taller than Ed remembered, and said, "How are you Julia? Nice to see your pretty face again."

"Hi Willy. You are looking good. Taken a few pounds off I see," she quipped back. Then quickly added, "Meet Ed Adams. He just picked me up in the Museum. He can putt better than I can."

"I watched him hit balls this morning and he can golf his ball. You two should hit it off. Doubt if he is good enough for you but you never can tell," was accompanied by laughter from the two of them and a smile from Ed.

Ed came back with "Have a seat Willy, and a doughnut. Your not so little, Willy."

Chapter 7

Willy took a long look at Ed. Then he smiled and said he needed to make a short call. Taking out his cell phone, he punched a speed dial, waited a moment, then said, "Ben, might be a good time for you coming over here. Ed and Julia are with me," a pause then "Good, we are out behind the museum."

"Did you just call my grandfather?" was Julia's quick response with the question and also the look on her face.

"Now Julia, it's not what you think. I like Ed and what Ben and I need to talk about is only about him and us. You just happen to be here. And maybe it is a good time for you to be here," was Willy's answer which was long enough to surprise her.

Julia's smile was so bright that Ed couldn't understand it's meaning. She then let him know.

"Those are the most words I have ever heard you put together at one time Willy. What's going on here? What have you and Ben cooked up with Ed Adams?" was said with such enthusiasm that it was now Ed's turn to wonder what his life was about to be, but he was sure it was going to be much better. Just watching Julia and Willy exchange conversation and looks made him understand this was a family that he may be asked to join.

Ed Adams Chases a Dream

Ben arrived in minutes and greeted them with a smile and seemed completely relaxed. He pulled up a nearby plastic chair and the four of them were tightly bunched around the small round metal table. Julia was on one side of Ed and Willy was on the other. Ben directly across from him. Julia had brought out a box of doughnuts that had been in the museum refrigerator a few days too long and the coffee was from the range's machine. The doughnuts tasted like cardboard and the coffee matched them perfectly. Ed didn't care and it seemed okay with the others.

There was a brief silence as what was to be said required a start and none of the four knew who should start it. Ed took the lead.

"You two know what's going on and why I am involved. Morris Cornith's sister-in-law pretended to be his widow and sold me the clubs for 50 dollars, with the condition that I can never sell them and of any money I win using them twenty percent goes to charity. She also let it be know that Little Willy told her I would be stopping by Saturday morning." The last sentence he said while looking directly at Willy, who smiled back at him. "So let's start there."

Ben smiled. Willy smiled. And Julia looked like she had never had so much fun in her entire life. Ed almost could not contain the good feelings he had.

"Ed you already know what is going on between the three of us. Julia being here was not part of the plan but both Willy and I are glad you met and she will now be part of the team. There is only one member missing and he will remain anonymous for now. He is funding the enterprise and wishes to leave it that way at this point."

Ben paused to let this sink in and then continued.

"It all starts with Morris Cornith. Our sponsor, myself and Morris were all IBM employees. I came out here later in the early eighties and Morris and Hank, I will call him, retired here in the early seventies. Morris was already in a wheel chair by then. Both had bought into IBM's employee stock options and both had bought more stock as the years went by. They both retired but Hank went into real estate investing, got really rich, and Morris made golf clubs in his garage, using scientific methods only. Hank loved playing golf and as far as I know Morris never hit a golf ball. I liked both of them and they liked me. Neither had children and I guess I was an adopted son. When I retired a little over ten years ago they convinced me to settle here and the relationship continued albeit Morris passed away three years after I moved here. Willy was Hank's caddie while he was still playing and, can I say it this way, was and is best friend, confidant, helper and consultant." Ben took in a lengthy breath then looked at Ed. "Don't you ever underestimate Little Willy. He is the best man you will ever have the pleasure of knowing."

"To finish up here we three have banded together to bring Morris's golf clubs to life. It is as simple as that. Willy and I work here at the range waiting to find the right golfer, not just any good golfer, the right golfer to pull it off. Ed, you are the chosen one, so to speak. We want one win on the PGA tour using Morris's clubs. That is what this is all about. That is what is going on."

Ed had suspected something like this but to hear it laid out in such detail cleared everything up except he knew something the other three didn't. The clubs were more than just one man's effort to create something just for the joy of creating. They had a magic for him that was special. A golfer occasionally has a feeling of being at one with his clubs but it is only fleeting. He was having a much more significant reaction, one that seemed almost mystical. That would be his secret and he would run with this opportunity as long and far as he could.

"I am in one hundred percent. Tomorrow morning will be driver and fairway clubs at eight thirty. Everyone is invited and I am looking forward to meeting Hank," Ed saying this with a knowing smile but was looking at Julia. He couldn't help himself.

Chapter 8

Willy stood up and leaned down to give Julia a kiss on the cheek, which she returned with one of hers, and he bid his farewell to Ed with "Tomorrow at eight thirty, my man." Ben did about likewise and that left Ed and Julia looking at each other knowing one or the other had to make the next move.

"Since no one has been to the museum this afternoon, other than a handsome golf hustler, I think I will close a little early this Sunday. Do you have enough time for another shot at putting with Calamity Jane?" Julia asked with a hustlers best dialect.

"I think I have just enough time open on today's schedule for just such a contest. There has to be a bet on the game. How about if I win you have to go to dinner with me tonight to a neat little Mexican restaurant I like and if I lose you still have to go with me to console me on my loss," Ed asked with at touch of hope that was obvious.

"Two out of three. Three games, three balls each at fifteen feet," Julia shot back with no hesitation.

It took three games and Ed lost by missing one putt. It was not on purpose and Julia liked that. She called Ben to tell him she was going to have dinner with Ed and would be home by nine. Ed liked that.

Ed Adams Chases a Dream

It was 4:30 pm when they walked over to Ed's apartment building and went directly to the garage. When Ed opened the door of the Porsche Julia smiled and remarked, "It's a 1958 or 59 isn't it. The tail lights say it is a 59. What a nice surprise. I love it!" and she slid into the passenger seat. All Ed could think was how good she looked seated in his car.

It was a 20 minute drive to Pedro's Gringo Cafe. A small 15 table place that Ed thought served the best Mexican food he had ever eaten. As they walked in the door a short rather over weight Hispanic wearing an apron, which showed he was the cook by the front stained by today's efforts, greeted Ed with a genuine smile and handshake. He then took a admiring look at Julia and turned to Ed. "It is about time you brought a beautiful guest to my restaurant instead of coming here alone all the time," and then to Julia "Welcome and do I dare ask your name?"

Julia answered in Spanish and other than "Julia" and "Gracious" Ed didn't know what was said. Pedro beamed his pleasure and they got the window table. It had a view of the 1959 Porsche in the parking lot. A good table Ed thought.

One Margarita each, followed a cold Cerveza with dinner. Pedro served the plates with much flair and spoke in a mixture of Spanish and English. The table was covered with a plastic red and white checkered oil cloth which was worn and not totally clean. One should always check the silverware and if served water a straw was wise. But the food was the best and Julia radiated a happiness that was genuine. Ed was totally in love in less than 6 hours.

It was a fun evening and as they neared Palm Desert Julia suggested they drive back to his apartment, park the car and they could then walk to her Grandfather's house from there. Ed thought that would be a good idea. He knew this was too good to spoil by rushing and he would let her guide the course of the relationship if there was to be one.

Getting out of the car, locking the doors and exiting the garage there was no hesitating walking towards Ben's house with Julia guiding the way. After two blocks she reached for and clasped Ed's hand. He turned toward her and said, "Thank you." Another two blocks brought them to Ben's home and they walked up to the front door. It was a private entryway and Julia reached up with her free hand and pulled his head towards hers and kissed him on the lips. A real kiss that lingered and then she whispered, "Don't you dare break my heart." She turned away to the door, opened it and disappeared behind it's closing. It was exactly nine o'clock.

Ed stood still. He knew nothing about her and she really didn't know much about him. They had just spent a few hours together and had talked mostly about nothing of real importance. That would come later and only make him want to be with her even more. He knew to be so sure was foolish but he didn't care.

As he walked back to his apartment he thought of what had happened in the last two days. His entire life had changed. From the moment the little, elderly lady flagged him down in front of the house with the almost empty garage until this moment only 36 hours had passed. It wasn't a dream. He now had a purpose. He had new friendships, real friendships. He was in love for the first time ever. He could hardly wait for tomorrow to come. He wasn't afraid of anything. What a good feeling it was to have so much to look forward to.

Chapter 9

Ed decided to include the three 7-irons in his bag and was walking through the portal between the range office and the museum shortly after 8:00 am. He went straight to the patch of grass he had hit from yesterday morning. Willy was there arranging several plastic chairs and waved to Ed as he approached.

"Good morning, good morning," he sang out the words. Then a big smile and, "You feeling any pressure?"

"Not a bit. I feel so good this morning that nothing can go wrong," was Ed's answer. He then thought he shouldn't be so cocky. That thought disappeared immediately and he knew this was going to turn out well.

"We are going to have a good gallery today. The four of us and your new friends the Finegolds. Surprise," Willy offered.

"I thought about calling them but was afraid it might be a bit too much for them to come out here this early. Did Ben call them?" Ed asked.

"Yes indeed. You better understand there are a number of folks here that knew and respected Morris Cornith. Every one of them were curious if any of his golf clubs would ever be played. Many have died off not knowing but there are still a few left. Ben is the youngster in the group. I am the new kid on the block. Only ten years wondering. Hank will probably show up but will stay in his car. Once the news gets out there are a dozen more geriatrics that will hobble out to watch you practice. They don't have much time left so the pressure is on you, my friend." Willy had to stop for a breath. He wasn't used to making long speeches but he got out one more important line. "You and Julia. Don't you ever do anything to hurt that girl. You understand what I am telling you?"

One look at Willy's face told Ed exactly what he was telling him. "I give you my word. Willy, I will never hurt her. Never," and he meant it as a promise he would keep as long as he lived.

"Well look who is here. Harriet it is so good to see you again. You have already met Ed," Willy said laughing. There stood the little lady that made the sale. Ed said hello and a quick conversation took place and was interrupted by the sight of Harold and Carolyn making their way out to the practice area. Next came Ben and Julia and Ed's attention was being demanded in every direction. He made the appropriate rounds and in saying "Hi" to Julia, the others had to be blind to not know what was in that simple greeting.

The final gallery member drove up in a 1958 metallic gray Lincoln Continental. The big rear window facing the practice area was rolled down and a craggy tanned face appeared and the gravelly voice demanded "Let's get the damn show going."

Willy got the three seated that needed chairs. Julia and Ben stood behind the chairs and Willy stood by Ed's bag and pointed at the clubs.

It was now Ed's show and he showed no reluctance to get it started. "I will start with the 7-iron that has the felt tip mark 7S on it. Willy." Willy handed him the club. The partnership of player and caddie had begun.

"This is the first of Morris's clubs I touched. The first I gripped, the first I waggled, swung and the first I hit a golf ball with. The thing I want tell you about this club is that it looks odd, certainly nothing like today's cavity back styles," and Ed waved it around and then realized most of his audience had seen this club years ago and maybe had actually held it. "You probably already know this but what you don't know is how good it feels to me when I hold it. If you play, or have played golf, you may once or twice held a club in your hands that you knew, absolutely knew, you would make a good shot with it. That is how I feel holding this club."

Ed did some stretches and swung the club in three quarter swings with a slow tempo. Then a few more aggressive swings and thought he was ready. He went over to the basket of range balls, noting they were brand new, and spilled about twenty on the turf. He turned and faced his small audience. "Willy has placed the red flag at 160 yards. I will hit three shots to land at 155, take one bounce and stop near the red flag." There was no bragging, just a calm statement of fact. He was sure he could do this. It was an strange feeling to have and one he was not used too but today he was sure he could do it.

With the club he pulled a ball over from the group. Moved it to where he wanted and took his stance. Then he stepped back and behind the ball facing the target. One look then back to the address position. A last look, a small forward press, full turn and a smooth swing taking a small divot just in front of where the ball had been.

Ed Adams Chases a Dream

The gallery was silent. Nothing needed to be said as the ball made a perfect arc to land 5 yards short of the target, one bounce and then stopping one foot in front of the pin. Ed pulled a second ball and repeated the sequence and then a third. Each of the shots looked identical and three balls lay within a 3 foot circle in front of the flag.

Harold, Carolyn, and Harriet's eye sights were such that they couldn't see the small circle but they knew the shots were good. Ben and Julia couldn't speak and Willy just had a big grin on his face. He had seen this yesterday morning and now he knew for sure his man could make the shots.

It was the voice of Hank, in the car holding big binoculars out the window, that spoke out and broke the silence. "Jesus Christ, did you see that!"

Chapter 10

Ed asked Willy for the 7-iron marked with 7F. He executed three beautiful high fades, each identical, landing 10 yards short and finishing on the direct line to the target. He smiled and knew how good the shots had been. Without speaking he handed the club to Willy who had already pulled the 7D marked club and made the exchange. Ed made three perfect draws at 10 yards beyond the marker and in line with the others.

It was quiet. Each in Ed's gallery knew golf and knew what they were seeing. Willy's smile had been replaced with a businessman's look. Julia was loving what she was seeing and just had an inkling that love might be possible with who was doing it. Ben, Harold, Carolyn and Harriet were each ready to adopt Ed into their family. Hank was hanging out of the window of the Lincoln with his binoculars focused on Ed's every move. Ed was in his own world as he took the 5 metal wood from Willy, looked on the sole noting the 5S, and pulled a ball from the group. He calmly said, "The blue flag is 240 yards. This should stop next to it."

There are some golf clubs that give you feed back as soon as contact is made. Morris's clubs were that kind. You knew immediately whether you had hit the ball right and knew where it would go. Looking up after the ball is gone you know exactly where to pick up it's flight. Ed's first stroke with the 5S metal wood was like that. He watched the ball arc and then fall, three bounces and roll to within 6 feet of the blue flag. Every golfer knows it when it happens and Ed was now expecting it to happen on every shot.

He and Willy went through the clubs, three balls each. Straight shots, fades and draws. Each the same, each perfect. The metal drivers provided a little additional excitement as after Ed had made his three shots each he asked Willy for the DS again and announced he would hit a few at one hundred percent. Three more range balls landed 30 yards past the blue flag and were still rolling when they hit the driving range fence 300 yards away.

Ed turned to Willy and handed him the driver and smiled. "Partners?" was all that was said. Willy smiled and nodded his head in agreement. He went over to the three seated guests and thanked them for coming. Then he continued, "Nine of Morris's twenty seven clubs have now been put to the test in my hands. I don't understand how I can hit shots like what you have just witnessed unless it was meant to be. I have never been able to do anything near to that and frankly I don't think it is really possible. Morris had to have some magical powers to have made clubs like these. He must have known that at the right time in the hands of the right person they could be put to the test. I will spend the rest of this week practicing with all the clubs and then decide what to do next. Willy will be my partner and help me make that decision."

Ed looked towards the Lincoln and could see Ben talking with Hank still seated in the back seat. Ben straightened up and slapped the car's top and waved as the long body with the big spare tire cover mounted on the trunk slowly worked its way out the rear fence gate, passing through it and turning right, as the gate closed. He then came back to the group with a smile that said something good had happened.

"Ed, you have a sponsor. Willy, you have a new job. And for myself I have a new project to work on. And for you Morris," he said looking skyward, "your clubs are going to hit the big time if all this works out."

Ben then addressed the assembly. "Let's all have lunch together and I will tell you the whole story. It will be my treat."

Julia thought this a great idea and Ed could hardly believe that in only 48 hours his whole life had changed. He had more to look forward to now than he could ever had thought possible. He then looked at Julia and the smile she gave made him think he must double that thought.

Chapter 11

Ben suggested the California Pizza Kitchen and all agreed. Harold and Carolyn would drive, Harriet and her driver would follow in her car and Ben, Julia, Willy and Ed would walk. Carolyn would secure a table and Ben asked her to get one of the corner booths. It was just 11:00 o'clock so that shouldn't be a problem. The four walkers enjoyed the stroll. Ed the most as Julia took his hand without hesitation and Willy carried his golf bag.

Carolyn had chosen the best corner booth and it was being set for eight when the walkers arrived. Ben took the outside seat so he could face the rest. Orders were taken and everyone had water as their choice of beverage. One of the waitresses stopped by, commented on what a happy group they made and then whispered to Ed, but loud enough to be overheard by Julia, "Glad to see you with a pretty girl instead of always by yourself. Us girls were afraid you might be gay," and she walked away with a sexy motion of very attractive hips.

Julia poked Ed in the ribs and moved a little closer to him on the bench. "Thought you were gay. That's not true is it?" she whispered in his ear.

Ed almost choked but managed a light pat on her thigh and smiled. He knew what was happening to him out of sight under the table at that moment but that would stay where it belonged until the time was right. His life was so good right now he wouldn't do anything that might risk it.

Ben stood and made the usual speaker's rap on his water glass. More like a clunk, as the glass was full, but that made no difference. All at the table knew that something was to come that involved plans for Morris's golf clubs and that they might included.

"My talk with Hank after Ed's exhibition was short and sweet, as it is always short with Hank, but not always sweet. It was sweet this time. He will sponsor Ed and we will be the team. All of us. Maybe even Harriet's driver if it can be worked out." The driver, Jimmy Lee, smiled and his eyes suddenly lost their glazed appearance. Ben took a sip of water and the rest waited for what was going to come next.

"Here is what is proposed by Hank. It is simple in words but not so simple in execution. Namely, a week from tomorrow Ed is to play a round of golf at Hank's club, Tamarisk, with the Club Pro. Willy will be Ed's caddie. Julia and I will make up the foursome but are not to get in the way. The Pro will only know at the time that we are guests of Hank and are to be treated well. There will be tremendous pressure on Ed as this will determine the sponsorship." Another sip of water. A look at Ed and then another smile.

"If it is a go, meaning Ed plays to the level seen today, we will form a small business to pursue Ed's future on the PGA Tour and see how far we can take this rather unusual opportunity. If it goes as it could there will plenty for all of us to do and it should be a fun adventure. There is a condition which Ed has already described to me. He cannot sell the clubs, ever, and twenty percent of all earnings using them are to go to charity." Ben nodded to Harriet who smiled back. "That should not be a problem for any of us and it is not a problem for Hank."

The orders had arrived and the party atmosphere continued through out the meal. Carolyn and Harold were particularly happy as life was becoming somewhat of a bore for them and to do just about anything that could take some of their time was welcomed. Harriet was almost beside herself to see that Morris's years of effort might come to fruition in such an exciting way that it made her blue eyes sparkle. Willy was just plain happy to be Ed's caddie, knowing how important this would be. Next to Ed, his part in this was going to be critical. Ben was the manager and it was exactly what he was good at and enjoyed doing most. Julia would be his assistant and already knew she was going to have an important role to play in making sure everything ran smoothly. She had another thing on her mind and hoped that would not complicate things. She already trusted Ed and hoped what she saw in him was correct. Ed was in a daze. Everything in his life since he first swung that 7-iron on Harriet's borrowed front lawn had seemed to be a miracle and he was in love. He thought "Don't let me wake up. Please. Not yet."

Willy asked Ed if he wanted him to keep the clubs until tomorrow but Ed declined the offer. "I think I will keep them close to me. Maybe sleep with them tonight. Anything to keep them happy. What do think?" Willy offered, "Oh sure," but then in a more serious note, "Don't forget what I told you."

Ed smiled and nodded to Willy while Julia

watched the play of words between them. She knew there was more than golf being talked about and would ask Ed about that later. But right now all was good in her life and she was happy.

Ben picked up the tab and the group parted ways with the knowledge that their lives may come back together in a way that each needed right now. The goodbyes and see you laters were made. Ben and Willy headed back to the driving range with Ed telling Willy he would be there at 8:30 in the morning with all the clubs. They could start the complex sorting to get down to combinations of 13 or 12 of them as Ed would keep his putter and may also want to put his favorite sand wedge in the bag.

Julia stood aside as all the partings took place. She then walked over to Ed and asked to walk back with him, and after he dropped off the clubs at his apartment would he walk her back to Ben's place? Ed hoisted the bag and they walked along El Paseo and then down the street to his apartment.

"I would like to see the rest of the clubs," Julia trying to say this in the right way. She wanted to see the clubs but really wanted to see how he lived. She wasn't ready to commit to a relationship yet and she hoped he would understand, not pushing her into a refusal and an awkward situation.

"Sure. Don't expect much in the way of furnishings. It's a studio so what you see is what I have." It wasn't embarrassment, as that was not one of his traits. He also knew this was not the time or place to advance their relationship. He would not make a mistake now. Too much good was just in front of him and in no way was he going to jeopardize it.

46

Chapter 12

Ed went up the stairs first and led the way to his apartment door. He suddenly had lost a little of his confidence. The stairs and landing had the worn look of a forty year old building. The rent was reasonable by Palm Desert standards and you got what you paid for. He did keep his room some what neat and had made his bed and washed the morning dishes. The bathroom was acceptable. Julia was beautiful, dressed in nice Palm Desert style, and did not look like she should be here at 2:00 in the afternoon on a Monday. Or for that manner be here at any time.

He unlocked the door and opened it going in first swinging the golf bag to clear the entrance. Turning to face Julia he started to speak and found he couldn't.

"Are you going to invite me in or should I just push you out of the way?" Julia said with a smile and not the least bit embarrassed.

"Yes. Yes of course. Please enter the palace of your dreams, my fair lady." He managed a smile and Julia came in and looked around. She saw what was there. A chair, a bed, a tiny kitchenette, a small table with two chairs and a door to what must be the bathroom. It was clean and the front windows let in enough light to keep the space from being gloomy. Against one of the two walls unencumbered by any pictures or art work was a long row of golf clubs.

In the middle of room was a big staff golf bag and Ed had just put his stand bag in the only corner available.

Julia turned to Ed and smiled again. "It is a fine place to start from when your life is about to get so much better. You believe that, don't you? I can sense it and I want to be part of seeing it happen. Okay?" Julia was now serious and was trying not to start crying. She came to Ed, put her arms around his neck, and softly said "Not now, not yet. Here will be fine but not yet," and kissed him in a way that made Ed's knees go weak. He held her against him and felt that this was as it should be for now and he could wait until it was time.

She backed away brushing her hair back as she turned her head away. She then turned back to him and said "Thank you for understanding. After we look at these clubs we can go to grandpa Ben's place, sit by the pool, and tell each other our life stories. I want to know yours and you need to know mine. Is that good with you?" Ed could only smile and nod his head in agreement.

Going through the clubs went quickly, but it was not careless. Julia picked one after another and gripped and waggled each. Her reaction was the same for each one. "It doesn't look or feel right in my hands. I don't think I could make a good swing with any of them. I don't see how you can get the results you do. You must like their feel and swing weight. You do, don't you?" and it was a serious question from one who knew golfing.

It surprised Ed. He knew she could putt but to understand swing mechanics meant she must be a good golfer. He answered that he did and that he had never swung any club that gave him the confidence that these gave him. Then he asked her a question. "What is your handicap? Tell me the truth."

"Ed Adams, do you really expect me to tell you my real handicap before our first match?" She paused, then added, "okay, it's a three."

Ed was again almost speechless. "A three! You have to give me three strokes. No way!"

He then smiled as another question was answered. Not really an important one but finding out that the beautiful woman he was falling in love with could not only play golf, but was the better player.

Julia was now confident she could trust Ed and gave him another embrace and kiss and suggested it was time head to Ben's place. And that is what they did.

Chapter 13

Ben's house looked from the outside most unob-trusive and it blended in with the moderately upscale neighborhood. Entering changed one's mind. The entrance was into a nicely appointed hallway with framed art and personal photos. A narrow table was on one side and a display rack on the other had a collection of at least fifty antique hickory shafted golf clubs. They passed through too quickly for Ed to take a good look at the photos but he did spot Ben photographed with a least two Presidents.

Julia tugged at his hand and told him he could look at this stuff later as they had some important things to discuss first. Glancing left and right Ed saw a den/office, a guest room, bathroom, kitchen and dining room. A spa-cious living room was next having a connected hallway that must lead to more bedrooms. They then went thru the living room's big french doors leading to the veranda and a pool with a cabana surrounded by a fabulous garden. Ed's only thought at the moment was that this was the Ben that handed out baskets for range balls at a rather funky college driving range. It then dawned on him why Ben would have been there, and also why some one like Willy, "Little Willy", would also be there. There was a big pic-ture starting to be painted in his mind and he knew he was in it.

Julia arranged the deck chairs so they would face each other. She sat close, knees almost touching, and said to Ed, "You first. I want to know everything." She reached out and touched his arm and Ed was just about to start when Ben came out and greeted them. Julia looked at Ed, smiled, and asked Ben to join them. He pulled up another chair and they arranged the seating in a triangle. Julia spoke first. "Ed was just about to tell me his life story. When he is done I promised I would tell him mine. Do you want to sit in, at least for Ed's?"

"No, but I need to tell you both a little more about our little project. Some you have an inkling of already, but if not to make sure you understand what has happened so far. It will only take a few minutes and then I will leave you two to find your own way. Ed, plan on dinner here tonight if you would like."

Ben leaned back and was relaxed. Ed now saw this wasn't some volunteer at the College Golf Center, this was a high level, professional executive.

"My involvement with Morris Cornith goes way back. I was your age Ed when I first met him at IBM almost forty years ago. Morris was the smartest and most intelligent man I have ever known. We worked together on all the major breakthroughs in computer technology of the time. Hank Morgan was our supervisor. We became known as the big three. Hank and I were the best golfers at IBM for years but Morris wasn't into sports. We were best friends. After Morris died Maureen asked us to take his golf clubs and do something with them. She hoped somehow all the time he spent making them would turn out to have been worth while for someone."

Ben took a moment to look at Ed and then at Julia.

"You two are starting to get the picture. Hank and I have been trying to figure out what to do with the clubs. Neither of us thought they had any value as they didn't feel or look good to us. But there was something about them that wouldn't let us just ignore Morris's belief in his work. We owed him at least one real try. Hank felt he didn't have much time left so he ventured the plan to see if we could find the right player for the job. Willy had been our caddie for years and is smarter than most and better than any. I took the position at the range and hired Willy to volunteer. Each time I, or Willy, saw a youngster that had the swing we thought was needed I would notify Hank and he would do the background check. And trust me when I say Hank can do a background check. Ed, we know more about you than you do. Hope you are okay with that."

Another pause, and Ben continued, "Ed you were the first one that made the cut. Ever since you checked out as first class all this has been planned. Only Julia, the Finegolds and Harriet's driver were not into the project. They have been checked out and can work with us. And of course Julia is in the place she should be in right now and I, in particular, want her to be here with us."

An even longer pause. Then Julia broke the tension. "Grandpa, does Ed meet your approval?"

"Yes little one. You will have to make up your own mind about him but Hank and I approve. And that's enough for now. Stay for dinner Ed," and Ben stood up and excused himself.

There was another pause in the conversation. Then Ed took the lead. "This doesn't bother me in the least. In fact I like what has happened. It puts me in a comfortable place. They know all about me and all I have to do is hit a little white ball around a green garden and into a hole using clubs I feel at one with. Such a simple task. Let me tell you what your Grandfather, Hank and Willy already know and after I am done it will be your turn."

Chapter 14

Ed had moved his chair to sit directly in front of Julia. He looked at her for a moment and held his breath. She was the most beautiful girl he had ever been this close to, at least one of his age group. His mother had been a beautiful woman and what had been more important a beautiful person. What he wanted to find out now about Julia was if she is also a beautiful person. He thought so but this was what he had to find out before he made what he considered would be a life long commitment.

Julia could see Ed was in a deep thought about something and was enjoying his appreciative gaze. She started to say something then thought the better of it and waited.

"About me," Ed finally began his story. He told Julia about his father's marriage to his Vietnamese mother causing his devout Catholic parents to disown him, and that he seldom had contact with his grandparents. His mother had been a war orphan and had no relatives. It had left his family pretty much alone as far as relatives were concerned. Both his father and mother were intelligent, ambitious and scholars. Both had become college professors by the time he was born and were teaching at UCLA. His mother had achieved a PhD in international studies, spoke five languages and was constantly in demand as a consultant by the U.S. Government. She was also a beautiful woman in both looks and being. Likewise his father, with his PhD in Mathematics, had a presence that matched his mothers. Ed had to stop for a moment as he knew he had to tell Julia what happened to them next and he knew he would not be able to hold back the tears.

Julia sensed something was causing a problem for Ed so she reached out and took his hands. "Take your time. Tell me about your childhood, grammar school and high school. Just the good things, the fun things."

That was what Ed needed so he started with his childhood which had been good. So good he had taken it for granted that it was nothing special until later when he realized how good it had been. How both his parents had been there whenever they needed to be with support and guidance. That they had provided him with every opportunity to learn and enjoy what was available and needed. He wasn't spoiled and was carefully taught he needed to earn what he accomplished. Golf came along after he discovered he didn't like team sports. He was an excellent athlete but did not care for competition against his peers, either in a team or as an individual. Competition to himself as against a golf course made golf his choice. By the time he graduated from high school he was good enough to be recruited by half a dozen colleges and he chose Stanford.

Ed had to pause again and then he told her of the car accident that had taken his parents from from him and almost destroyed his life. A life he just now thought was worth living again. He couldn't hold back the tears and Julia moved in close and held him in a tight embrace. Tears came for her too as she felt his pain and thought of her mother, and grandmother, that she would have to tell him about soon.

Ben had come out on the veranda, saw what was going on and was sure he knew what part of Ed's story had just been told. He also knew Julia's story, which was also his, would become part of this mutual love story. He was ready to start preparing dinner and wanted the two of them to be in the kitchen with him but that could wait. He retraced his steps and went back into the house.

They held each other as the tears subsided and then Julia pulled back and looked into Ed's eyes. "That is enough for now. You can tell me about the last ten years later. I know what I need to know for now and I will tell you my story later. Ben will want us in the kitchen as he prepares dinner. Cooking is another of his talents and he will want to show you his skills. He is a kind man and a good man. He is all what is left of my family, along with Hank and Willy, and I will explain that to you when the time is right."

She kissed him again. It was a long and passionate kiss and it lifted Ed's spirit such that a smile came to his tear streaked face. They rose together and headed for the kitchen with arms around each others waists.

Chapter 15

Ben was at the six burner gas range and was stirring a sauce on low heat. Scattered about the counter top were a variety of small glass dishes with herbs, chopped scallions, salt and pepper, lemon peal, and the like. He was wearing a white apron and when they entered he stepped over to a rack and quickly doffed a chef's hat. Julia started to giggle as Ben took a formal bow.

Ed joined in with, "This kitchen could compete with Pedro's Gringo Cafe's. In fact is that Pedro?" pointing at Ben. Julia couldn't stop her laughter and Ben joined in and then added, "You may not believe this but Pedro and I are on a first name basis." There was more laughter as the joke was on all three of them.

Ed looked at Julia and came out with, "You have been there before. You and Pedro played a game with me." Julia came around the cooking island and kissed him on the cheek. "You have a lot to learn about me, and women. I like that."

"Set the table," was directed by Ben then, "Ed, could you fill the water glasses." Julia was off to the dining room and Ed went to the counter and picking up the first glass knew he was handling fine crystal. He set it back down and picked up a heavier pitcher and filled it from the refrigerator spigot and then in turn to the glasses.

He couldn't see Ben's expression but it was nod toward him of approval.

Then things went very fast. The veal cutlets were browned in butter in a skillet while Ben took the sauce he had been preparing off the low heat. On three plates small new potatoes appeared with sauteed asparagus spears. The cutlets were plated and the sauce poured over them. Julia had returned and removed three salad plates from the refrigerator cool box and set them on the counter, quickly spreading small croutons and grating Parmesan cheese. A little salt was added as was ground pepper and it was off to the table. Ben carried the three plates, two in one hand and one in the other, and the table was set. There was a basket with a small baguette neatly sliced. Ed watched all this in disbelief.

Dinner tasted better than it looked, and it looked perfect. The table talk was brief and enjoyable. Ed was made to feel that he was family and by the end of meal he realized how much he had missed that feeling. He knew he dared not express his appreciation to Ben for what he had just given him. He had all but drained himself of emotion and was afraid he would have no way to control it if more came up.

Julia quickly cleared the table and came back with small crystal dishes filled with coconut ice cream and two small cookies tucked neatly on the edge. It was a perfect finish to a fine meal. Ed was able to get out a coherent sentence on how good it was. He almost mentioned what a good cook his mother had been and then thought better of it.

As if some clairvoyance had communicated around the table, Julia suddenly excused herself and left the room.

Ben's demeanor turned to sadness and he looked at Ed a gave him a weak smile.

"She will be okay. A dinner like this reminds her of the one's my wife and I would put on before our daughter, Julia's mother, died. My wife passed away less than a year later. That was five years ago and it might as well been last week as far as the hurt is concerned. You know all about that so I need not say any more. You were just telling Julia about your parents when I first came out to tell you I was ready to fix dinner. I came back and waited until I could see you getting it back together."

"Ben, you are some kind of man and father. That I could ever equal that would be as great a gift as meeting you and Julia has been. I will try to live up to the honor." Ed had to stop there as his control was starting to wane.

"I will tell you a story. Julia has heard it many times. It is how I met her grandmother. I was on a graduate program in the mid nineteen fifties at the Sorbonne in Paris. It was fall and just getting a bit chilly. I was staying in a small apartment just off Rue du Champs de Mars in the Rue Cler district and in early afternoon one day stopped in a boulangerie, a bakery, to buy a baguette. At the counter was a staggeringly good looking french girl and like the idiot I was at the time I asked her if she would like to share it with me. I had some cheese, just purchased, and a small bottle of wine in a sack. There were three tables out side with a few chairs scattered about, none occupied. Miss Natalia looked over to the lady at the cash register and they quipped in French something like 'He's an idiot American, why not.' She smiled, I smiled and we spent the next hour, nearly freezing, in deep conversation. I asked her to dinner for the next evening and we married the day after. Or at least had some kind of French certificate to that effect."

Ben was smiling again and Ed sat still, enjoying the well told tale but not knowing what to say.

Julia returned with a happy look and clear eyes. Ed fell deeper into where he was going.

Chapter 16

"Would you like to have a cup of coffee?" Ben offered. Julia, who was still standing next to the table, answered for both herself and Ed and rushed off to the kitchen. "We will be in the den," was said to her back. Both Ben and Ed watched her disappear around the corner into the kitchen.

"She is a beautiful girl, or woman I should say, just like her mother and grandmother were," Ben said in a low voice. "Ed, I have been blessed by having three extraordinary women in my life. Not only beautiful in presence but beautiful in person. My wife and daughter were taken much to early in life by cancer and I am now left with Julia. I am sure you can relate to how important she is to me. She has her life to live. I respect that and try not interfere, but I didn't interfere with her mother the one time when I should have. And even there I cannot judge myself wrong as Julia was the result of her choice of a husband."

The grandfather and prospective grandson-in-law sat quietly. Each understanding, and acknowledging, what had just been said. It was Ed's turn to respond.

"Ben, just this morning, just before you all arrived for the demo, Willy took me aside and I quote you what he said. 'Don't you ever do anything to hurt that girl. You understand what I am telling you.' I understood clearly and gave him my word that I would never do anything to hurt her. I give you the same promise. Never. Never."

Ben's "Thank you" was interrupted by Julia's call that coffees were in the den.

It was a comfortable space. The big desk and book cases still left room for a small table surrounded by three comfortable leather chairs. Probably not the right description Ed thought but cozy came to mind. The coffee was excellent. He looked at Ben, then towards Julia and then around the room. He wasn't sure he belonged here but he could only think there was no where else he would want to be. He had just realized that he hadn't felt safe since his parent's accident. That was what had been missing in his life since that awful day. Being alone and afraid was no way to live. He now had the chance to make the change and with these two, and their group of friends, it would be possible.

"What deep thoughts you must be having Ed," Julia posed with a smile and waving gesture to get his attention.

He smiled at her and offered a guarded response. "I was thinking. Not sure I should share it with you but in essence it is that I feel at home here and you may have trouble getting me to leave."

"That's a good answer Ed and you are welcome to stay," Ben said a bit quickly then added, "Maybe not tonight, or tomorrow, but at some time in the future."

Julia flushed but made no response and actually thought she wanted him to stay tonight. Wanted him in her bed and to sleep with her. She managed to hide this from Ed but Ben could read her thoughts.

There was a silence and the coffee was finished. Ed realized that it was time for him to go so he started to make his good nights and stumbled on the words. "I should be going. I have a big day with Willy tomorrow. We have to figure out how to utilize these clubs on a course." Then to Julia, "Can you help out? There will be a lot of note taking and I am not sure either Willy or I can keep it all straight."

Julia was disappointed that Ed was about to leave and Ben was relieved. Ed stood up, as did Julia, but Ben remained seated. He accepted Ed's handshake and said he would remain here for a bit and would stop by the range tomorrow before noon to see how things were going. Julia took Ed's hand and they headed for the hall way. Once there Ed started looking at the photos on the wall and Julia didn't rush him.

"Is this your mother with Ben?" Looking at a beautiful lady standing next to Ben in semi-formal wear. Julia smiled and gave Ed's hand a squeeze.

"That is my grandmother. Pretty, isn't she?"

"Beautiful, You look just like her. Amazing, just like her." Ed was looking at Julia intently. He didn't want to move. He wanted to stay here in the house with her. The thought of going back to his apartment filled him with despair.

Julia leaned into him and they kissed. There were no doubts left. None for either of them. It wouldn't be tonight but it was going to be soon and they both knew that it was going to happen.

"I will be there in the morning and the next morning. Be there for me," Julia said as she opened the door and Ed stepped out into the evening coolness of the desert.

Chapter 17

As Ed walked back to his apartment the day's events went through his mind as if trying to re-member a dream. The demonstration had gone well. He had done his part and all his golf shots had been remarkable. The confidence he had even surprised him. This was the key for his future in golf at this level. He could look forward to tomorrow.

The luncheon was nice. To see this small group interact was something he could also look back on with pleasure. Each could gain from the success of bringing Morris's clubs to life. It wasn't just the golfing but the memories of Morris and Maureen that were important. Again he wanted to be a part of this and have it be a success.

As he made his way along El Paseo, two young women walked past him, slowed and turned to face him. They were good looking, dressed and made up to make the rounds of the Palm Desert bar scene. Unfortunately for them there wasn't much of a bar scene along El Paseo. One smiled and asked him where they should go to find a good time and would he like to join them. He politely declined and they looked disappointed. As they turned about one said to the other "All the good looking guys around here are either married or gay. Let's head for Palm

Springs. There nothing going on here."

Ed smiled at that. "Good luck in Palm Springs," he whispered to himself.

Then Julia came back in full focus. She was now totally dominating his thoughts. Her visit to his apartment was as it should have been and he thought it had gone well. Dinner and his time with her and Ben would be a memory that should last forever. He had already decided that she had to be his future wife. Ben's story of finding his wife in Paris and marrying her three days later was not lost on him. He didn't know the story about Julia's father yet but was sure he would know soon. As Ben had alluded, he had done his part to conceive Julia so he must have some good qualities.

Julia looked just like her grandmother in the photograph and Ed had no doubt her mother looked the same and passed those looks along to her. Tall, slender, blonde with a perfect complexion and blue eyes that could melt your heart. Add to that from what he had seen and felt was a feminine and athletic body so desirable he was starting to have trouble keeping his desires hidden. All that was nice but it was her demeanor and personality that suited him so perfectly. He knew they would also become best friends.

He could wait but he thought that Ben was almost encouraging them to couple. The suggestion of an invitation to live in his house, and by inference with Julia, was an interesting one to contemplate. There was much going on in his life right now that he did not fully understand but he knew he had to chase the dream as far and as best he could.

As he entered his apartment and turned on the

lights the sense of all that was so good in his life seemed to disappear and he retreated out to the landing in front of his doorway. Life was going on below and all around him. Other peoples lives who he had no interest in. The sky above was full of stars. It was a clear night and the skies sparkled. He saw the lights of an airplane taking off from Palm Springs Airport headed somewhere, no doubt full of passengers living their lives. He wanted to be living his life with Julia. He didn't care where, or what they were doing, just to be with her.

The next morning as he carried the big bag, with the 27 clubs weighing twice as much as his usual carry bag, through the driving range portal the first person he saw was Julia. Nothing had changed. The desire for her to be with him last night, even in his humble apartment, had been almost more than he could bear. The smile he craved to see so badly was now his again. The greeting was not just a "Hi" but a hug and a kiss. His day had started and he suddenly felt ready to be the best he could be.

Chapter 18

"You better be ready. Willy has been here an hour and has things ready to go. What, I have no idea," were Julia's first words as they walked toward the teeing area that now seemed to have become their private turf. Willy had set up a small table that had a golf club lie and loft gauge, two clip boards, four or five Sharpie pens and assorted other small items.

"Good morning, my man, and it is a good morning," was Willy's greeting and his smile said he was more than ready get started. "Set that bag next to the table. Get me the three 7-Irons and take one of what looks like a 5-Iron and warm up. Take your time. Do some stretches just like before the first tee at a golf course. Julia, I need your help."

Ed thought, "Okay, I now know who is the boss. At least for now and it is as it should be. I can handle a set of regular clubs but not this bunch," and he did as he was told. He was only a few feet away, starting his stretches, when Willy gave Julia her first instructions and explained what was on the clip board he had just handed her. "Listen up Ed as you will need to understand this too. But keep up your routine." That wasn't going to work so he joined them.

Willy started by telling Ed and Julia that Hank and

67

Ben knew a lot more about Morris's clubs than they had let be known. Morris never would let them hit any balls with them. Not even swing one. But on the technical side he had explained what he was up too in great detail. It was a simple concept. Let one club be slightly altered in lie, loft, weight, open or shut, shaft length, flex and grip size into the design to result in three clubs with about the same loft that could naturally give you three different shot shapes and distance. Creating a set of four in three club combinations would give you twelve clubs that could cover all the needs of iron play. Pitching, chipping and sand wedges would only require one each. The drivers and fairway metal woods would likewise develop in three styles. The 7-Iron set was the first one made. Morris was so sure of his design after that he made the rest which were now all in the big bag.

"We are now going to find out what he did and how we can use the clubs on a course. Narrowing it down to the 14 clubs allowed will take some figuring. Clubs for the course will be our guiding motto. This going to be fun." Willy was almost jumping up and down with enthusiasm.

Ed let it be known that he didn't want to miss out on any of this and told Willy he wanted to go through the 7-Irons with him and Julia. The clip board Julia was holding had boxes with rows for 3S, 3F and 3D at the top with columns LOFT, LIE, WT, OPEN, SHUT, SHFTL and GRIP. The next nine rows were made up for three rows each for 5, 7 and 9-Irons with each having a S, F, or D. This meant 12 clubs and 84 measurement sets.

They started with the 7-Irons. 7S, for straight, was the first to be measured. It turned out to have almost the standard loft of 35 degrees and lie of 63 degrees. The shaft length of 37 inches was one half inches longer than standard. Neither open or shut and a standard grip but with a reminder bead aligning the club head to neutral. It was what came next that explained what was to make the same lofted club play so different. 7F had the loft and lie both half degree greater, the shaft at 36 and 3/4 inches, open by the reminder grip positioning opening the club face at address.

"That is what promotes the natural fade and the higher trajectory," was Willy's first comment. That was followed by, "The reminder grip design is so subtle the increase of ½ degree lie you would hardly notice the difference in the club at address." He looked at Ed for a comment.

"I never even felt the reminder and the clubs at address looked exactly the same. Unless you were looking for it, a half degree open wouldn't register. I bet the face grooves are the next design point that makes a difference. I did notice that each of the three 7-Irons have a slight difference in groves." Ed was now as excited about the subtlety of the club design as were Willy and Julia.

It took two hours to go through the twelve clubs as not only the measurements were taken and logged, each was visually examined and handled. Both Willy and Julia came to the same conclusion, neither could ever play decent golf with these clubs. For Ed they felt perfect and his confidence in hitting good shots was such that he was beginning to think that the clubs were in control of his swing.

It was at that moment Ben walked up to join the merry group. He already knew what they had just discovered and understood their excitement. He let them explain in detail everything they had just learned and showed, at least to them, his undivided interest.

He then turned to Julia and quietly said "I have to go to Far Hills, New Jersey and won't be back until Friday. You can take care of things at the house. You are okay with this, aren't you?"

They walked back toward the range entrance together. "Yes Grandpa, I can take of things. Far Hills is the USGA headquarters, is it not?" Julia answered while looking back towards Ed.

"You never miss anything. Just like your grandmother. Also it is time for you and Ed to have some time alone together and my house would be a good place to spend it. He is a good man, Julia. Don't be afraid, just be careful."

Ben kissed his granddaughter on the check and waved to Ed and Willy. He didn't mention to Julia he was also seeing a urologist he trusted in New York.

Chapter 19

The afternoon was busy. Almost an assembly line. Ed hitting shot after shot. Willy handing him the clubs and calling out to Julia which one. The shot shape was noted and with a Sharpie the club was marked. They were focusing on distance and Ed took three shots with each club. Willy had placed flag sticks at 10 yard intervals, in several directions, and was accurate in judging the distances where the ball landed and the roll. The line was merely noted if it was more than 10 feet one side or the other. Left or right.

By early afternoon they were finished for the day. Tomorrow they would go through the rest of the clubs which included the drivers, fairway metal-woods and the single pitching thru sand wedges. For those only the lofts could describe the club's performance and Ed would experiment with them to determine where they would fit into his play. The metal woods would be the big treat of the day.

Willy told Ed and Julia he would pick up the area and take the clubs home with him. Ed at first was reluctant at losing control of the clubs then decided carting them back and forth to his apartment was a pain and Willy had his big van just a few steps away.

Ed asked Julia what she would like to do for dinner

and if she would like to go out. He had not overheard her conversation with Ben but Julia knew that it was time and the place was the guest bedroom. Ben had implied this was right by him and it was what she wanted.

"Let's go by your apartment and you can pickup some fresh clothes and your bathing suit. We can then go to Grandpa's, take a swim and relax. Go out if we want too, or eat in. Okay with you?" was her answer which Ed thought to be perfect.

When they entered Ben's house Ed had the feeling that he wasn't there. Why, he didn't know and didn't ask. But he was sure of it.

"I could use a shower before going swimming. Would that be okay? Is there one in the guest room I can use?" Ed asked a bit sheepishly.

"Oh sure," and she guided him into the guest room which was actually another master bedroom.

"This will be great. Just take a few minutes. Shall I meet you in the pool?" Ed asked hoping it would be some where else.

It was a big shower and open to a very large ancillary area with tiled floors and high glass block windows for light. With the shower running full he had just finished soaping up and was starting a rinse when he felt Julia's arms encircling his chest and could feel her body against him. Except for one part of his being he almost couldn't function. He could barely breathe and his pulse rate had skyrocketed. He wanted this, imagined it happening, knew it would happen eventually and now she stood right behind him holding him to her.

She hugged him even tighter for a moment, then loosened her arms and he slowly turned around to face

72

her. She released him and stepped back. "My God, you are so beautiful," Ed whispered looking at her body in appreciation of something he could only dreamed he might ever see. He then took her in his arms and kissed her lips, then her cheeks, neck, to her shoulders and down further.

Julia held his head and then brought him back up to her and whispered "It is time Ed. It is time for us. For me. Ben will be gone for two days. He knows we are here. It is time for us to make love. Make love to me Ed. Make love to me now."

At 8:30 am the next morning Ed and Julia were walking up to meet with Willy for the days experiments. The night before and this morning had been so good for them both that they vowed not to let anything ever come between them. Before breakfast, still in bed, neither could stop smiling. Just a look brought on laughter and touching. Anywhere would do. Just a single touch was needed which would lead to more. Life could not be any better for two people who were so ready for each other.

Willy knew when he first saw them coming up the walkway to the practice area that it had happened last night. Ben had told him it would and that he wanted them to be lovers. He was hoping it would turn out to be true love for them both. He needed someone to care for Julia and he was sure Ed was the right man. Willy knew the real reason for Ben's trip to New York and it didn't have any thing to do with golf. He wiped away the tears that had run down his cheeks, sucked in his belly and called out a cheerful sounding welcome to the happy couple.

Chapter 20

There were 6 iron clubs in the bag with the lofts of wedges. It was a strange assortment and none really matched the numbered clubs tested yesterday. Willy started with, "What do think, my man. I don't know where we should start."

Julia started laughing at the sight of the two men staring at the weird clubs seemingly to be lost as to what to do. She reached over, pulled one from the bag and handed it to Ed. "Go hit a golf ball and see where it goes."

"That seems like a very good idea. I will do just that!" Ed said as he looked at Julia in such away that anyone paying attention would have known he would do whatever she asked. He did some simple stretches and then gripped the club and took a few gentle swings back and forth. It was an ugly club, looking heavy with an odd shaped sole. The face was almost normal but the groves were not parallel, or even. Still, it felt good in his hands.

He pulled a ball over and made his address. As part of his routine he then stepped back behind the ball and sighted his target. It was a blue flag at 50 yards and he concentrated on the bottom of the flag stick. Returning to his address position he looked once more at his target, then at the ball, made a very small forward press and swung. The clank the ball made as it struck the bottom of the flag stick startled all three of them.

"Well I be damned," Willy almost shouting and then adding, "Did you see that ball flight. It was pure."

Julia joined the chorus and clapped her hands. Ed pulled another ball over and without any more time than for a look at the target he swung again. Two feet from the base of the flag the ball landed and sat dead in its own mark.

"Man oh man! You children I have seen the light," chortled Willy with the appropriate accent. He reached for another club at random and handed it to Ed taking the first one from him. Ed looked at the loft and guessed it to be a little less than the first and picked a red flag target set at 60 yards. A quick look from behind the ball, then address and swing. One yard short directly in front of the flag stick with spin that returned the ball 15 feet.

"My God, what are these things," was Ed's reaction. He had never, with no real thought, been able to hit a wedge like that. The feel of the club, the feedback so strong and correct, the ball flight and it how landed. Never in his life had he had such an experience with a golf club.

They had six clubs to test and get familiar with, each different but all rather strange looking. It took the better part of the day to test each one. In the practice sand trap, which was in pretty rough shape, the sand flew and the golf balls seemed to float to their targets. It seemed it made no difference which club was in play, or where it was played from, Ed hit one perfect shot after another.

Julia couldn't believe what she was seeing. "This must be illegal or magic. One or the other, or both." She tried to hit a modest pitch with one of the clubs and it squirted off the club like it had been a shank. Willy had no

75

better luck. He tried three different clubs and was not able to make one good strike. "They are your clubs Ed, nobody else will be able to use them. How are we going to start a golf club company if the only person in the world that can use the damn things is you," was said only part in jest.

That would be enough for the day. Tomorrow they would work on the drivers and 5 metal-woods and then they would start the task of filling the bag with the 14 club limit. They would use the Tamarisk Country Club's course as the first objective.

Organizing their things they packed them and the big bag of clubs in Willy's van. Julia asked him if he like to go for a beer or soft drinks and some happy hour snacks but he declined saying he had some things that needing doing at home.

As Ed and Julia started their walk back towards Ben's he asked her if she wanted get a snack along the way. She smiled and answered, "I would rather take a swim in the pool."

Chapter 21

The next day with the drivers and 5 metal woods went just as the before with the irons. Ed was almost beside himself with the way his shot making was developing. It seemed he couldn't hit a bad shot. He knew one should never think this way but for now he would ignore that bit of wisdom. The distances were longer than he had ever achieved, the accuracy even better. Each club had a built in straight, fade or draw with beautiful ball flights. He was ready to start with Willy and Julia figuring out how to match up clubs to courses. Weather conditions could wait until later but would also play a part in the selection decisions.

The swim in the pool never happened but Ed didn't particularly like swimming anyway. It seemed so comfortable for the both of them, so evenly matched in their desires. Then the telephone rang and Julia rolled over on his chest and answered. After saying hello she immediately sat up and pulled the sheet to cover herself.

"Hi Grandpa, are you alright?"

Ed could hear Ben's voice clearly. "I'm fine, sweet stuff. Is Ed with you?"

Julia was surprised by the question and looked at Ed. He whispered, "Say yes. He will understand."

"Yes, Grandpa. I am in love. Don't laugh at me."

"I will never laugh at you. And I am happy you are happy. That is what life is about. Achieving happiness," Ben responded without hesitation.

There was a pause and both Julia and Ed knew the reason for the call was coming next and might not be so cheerful.

"I will be here a couple of extra days. You might as well know why and don't you worry about it. It was expected and even anticipated. I came back here to visit an old friend who is still a practicing urologist. My prostate is acting up again and I may have to have some surgery in the next few months. Again, it was expected that this may happen and the planning to take care of it is already underway. I will have a biopsy procedure done tomorrow and my doctor friend thinks I will need two days rest before flying back."

"Oh no Grandpa. Don't let it happen. I mean . . . I mean, I don't know what I mean."

"Julia, I am okay. I will be playing the demo game at Tamarisk next week. Willy tells me progress is such that in the next few days the clubs will be sorted out for the course and you three may go out and do some practice and walk the course. I miss being there to watch what Ed is up to." Ben was good at the messaging. Julia was satisfied and starting to relax, but Ed had his doubts that all was being revealed.

"I will call you tomorrow evening to give you my flight plans. Probably be Saturday or Sunday. Should be ready to play some serious golf by the middle of next week. Now I don't know where you two are at this hour, but try to spend a little time together."

"Grandpa, you know all so don't try to smooth talk

me," and the laughter had come back and her eyes almost sparkled, but not quite. Ed watched her as the good nights were exchanged. Julia then rolled over towards him and the sheet fell away. She then said something he would always remember. "It is a lot more serious than he told us," and she started to cry.

Ed didn't want to move or say anything that would cause her more sadness. He reached out gently touching her cheek, carefully wiping away a few of her tears. She looked at him and in her eyes he could see the thoughts forming. Then she said "I am so glad you are here with me. I need you to be with me. Grandpa is the only person I have left for a family. I need you to become part of my family so I can go on living if anything takes him away from me." And tears came back in earnest.

Ed pulled the sheet up and wrapped it around her shoulders. There was a guest robe in the closet, he crossed the room and put it on. Coming back to Julia he picked her up and carried her around the house, the ends of the sheet trailing behind. She nestled her head into his chest and quietly sobbed for a while longer as he carried her about her home. The sobbing finally stopped and she reached for his face and pulled his toward her. It was barely a smile but it was a smile.

"Thank you Ed Adams. I love you." and she kissed him softly.

"Julia, you have to believe what he said. What little I have read about prostate cancer cases most have cures and treatments if caught in time. Years more of life, a good life, can be expected. Let us plan on that for him and his being around for a long time to come."

"Carry me back to my bedroom and I will put on

some clothes, you can get dressed, and I will fix us something for dinner. After that we will take a walk outside and come back here and start our night together over again."

Chapter 22

Julia fixed a good meal from the refrigerator left overs and it was decided they would go to the ice cream shop for desert. A double scoop of pecan on top of coffee on a sugar cone was shared as they walked along El Paseo and were just returning to Ben's house as the sun set. It had been a nice walk and Julia's spirits had been lifted.

"Let's go sit by the pool and enjoy the nice evening." Julia suggested and with Ed in tow she got them seated. The evening chill was a few hours away and the cushioned deck chairs were comfortable. They sat side by side holding hands.

"You still owe me your life story. Would now be a good time to tell it to me?" Ed asked, unsure if it was a good time but hoped it would help her to talk about herself rather be thinking about others.

Julia looked at Ed and gave him a smile. "You remind me a little of Grandpa. Don't take that the wrong way. Just that he always seems to know when someone needs some help and knows what to say or do. So yes, I will bare myself to you," which was followed with some laughter.

She started with having a good childhood here in Palm Desert. She never knew her father, Peter Renquest. Her mother kept the surname, rather than use her maiden last name of Shea, after the official annulment. Janice Renquest apparently had sounded better to her. Julia was one year old when Carl Renquest decided male companions were more appealing to him than a woman with a child. He moved to San Francisco first and a year later disappeared. Ben had tried to find out what had become of him but never found a trace.

Julia continued with how her mother had met her father here in Palm Desert when she had joined her parents on their two week vacation which had coincided with her college's spring break. It resulted in a quick engagement and marriage. Julia blushed, and added that she had arrived a few months early.

Carl Renquest had been a high school advanced math teacher, was good looking, friendly and likable. Her parents, even while troubled with the events, looked kindly on the marriage and Julia's birth. A year later they would be supporting their daughter and granddaughter for a number of years while she grew up here in Palm Desert.

Her mother, with Julia twelve at the time, moved in with her parents into this house when Ben retired and they moved here. Her grandfather would become her surrogate father.

She went through the school system with a number of both scholastic and athletic honors. She was senior class president and one of the top high school golfers in the state her senior year. It had been a good life. She had friends and the boys chased her for dates but she never found any of them likable. All they seemed to be interested was sex and it was never given to them. They stopped bothering her in her last year of high school and she seldom dated.

She had been offered several golf scholarships and choose the relatively small college of Pamona just over the mountains. Her mother got sickly in 1985 and died of beast cancer in1988 after a long and brutal battle with the disease. It was terrible for her grandparents and then her grandmother died from the same disease a year later.

Julia eyes started to tear up and Ed moved to sit next to her on the arm of the chair and she snuggled up to him and the tears came again. He was amazed that their lives had so many parallels. The loss of parents is hard at any age, but Ed thought for young adults it was especially hard.

"Ed, take me to bed and hold me until I fall asleep. I promise I will be better company in the morning," Julia whispered.

He picked her up, liking to hold her in that manor, and carried her to the guest room. She slipped out of her clothes and into a night gown. Once in his briefs and a T-shirt he slid in next to her and his arms went around her in a comfortable embrace. She soon fell asleep and an hour later sleep came for him. They woke in the same position. Ed was first which gave him the chance to watch her as she slept. The sight of her face and the rhythmic breathing he could not only see but feel against him brought a sense of closeness that overwhelmed him. She slowly opened her eyes, looked directly at him, and smiled.

There was some contact between the sheets but just with hands and lips. It was a new day and they had some work to do. Breakfast of dry cereal and fruit with a glass of orange juice was enough and they walked to the College Golf Center. Willy was there and wished them a good morning. He looked tired and somewhat sad.

"You had a call from my grandpa last night, didn't you?" Julia demanded.

"Yes I did. He should be back on Saturday and says he will be ready for our game at Tamarisk midweek. You know what's going on?" said Willy almost in tears.

"We think he will be okay, Willy. He has to be. I won't think otherwise," Julia got out before she started to tear up.

"You probably don't know this but your grandpa saved my life. I was your age Julia, and a lost soul more lost than I was couldn't never have been. I had no family, no friends, no job and no future. I was sitting right over there on the cement where I had spent the night when he came by. He ask me to shag a few balls for him. It was a Sunday and the range was closed. Sent me out to about the 150 yard flag and told me when he waved to pick up the balls and bring them back in. He spent three hours hitting balls to different targets and then called me in the last time. Took me to lunch for a hamburger, fries and a coke. We ate together and talked."

Willy had to stop for a minute to compose himself. "He then ask me to caddie for him the next day. He and his friend Hank had a game going and he didn't want to carry his own clubs. You know Hank. He needed a new man to drive his Lincoln and do chores as the last guy had just quit. Man what a job that was. The two of them taught me how to play golf. I got pretty good and started making some money on the side teaching black kids to play. I married a good woman who works full time and we raise foster kids. It's been a good life. I want Ben and Hank to hang around. They are my best friends."

Willy rubbed his eyes, took a deep breath and

announced, "It is time to plan how we are going to use these damn clubs!"

The golf museum had a small meeting room with a big conference table that Willy had gotten the okay to use for the morning. He had already placed some sheets of letter size paper around the edge of the table, 9 on each side, 18 in all. Each had a line drawing of a golf hole with a few details depicting bunkers, traps and water hazards. He had the Tamarisk yardage book which had similar drawings showing yardages from various locations to the center of the greens.

"I drew these up last night and the three of us can start by plotting shots using the stats we have on Ed's shots with the Morris clubs. What do think?" Willy finished with his question.

"I think that is a great idea," was Julia's immediate response.

"I like it too. Nice drawings, Willy. We can plot the course and when we play it see how good we are at the club selections. Then repeat it for any course we play," Ed said this and was smiling at Willy. He was reminded of Ben telling him to never underestimate him.

They pulled up three chairs in front of "Hole 1-Tamarisk CC."

Chapter 23

Willy sat in the middle seat with Julia to his left and Ed to his right. "Hole 1 is a short par 5 of 478 yards. Almost straight with a slight bend to the right. A good drive just right of center of 280 to 290 leaves a doable 198 to 188 yards to the green. Big bunker mid-green on right and another left front. Should be an easy birdie or maybe an eagle." Willy ran through what showed in the yardage book and as he did this pointed to the highlights on his drawing.

They huddled close together and Ed suggested the straight driver and the draw 5 iron for the second. Willy thought that would be a long 5 but the draw would bring the ball in on the right path. It would need some roll if the pin was in the back portion of the green. Julia jotted the club selections on the paper and they looked at Hole 2.

"Hole 2 is a par 3 at 170 yards. A bunker on the right front and water short to the left. Difficulties on the green so pin location is important," was Willy's description and Ed promptly said 7 iron straight or 5 iron fade. Julia made the notations.

It was then on to Hole 3, the number one handicap hole on the course. "It is a long par 4 at 442 yards. Fairway bunkers both right and left and a large green protected by bunkers," was Willy's summary. Ed said straight driver and 5 iron draw if the pin was all the way back or 5 iron straight if nearer the front.

The rest of the morning they kept up this protocol until all 18 holes had been marked up. The first club chosen was the straight driver. There was only one real dogleg hole and a good drive would take care of that. Ed was inclined to put all three 7-irons in the bag, straight and draw 5-irons, straight 3-iron, straight and fade 9-irons, straight 5-metal wood, 3 wedges yet to be determined and his trusty putter. 14 clubs in all. They would be marked with red Sharpie on the back of the heads except for the two metal woods. Identification of the wedges would be by use and they would decide on that later.

It was time for lunch and the three headed for the California Pizza Kitchen and ordered a large pizza and soft drinks. The conversation was good and Ed was coming to realize how much he liked Willy. They could be brothers had Willy not been 4 inches taller and 60 pound heavier. And also black. But they were becoming good friends which was good enough for both of them. Julia like seeing this happen. Both men needed friends and other than her grandfather, these were the two most important people in her life.

Willy suggested they take the weekend off. They could go over to Tamarisk and practice wedge shots and do some putting on Monday when the course was closed to play. Maybe even walk the course and take notes. They were planning to play with the pro on Tuesday but Wednesday might be a better choice for Ben. The schedule was approved and Willy took off for home with all the equipment and Julia and Ed headed for Ben's house.

Entering the house there was a moment of awkwardness between them. They both knew what they wanted to do right then but it was just after two in the afternoon and neither spoke the words. Ed looked at Julia and smiled. She took his hand and a minute later they were on the guest room bed with the clothes they had been wearing scattered on the floor. Ed was almost beside himself having this beautiful woman his soul mate. His only thought was to never let anything happen between them that would spoil their relationship.

At five Julia suggested a shower together then order take out Chinese, come back here and have dinner by the pool. The shower was better than could be believed and the Chinese take out was good enough.

Chapter 24

They sat opposite each other with the Chinese dinner between them on one of the small pool side tables. The large single dinner serving had been chosen. They each had a fork and it soon became obvious that it would be more than enough. The sun had dropped below the mountains and the colors of dusk surrounded them. It was very pleasant and they had a weekend to plan. Golf was to be put aside for a short while.

Julia then asked Ed, "Why don't you bring some of your clothes and personal items over to the house and we will make the guest room our bedroom."

"Ben, Grandpa, will be okay with this? I know he implied it but do you think he really meant what he said?" Ed asked, already knowing the answer.

"Of course he does! He will and it is what he wants for me. He never says anything he doesn't mean. I won't question how we met because it just happened and wasn't planned. But he knew all about you before. I think he is happy about how it has turned out. So am I. You do know that!" Julia saying this with such conviction that Ed had no question about making the move.

"We, or I guess it should be I, will do it tomorrow morning first thing. Almost first thing that is," Ed got out before he could hide his smile and starting to laugh.

Ed had been thinking it might be fun to take the Porsche for a drive tomorrow and was about to suggest that when the telephone rang.

Julia quickly picked up the pool phone. It was Ben and Julia's "Grandpa, how are you? When does your plane land?" were asked almost before he could say his hello.

"I am fine. The biopsy went well and nothing was found that wasn't expected. My friend, the urologist, gave me a second opinion and that my doctor in Palm Springs is correctly handling my case. That it should be pretty much a routine surgery and it is not needed to be done immediately. In the next thirty to sixty days would be okay. That's a relief. I am a little sore in a place we don't have to talk about. I am flying back Sunday evening, arriving 10:30. Willy will pick me up."

"We can come get you. Grandpa, I just said we. Oh my, has my life changed," Julia said not knowing whether to laugh or cry.

"That's my girl. Let Willy come up. I talked to him an hour ago and he told me you all were taking the weekend off. Why don't you and Ed take a trip in that funny little car of his. La Jolla would be a fun overnight," Ben offered making Ed think he could read his mind over the telephone.

"I will ask Ed next time I see him," Julia shot back looking at Ed.

"See you two Monday morning unless I wake you Sunday night. Love you Julia. Bye," and the connection was broken.

Julia jumped into Ed's lap and began kissing him with a joyful enthusiasm.

"I think I am in the mood to share an ice cream

cone. Maybe the scoop of coffee should be on top of the pecan this time. What do you think my best friend?" and she jumped up and pulled Ed out of the chair.

The walk was good, the ice cream perfect and they decided to stop by Ed's apartment to pick up his things. His meager collection of sport clothes went in a duffel bag. Julia found a hanger bag in the closet and unzipped it. It had Ed's "gallery manager" clothes and she whistled when she saw the jacket, slacks and dress shirts with several ties hung around the collars. In the bottom of the bag were his dress shoes.

"Well mister Ed I may be able to take you out in public places other than golf courses, after all. You are going to have to model these for me to make sure you look as good dressed as you do undressed," she said with a sly smile. Then added with a not so sly smile, "Let's stay here for a little while."

They did. Two hours later they walked back to Ben's and Ed hung his sports shirts, pants and shorts in the closet. Then his hanger bag next to them. His tooth brush and electric razor were next to the right side sink in the bathroom. He climbed into bed next to Julia.

"Welcome home," Julia whispered.

"It is good to be home," Ed whispered back.

Chapter 25

At breakfast the next morning Julia and Ed decided the overnight to La Jolla would be a fun trip. They packed a small travel carry bag and put a few things on hangers. By 9 o'clock they were headed west on Highway 74 and the Porsche was making the trip up the curvy mountain road a pleasure. Julia had a permanent smile on her face.

"You are going to let me drive it one of these days, aren't you?" she asked.

Ed was ready for this. "Yes, it will happen but not today and maybe not tomorrow, but sometime soon. I will first have to explain to you my relationship with this car. When you sit behind the wheel and start the engine for the first time you will know that you have gained complete control of my life."

"I can live with that. So I have another challenge. I like challenges," and she reach over and ran her hand up and down his thigh. Ed had to concentrate on his driving as they had an open road and he was driving fast.

They were in La Jolla in about two hours and drove in near the Cove and parked next to the park. They walked along the walkway out to Rocky Point and then back along the shore path to the Cove overlook. It was early enough not to be crowded and they walked slowly holding hands. The views were spectacular as long as you faced the ocean. Looking east was nice if buildings were your thing. To the north was the long beach of La Jolla Shores and you could see the green areas of Torrey Pines Golf Course on the bluffs above.

"This is a beautiful place. Would you like to live here?" Julia asked Ed.

"I am not sure. It is really expensive. There are too many people. You have to drive almost everywhere and the golf courses are crowded and expensive. But then there is the weather. What about you?" Ed countered.

"I can think about it," she answered as she pulled Ed to her and kissed him. Then, "I want to be wherever you are."

They walked about some more and then Ed suggested he should call Harriet and see if they could pay her a short visit. They spotted a public phone and Ed made the call. She answered on the second ring. Ed explained the last minute call and that he and Julia were doing a no planning weekend road trip.

"Where are you, then," Harriet demanded.

"The La Jolla Cove park," Ed answered.

"How much time do you have on the parking meter?" another demand.

" Probably an hour left."

"Get back there and fill it up with quarters. Get yourselves opposite where Cuvier Street comes into Coast Boulevard and Jimmy will pick you up in ten minutes. I will see you in fifteen," and she hung up.

They did as told and fifteen minutes later they had been chauffeured by Jimmy to a nice apartment building and were standing in front a door that was opened by none other than Harriet. A hand shake with Ed and a hug for

Julia.

"Come in, come in. It is so good to see both. You are together. In love. We all knew it was going to happen. Knew it for sure." Harriet was vibrating with good cheer. "We have an hour and a half to spend before you need to get back to that awful meter but that will be just about right. Come over here and sit at the table. Jimmy will fix us a good salad and we can lunch and talk at the same time."

Looking out the big picture window the view of the Park, Cove and the blue Pacific Ocean stretched out in front and below them. It was spectacular from this vantage point.

The conversation immediately went to the Morris golf club project. It had just been six days ago but Harriet wanted to know everything that had happened. Especially how many days it took for Julia and Ed to get together. And she didn't mince words on what she was asking.

Jimmy served up a shrimp salad that would challenge any fine restaurant. A cold white wine and a sliced baguette, with butter on the side, that could have just come fresh from a Paris bakery. They talked about everything that had happened so far after her visit at the demonstration. That the big golf game at the Tamarisk Country Club was to be on Wednesday. Harriet chimed in with, "Don't you worry about Hole 3, just take that driver you got and lay into it right over the fairway traps for an easy approach."

"Okay, I will do that and if I birdie the hole I will tell Willy that Harriet told me do it!" Ed announced.

Then Harriet smiled and looked at them both, one at a time. Then showed a devilish little grin with her blue eyes dancing. "It happened Tuesday night, didn't it?"

Ed sat frozen and Julia broke out laughing. "How can you old people be so smart. You know everything and pretend you don't know anything," and she continued to laugh and was poking Ed in the arm. He suddenly got it and joined in the laughter.

Chapter 26

Ed excused himself and asked Harriet if he could use the bathroom.

"Of course dear boy. Down the hall and first door on the left. Don't you get lost now," was said quickly and she turned back to Julia and took her hands. "What a nice boy you have caught, my dear. Now tell me . . ." was what Ed could hear as he left the room.

The hall was long and both walls were covered with photographs, mostly black and white 8 by 10's, nicely matted and framed. Most were of people but many were of places. All were professional in quality. Ed knew he would have to take a closer look at them after he had done his duties.

When he returned to the table Harriet's greeting was, "You had to stop for a while and look at my history, now didn't you?"

"You have quite a history, don't you. I saw a few presidents and several movie stars. Was that you sitting on Bob Hope's lap with Bing Crosby looking on?" asked Ed in a teasing manner.

"You have a good eye and good taste young man. Julia and I have been talking about you and she has told me everything, even the most personal details. Shame on you for the way you treat her so poorly," she spoke in a serious tone until the laughter came. Her eyes were dancing again, Julia couldn't stop smiling and Ed joined in the teasing.

"You better get going or you will have an expensive ticket on your windshield. Let me point out one photo you must see before you go," and she hustled them into the hallway.

"This one. You see who is there?" pointing at a family group. A couple stood with a baby next to another couple. It took only one look and Ed knew. Julia took a little longer and then reached for Ed and started to cry. They were very attractive people and well dressed. A young mother holding her baby with the father standing by. The other couple were the parents of the baby's mother as there was no doubt as the resemblance was clear. Julia looked exactly like the mother and the grandmother and the older man was a younger Ben Shea. The other man was Julia's father.

Harriet reached out to Julia and took her in her arms. "You have never seen a photo of your father, have you? Take a close look. He was a handsome man and seemed so nice. We all liked him and then he left and never came back. He broke your mother's heart but she never let you know that. I would let you have the photo but you could never let your grandfather see it because it would hurt him too much. So we will just let it stay where it is until the time is right for you to have it."

Harriet hustled them to the door calling Jimmy to get them to the park before the meter flag came up

Julia was still having trouble with what had just happened. They thanked Jimmy and Ed quickly put two more quarters in the parking meter and they had another

30 minutes.

"Walk me around for a while. That was a shock. I wasn't prepared for it. Did I thank Harriet for lunch?" Julia was searching Ed's eyes for an answer.

"Yes, you thanked her and she told me she was sorry to have startled you like that but you would realize later that it was a gift."

They retraced their earlier stroll and found an empty bench and took a seat. The sound of the ocean crashing on the rocks below provided a music that lulled the senses and Julia was feeling better. She liked it here and sat a little closer to Ed and they held hands.

"What's the plan for the rest of today?" Julia asked as if she was asking anyone that was near by.

"We could stay here or drive up to Carlsbad and spend the night. There is a good Mexican restaurant just off the freeway near the ocean," Ed offered but not too enenthusiastically.

Julia squeezed his hand even tighter. "Let's drive up there, then head to Pedro's Gringo Cafe for dinner and sleep in our own bed tonight."

"You know something, you can read my mind."

Chapter 27

They made it to Pedro's by 5 o'clock where they had a good meal and a fun exchange with Pedro. The drive back from La Jolla via Carlsbad had gone quickly and the Porsche made it fun. As they headed back into Palm Desert after dinner the sun had made it down behind the mountains and a soft glow of shadows had settled into the desert landscape. It was a pretty place. Summer was coming, however, and that brought a different look and feel. You had to change your life style then. It became a true desert.

Arriving at the house they decided on a swim, suited up and headed for the pool. The water felt good and Ed thought Julia felt especially good when they made several comfortable contacts. Laying on the chase lounges as they dried off they talked over the day. It had been a good day and a fun drive. Julia spoke of the photograph of her father and mother together. It was the first time she had ever seen what he looked like. It had scared her. When she looked closely she could see just a little hint of him in her look. Just in the eyes. She had been afraid of something that she couldn't understand.

They showered together and slipped into bed. This night they just talked and just before Julia adjusted her position for sleep she told Ed that she was glad she had seen the photograph of her father and mother. That Harriet was right to show it to her and that they should bring her into their lives while there was still time. She snuggled up to Ed and fell asleep. Ed would lay awake for some time.

It was just one week ago this morning he had spotted that small garage sale arrow and turned to follow it to his new life. He was laying next to a woman he could only have dreamed of being with as he was now with Julia. In a few days he may earn a way into a chance to play the game he loved professionally. He must be careful not to make any mistakes with Julia as she was the only part of this dream he couldn't live without.

There was just enough light in the room that he could make out the curve of her hip under the sheet as she laid on her side. As softly as he could he traced the contour with his hand. She stirred and he lifted his hand away and smiled. How could this have happened? Why has it happened? He had no answers and was sure he never would.

The next thing Ed knew was that the beautiful woman he had fallen asleep next to was astride him telling it was time to get the day started. Before he could react she jumped off laughing and headed to the bathroom. He waited and then followed in after her. She was partially dressed and gave him a long look. With an approving smile she said "It will be worth your while to be around here this afternoon, big boy, but this morning we are going to take a run along that trail you like. I want to see if you can keep up with me," and she then pulled on her T-shirt.

The run was good. Ed had done it many times and Julia appeared to know it as well. He was much stronger than she, but she ran in that effortless style of a true athlete and expended much less energy than he did. When they finished he was breathing hard and sweating while she seemed unfazed and cool.

Back to the house it was into the shower and a ritual they had started was continued. Ed thought his life could not get any better than at that moment.

"How about breakfast and then a slow walk around town. See if we can find some kind of excitement in our dull life?" Julia was radiant. Ed had no chance. He knew that she had him at her mercy.

"What ever you ask is my command. Somebody said that but probably didn't mean it," was Ed's offering to the back and forth. Julia gave him a long look and then came to him putting her arms around his neck. "I will never give you a command. Never. I will never do that to you." The kiss she gave him made him believe he could trust her on this for as long as they were together. Forever, he hoped.

The rest of the day slipped by and in late afternoon they drove over to the Whole Foods Market and picked out a rotisserie chicken, added a small potato salad and two ears of sweet corn. Back at the house dinner was served out by the pool and they watched the sun go down. They had met a week ago this day and both felt they had been together for years.

That night they made love slowly and were asleep by 9:00. Ed awoke at 11:30 as he heard Ben coming in the front door. He nudged Julia and whispered "Your grandpa is home."

He came into the room and walked over to the bed. Leaning down he kissed Julia's cheek. She sat up and gave him a hug and said, "Welcome home to a very happy house. I love you Grandpa."

"That's my girl, see you both in the morning," he said with a nod to Ed and left the room.

Chapter 28

The next morning they awakened at the same time. Facing each other they recognized the new day. Ed was first to speak. "That was nice last night when Ben came in to let us know he was home. There wasn't any embarrassment. I wasn't embarrassed, or made to feel that way. Nor were you, or Ben. How could that be?" he asked looking directly into Julia's eyes.

Julia reached out and put her hand on his cheek. "This is where you belong. We belong together. Just one week, or years from now, it will always be this way. It has to be. It is what I want and it is what Grandpa wants for me to have. It is something I never thought could happen but it has. That is all you need to know."

They had slept in night clothes and made no move to change. It was time to start the sequence of events that would mold their future and both knew it was important to get started. It was a quiet house and sound did not carry but the noise of a coffee bean grinder made it through to them. A good morning kiss would do this morning and it was made. Five minutes later they were in the kitchen saying good morning to Ben.

He had the waffle iron heated, the batter ready and the small kitchen table set for three. It looked like a photo in a cook book with orange juice poured, plates set, the butter dish and maple syrup pitcher full. He poured in the batter and closed the lid. Ed experienced the same feeling he had last night when Ben had come into the bedroom. He belonged here. He was expected to be here. He almost thought it wasn't happening. That it couldn't be real.

"You sit here and Julia next to you. I will sit on this side." Ben's voice brought Ed back from his foggy state. And the breakfast was the best he had ever experienced. Ben poured the coffee and the conversation of the day's plan was outlined. Willy would meet Julia and Ed at the course at 9:30. He had the clubs for Ed except his putter. Ben planned to come over around ten, or so, with his and Julia's clubs and they would do some putting and short game practicing. A lite lunch would be prepared especially for them and then in the afternoon Willy and Ed would walk the course, as could Julia if she wanted, but he would come back to the house.

Tuesday the club would be open and Ed and Julia could do some more practicing in the morning and, if they wanted to, have lunch in the club's restaurant. No plans for the afternoon had been made. On Wednesday the big match was to start on the first tee at 10:00 am sharp with two holes empty in front and two holes free behind. Ed and Gary Martin, the club pro, would play from the back tees and walk, Ben and Julia from the middle tees and have a cart. Willy would caddie for Ed and Gary had his own caddie. They would play at scratch, no handicaps.

Ed thought all he had to do was do what he was told and be on time. Just tie his own shoes laces, put his golf glove on, and hit a little white ball in the right direction and to the right distance. How hard could that be. He smiled at the thought but would not share it.

Ed Adams Chases a Dream

Breakfast was so good and pleasant none of them wanted to leave the table. Julia stood, went around and hugged her grandfather from behind. "You do everything so well. How come? Were you born that way or is there some kind of secret one can learn? I bet it is magic and you are a magician," she said with a laugh and headed back to her new bedroom.

Ed glanced at Ben and saw his eyes were watering. "Ben, you knows she is right. You do have the magic touch. You have touched me with it and I thank you." Ed said this as he started to pick up the dishes. Ben rose and did the same but said nothing. In a few minutes the table was cleared and it was then Ben who spoke. "I have meddled in your life Ed. Your meeting Julia was not in the planning. What I want you to know is that if I could have picked a partner for her it would be someone like you. I couldn't be happier with what has happened. The Morris's golf club project is totally different. No matter how it turns out it will have nothing to do with your relationship with Julia. You are welcome here and into my life and home as Julia's choice regardless of how the golfing goes. I can't emphasis that enough. You do understand what I am saying."

Ed was surprised by Ben's candor, especially it coming so early in their relationship. But then again he had an inkling that Ben was preparing for more than just a golfing adventure that had now included Julia. He was pretty sure there was more to Ben's trip to New York than just a needed second opinion on a medical condition from a doctor friend. He let that thought go with a thank you to Ben and how much he cherished his granddaughter.

105

Chapter 29

Driving due west on Frank Sinatra Boulevard they made the right turn into the Tamarisk Country Club and were waved through the entrance gate without so much as a glance. The silver 1959 Porsche had been approved and the occupants didn't matter. They passed the big club house to their right and then into the parking area. Willy's van was easy to spot so they parked next to it. Ed and Julia put on their golf shoes sitting in the car with the doors open. Ed hoped that there were no disapproving eyes watching them. He grabbed his Wilson Winsum putter and they headed to the driving range. They walked under the canopy of towering palm trees, passing the entrance to the club house, and then to the left to the practice range. Willy was seated under an umbrella nursing a coke looking like he owned the place.

"Pull up a chair and let's make up our game plan," was his introduction to the day's event.

Julia laughed and said "Grandpa laid it all out to us this morning at breakfast. He will be here in a few minutes with my clubs so you and Ed can get started on what you two have planned."

"Well Ed's clubs are over there," Willy said pointing out his carry bag standing by itself on the hitting area of the driving range. "The practice sand trap and chipping area are over behind the halfway house," pointing over past the 9th hole green. "I suppose I better help my boy. What do you think Julia?"

"I think he needs some help," was said as she looked at Ed and wished they were alone somewhere private. She blushed just enough for it to be noticed as she thought she didn't want to share Ed with anyone. Not even Willy.

Ed solved all problems by saying he would like to do a little putting first by himself. Maybe a half hour, or until Ben showed up. Willy jumped up heading for Ed's bag and returning with six Titleists. "Want me to line you up or tend the cup?" he asked.

"Not just yet Willy. Just a few minutes to get my mind on golf. It has been the best week of my life and I need to get my feet back on the ground."

"Gotcha, my man. I will romance Julia while your gone. Better not be gone too long," was accompanied with a hearty laugh.

Julia went to Ed and kissed him. "I understand. Take your time."

Ed needed these few minutes. He had been alone for so long he couldn't shake the fear that this could all end. He needed to concentrate on the little white ball and the stroke to place it in a small hole. Nothing else for just a few minutes.

He started with a putting drill he liked surrounding the cup starting at 3 feet making a circle with the balls. Usually he would use eight, but this time it was six. Six found the cup. He then moved to 5 feet and all six found the bottom of the cup again. He was half way through the next group at 10 feet when a shadow showed up on the green and he looked up to see a man, Ed judged to be in his late forties, standing there watching him.

"Hi, you must be Ed Adams. I'm Gary Martin, the club pro here. We are to have a game on Wednesday," he announced as he came closer with hand extended. Ed took it and it was a good handshake.

"You have it right, Gary. How much do you know about the why of all this?" Ed asked. He immediately liked Gary Martin. He also knew that was a prerequisite for a club golf professional. To be immediately liked.

"Not much. A long time member, Hank Morgan, has something to do with it and he has a habit of not always sharing information. I know the pay off for me and only that you are a friend of Ben Shea and Little Willy." Gary's answer was begging for more. Ed told Gary he had three more putts to sink and then they would go over to the driving range and sit with Willy and Julia. Ed quickly ran through his putting routine and holed all three.

"That's good putting but what kind of putter are you using. It looks older than Hank and just as beat up." Gary had a nice voice and a good smile.

"It's a Wilson Winsum, Willie Hoare design. It was my grandfathers, then my fathers and is now mine. It is the only putter I have ever used." Ed handed it to Gary, he took a quick look and handed it back.

"How old is that thing?" Gary asked with interest.

"I'm not sure. Probably early 1950's. It once had a leather grip with a reminder flange to fit the palm but the shape was deemed illegal by the USGA in the 60's so I now use the Lamkin jumbo. Still have the original and would put it back on if it was allowed."

They headed over to the range and sat around the table with Willy. Julia had gone into the clubhouse and the three of them passed a few pleasantries then got to the point. Gary was first. "Just so you know, Hank's fronting me 500 and 1000 more if I beat you," which was directed at Ed.

Ed mulled this over, but just for a second. "Sounds about right to me. My prize is a little less up front and won't be revealed but it might eventually be worth a lot more than yours. Especially if I am the winner. We will just leave it at that," was Ed's answer to what Gary was asking. Willy chimed in with, "Ed is playing with Morris Cornith designed clubs. He was a member here but was in a wheel chair. Ben Shea is promoting Ed and Hank is the sponsor. They got some big plans going on and your part is to try your best to outplay Ed here. Hope that's not putting too much pressure on you, Gary."

Just then Ben showed up and joined the group. Willy went to Ben's car and brought back the two bags of clubs and set them near Ed's. Julia showed up next and greetings were exchanged and Gary made his exit after some small talk with Ben and a hello to Julia.

Julia commented, and Ed took notice, "Gary is a pro. He is polite, knows every ones name, runs an excellent pro shop and Member and Junior programs. I'm not sure I like him. No reason. He has never done anything offensive but there is just something about him that makes me uneasy."

Ben looked at Julia and smiled. Ed was starting to recognize that smile. It came whenever Ben witnessed that his granddaughter was indeed an exceptional woman. Ed also was noticing how often she demonstrated that trait and he had started to take note when he saw this inter-action.

Chapter 30

They assembled on the practice range and started hitting balls. Tamarisk has a nice set up. Four greens, three of which have small sand traps, are presented at good distances. Willy had paced them off for Ed. Just to refresh his memory as he had known them all before when he was working for Hank. They were also posted at several places on the teeing ground.

Ed went through all the wedges, liked each one but each was different. He finally settled on three that gave different ball flights and distances. One he particularly liked as he could hit a low shot to almost any distance less than 75 yards that would take one bounce and stop dead. He was sure it was going to be his go to club when he needed extra control on difficult approaches.

He then made a mistake. He looked over towards where Ben and Julia were hitting from. Julia was just taking a full swing with a mid iron. It was one of the most beautiful swings he had ever seen. He watched her as she pulled the next ball over, take her stance, sight the target and with a just perceptual forward press take a classic full turn. The down swing was just as good and the ball took off on a perfect arc.

Willy walked up. "Stop watching her. You got a game to play and it does you no good to see somebody

110

swing a club like that. You got your own swing and that is the one you got to use, my man!"

Ed came out of his trance and looked at Willy. He smiled at him. "No wiser words have ever been spoken Willy. Let's go over to the sand and hit some shots where I can't see anymore of what I just saw."

Ed tried all three wedges in the practice sand trap. Two didn't suit him. The one he had chosen for the short high pitches did. Remarkably good. It had a large sole with a very slight curve, or bounce. He hit a dozen balls with various lies and they just popped out of the sand with so little effort from him he couldn't believe it. He took additional swings coming into the sand too steep and to shallow. It made no differences. He had his sand wedge.

Willy just stood by and watched. "Don't you let anybody see that club up close. I can't tell what it is but I've never seen one work that good. Maybe it is just you Ed but don't let any body touch it," Willy grumbled this out and was shaking his head. "Man, I've never seen any thing like that."

They had their clubs picked and headed back to the driving range. Ben and Julia were sitting under the umbrella and water bottles and a plate of sandwiches were on the table. Ed walked over to his stand bag and added the wedges. The Winsum was already in place and he counted the clubs. Fourteen. His bag was ready. They had already put in 6 Titleist Professional balls, 2 gloves, a dozen tees, a divot tool and the two silver quarter ball markers. He hefted the bag and smiled. Not too heavy and should be an easy carry for Willy.

Back at the table he sat next to Julia, as close as he could and not be too obvious, and the foursome had lunch and idle conversation. When they had finished eating Ben excused himself and said he would head home as he had a few things to do in his office and would see them at dinner which he would fix to be ready at six. Julia would stay to walk the course with Ed and Willy and asked Ben to take her clubs back with him. Willy put them in Ben's car and he left.

They had lots of time for the walk but Willy said he could use the late afternoon at home to help his wife out a bit if that would be okay. They started on Hole 1 that was directly in front of the big window of the club's main room. Willy got out his yardage book and standing next Ed between the black markers asked, "Do you see it?" Ed answered, "Yes," and they were off.

Julia had briefly looked back at the clubhouse and standing almost out of sight stood Gary Martin, watching them intently.

They walked all 18 holes. Willy and Ed talked back and forth about ball placements and strategies. Julia had played the course many times and her inputs were also noted in the book. On each green Ed would roll one or two balls toward the pin and watch the break. Willy would each time ask, "Don't you want to try a different line?" and Ed would decline saying, "This is where I plan to be putting from so it will be what I need." Willy, and Julia, gave him funny looks and as it turned out he should have listened to them.

By 3 o'clock they were finished. Tomorrow morning they would meet at the Golf Center at 10:00 am for a couple of hours to run through the bag and then they would be ready for the next day. Ed was so calm Willy had started to worry about his man. Julia was looking at him with even more curiosity. She couldn't understand how he could be so confident. They didn't know it yet, and wouldn't believe it even he told them. It wasn't him, it was the clubs. He was was swinging them, they would do the rest.

Chapter 31

As they drove back to the apartment to park the Porsche in the garage Julia kept looking at Ed. He finally said, "What?"

"I want to know something. Will you tell me?" Julia asked and he knew what it was about. He had just been mulling it over in his mind when it would be that he had to tell her about the clubs. He decided to be blunt and blurt it out and see how she would take it.

"It's the clubs."

"It can't be," she immediately answered.

"Julia, you have had a few times when your golf shots seemed effortless. When you picked your target and swung without thinking about swing thoughts and made the perfect contact."

"Yes, a few times. I can say that it has happened but not very often," she agreed.

"Well, that's what happening now with me. Every shot. I am afraid to even think about it for fear it will leave me. When I grip Morris's clubs, any of them, that is what happens. I am absolutely sure I will hit the ball perfect. Pick the target, swing the club."

"It might not be the clubs, maybe it's me," and she started laughing.

"I bet you're right. I had not thought of that so let's

think that is it," Ed said, relieved.

He turned into the apartment's underground parking and parked the car.

"Take me upstairs and let's make love," Julia suggested. Ed thought that was a good idea and complied with her wishes.

They were back to what was now beginning to be thought of as home for the two of them before it was time for dinner and spent some time at the pool relaxing. Ben joined them and the conversation was pleasant. They talked about the day's practice, how Willy had guided the walk of the course and plotted the management of the match on Wednesday. How they had decided that tomorrow they would spend a couple of hours at the College Golf Center going through Ed's bag hitting each club to keep his tempo right. Dinner was simple but fine and a long walk up and down El Paseo helped finish their day.

It was late in the afternoon the next day when Ben had a call from Gary Martin telling him they had forgotten that they had a Junior event on Wednesday morning. It should be over by 10:00 am but some of the kids and their parents might like to watch part of the game between he and Ed. Would that be okay with him? Ben told Gary he would talk to Hank and see what he thought of the idea. Gary called back 15 minutes later and said the event had been canceled.

Ben had been thinking that Martin might try a trick or two to upset Ed and he also thought he and Julia might be a distraction. He knew he he shouldn't be playing at the moment and had talked with Julia privately about not being included. She agreed and told Ed that she and Ben would be spectators. He understood and thought it might be better that way. He was getting the impression that Gary might not like what was about to happen to him if he played as he expected. Ed also was beginning to think that Julia was a very good judge of character.

Wednesday the sun came up right on time and ushered in another beautiful day. Waking up next to Julia was again a highlight for Ed and he thought he had never felt better about life than he did at that moment. It was one of those times you were sure that everything would happen just as you wanted.

Ben had another gourmet breakfast ready and they ate outside by the pool. By 8:30 am they were on their way to Tamarisk. Willy had called just as he was leaving his place and would meet them there. They gathered at the range and Ed and Willy made a last check of Ed's bag to make sure everything was as it should be.

As Ben headed into the Club a gray 1958 Lincoln Continental drove in. A special golf cart fitted with dark side curtains pulled up next to it and an elderly gentleman, with a cane and binoculars, exited the back seat of the car and entered the privacy of the golf cart. As the cart sped by Ben he waved to Hank but the cart didn't stop. Ben smiled and continued on to the Club House. Julia was sticking near Ed's side and watching everything that was going on. Not a dependent but as an assistant. She knew tournament golf and knew the first hour before competing was important. She wanted to make sure nothing went wrong or happened that could distract him.

Thirty minutes on the range had Ed ready. He was hitting shot after shot exactly as he wanted. A dozen, or more, golfers started watching and several who knew what pro golf looked liked started to take a keen interest.

A buzz started and more people seemed to be gathering in the practice area. Julia was starting to get nervous but Ed seemed to relish the attention.

About 15 minutes before ten o'clock Ed and Willy walked over to the 9th green. It was open and no golfers were on the fairway so Ed dropped a couple of balls and sent them toward the pin. They ran 5 feet past. Ed looked at Willy as he reached down and brushed the green with his hand.

"Ed, the green has been mowed twice and it's running way faster than the practice green. Take a few more putts and get the speed right. That is a nice trick of the Club Pro, don't you think?"

Julia indicated it was time to head to the first tee. It was a short walk and the three of them were quickly in position. Gary Martin hadn't shown yet but at exactly 10:00 am he arrived on the tee in a big hustle with his caddie and half dozen others. Ben calmly walked up and said something to Gary and pointed out the special cart with the dark side curtains. Martin quickly spoke to his friends on the tee box and they all left and found a place to watch off to the side.

Willy set Ed's bag just outside of the markers as the tee was as far back as it could be placed. Martin's bag was a big staff bag and was on the other side of the tee. Ed and Gary shook hands and the caddies handed their players their drivers. Several hundred spectators had gathered on both sides of the tee box and some had started to fill in along the fairway. The word had gotten out. Not about Ed but by a Club Pro that craved attention. Julia had joined Ben and they stood together beside Willy. "You have the honor Ed. Hit away," announced Gary Martin.

Chapter 32

Ed acknowledged the invitation and teed up his ball. He felt calm and his hands were steady. He took his address then backed away and completed his routine of standing behind the ball and visualizing his target. The landing area was so clear it even startled him to see it stand out like that. He smiled and returned to his address position. The club had never felt better in his hands. One last look down the fairway at the target, a focus on the back of the ball, a slight forward press and he swung. The sound of the club striking the ball caused a gasp from the crowd around the tee box. Ed didn't have to look. He knew exactly where his ball was headed. He picked up his tee, looked toward Gary Martin and motioned to the tee box with an open palm indicating it was his turn. Ed knew what would be going through his opponents mind as he followed the flight of his ball.

Martin stood absolutely still until Ed's ball stopped rolling. Over 300 yards just right of the center of the fairway in the perfect spot for an easy mid-iron approach shot to the par five opening hole. He saw Ed's gesture that it was his turn and the realization that this wasn't going to be some clown a rich old member had pushed him into playing was clear. He was a seasoned professional and had played in many tournaments, even some at a high level.

He knew he had to regroup quickly and forget all the plans for an easy outing and fast 1500 dollars. He took a deep breath and exhaled slowly. He went through his routine and managed to get off a descent drive although 30 yards short of Ed's and to the wrong side of the fairway. He would have to make two more good shots to have any hope of a birdie and may have to accept a par.

The game was on and the gallery started the race to get the best look at the next shots. The whole atmosphere had changed. Everyone knew something unique was happening and as if by some golfing telegraph was typing out headlines more spectators were arriving. Ben sat in his cart and smiled. He could only hope Morris could be watching. Julia almost fainted as Ed teed up his ball and went through his routine but the sound of the ball being struck had revived her senses as if she had been hit by lighting. She was walking with a confident stride along side Ed and Willy. Willy looked like he was walking on air and couldn't stop smiling. He, of all people on the course with the exception of Ed, new what was going to happen.

Martin's second shot was a fairway metal that was positioned well leaving a fairly easy chip to the front located pin. A birdie was still possible. Ed and Willy were approaching his ball when the cart with the dark side curtains drove up, a weathered hand appeared and handed Willy a sheet of paper, and then drove away. Willy took one look and said to Ed, "Look at this. He had all the pins changed from Monday. None of them are where they were." He handed Ed the pin sheet and took a closer look at the pin on the green. "The pin is on the front. Ten feet from the front. That's 15 yards less than what we were

119

expecting. That S.O.B. had them changed last night. OK, you like that 7F so much, put it right at 155 with the fade. Your drive was 15 yards long, remember."

Ed couldn't help but smile. He hadn't hit his second shot yet and knew for certain he needed Willy on his bag. It would be too easy to get caught up in a big drive like he just hit and forget where he was when he got to the ball. He had a good lie, the visual was clear. A nice high fade knowing the ball would stop where it landed. Willy handed Ed the 7F iron and Ed hit the exact shot he wanted. 3 feet below the hole.

Martin made a good chip and holed an eight footer for his birdie. Ed made his 3 footer for an eagle. One hole and a one shot lead for Ed. The game was on. There would be no more gamesmanship. Even Martin had enough pride to know this was true golfing now. Who could play the course better, hit the best shots, play the best golf.

The short par 3 was next. Hole number 2. On the tee Martin walked up to Ed and apologized. "I started this game wrong. I thought this was going to be some kind of joke, or a get back for something I had done. You being with Ben Shea and Julia I should have known that would not be the case."

One of the club's staff ran up on the tee and gave Martin a sheet of paper. He handed it to Ed. "This is the pin placements for today and the greens are running at 12. The rest of the way there will be no tricks." Ed gave him a long look, didn't mention he already had the pin sheet, and then offered his hand.

"That's good by me Gary. Let's put on a show for the crowd."

It was a good show and great golf. Ed shot a seven

under 65 to Gary Martin's 69. It was Gary's best competitive round in six years and he was delighted. Beside just golf there was one highlight to the day and that came early on Hole 3. As they arrived at the tee box, after both had birdied Hole 2, there was a little old lady waiting for them.

"Who is that? What is she doing there?" Gary Martin questioning out loud and Ed answered him.

"Oh my God, it's Harriet! Gary come with me and meet her. I am going to get some advice. Give me a break here and no penalty, okay?" Ed asked. Gary grinned and agreed.

"This is my hole Ed. I told you how to play it and I came here to see that you do it like I told you." Harriet's eyes were dancing and Gary's "Glad to meet you" was brushed aside with, "You can play it this way too, if you want to!" Then it was back to Ed.

"See that bunker on the left. Hit your drive just over the right edge. It's 286 from here and it slopes down on the back side and with the bounce you'll get another 50 yards right into the middle of the fairway. Makes the number one handicap a joke. Trust me and do it!"

Harriet stepped aside just outside the markers, putting her hands on her hips and impatiently waited. Ed shrugged and looked at Gary. He smiled and said, "It's your honor."

Ed had his driver in hand, teed his ball and went through his routine. One last look and he knew he could make the shot. The target was right there in front of him, a clear rectangle just over the right side of the bunker. He made a full turn and a maximum swing. He could feel the ball compress and he knew exactly where it was going.

121

Clearing the trap by five feet it took a huge bounce and when it stopped rolling it was where Harriet said it would be.

Gary watched all this and chose to place his drive in the fairway and his ball was 70 yards short of Ed's. When Ed looked to where Harriet had been standing he only saw her back as she walked away with Jimmy at her side.

Chapter 33

On the 18th green the handshake was made between Ed and Gary, and it was a good handshake of mutual respect. Ed had left a couple of shots on the course, but they were putts. He had hit every shot tee to green about as good as they could be played. Morris's clubs had been perfect and Ed, with Willy's help, had played them the same.

For Gary Martin it was a different reward but for him just as important. He had given up his dream of playing the PGA tour 18 years ago at the same age as Ed was now. Resigned to being a Club professional it had been a satisfactory life and his position here at Tamarisk was about as good a one as he could expect. His 67 from the back tees was the best he had shot since he had given up serious play in 1976. In two years he would be 50 and eligible for the Senior Tour. As he shook Ed's hand his thought was "I want to do this again."

After the accolades had been bestowed and the gallery slowly retreated, the small group of principals retired to the club house. A big round table was set in one of the private dining rooms and the group arranged themselves around the table. The atmosphere was electric. Ed, Julia, Ben and Willy sat next to one another and Gary Martin and his caddie were there. A couple of Tamarisk members, one of which Ed thought was the president of the club, several of Gary's staff and two of the club's junior golf team made up the party.

It was a big table and had room for all. The wait staff brought in drinks, mostly water, soft drinks and a few beers. Then several platters with finger food and small plates were brought in and set accordingly. The stories of the day's happenings began and then suddenly there was a silence. The door to the room had opened and the old man, with a cane and binoculars hanging around his neck, slowly and painfully made his way to the table. His craggy face had a smile and his bent body made it into a chair that was held for him. His first words spoken were, "I'd like a double scotch on the rocks!"

Ben stood and said, "I would like you all to meet my oldest and best friend Hank. No last name is needed. He is Hank to me and if you are lucky he can become Hank to you." There were several "Hello Hank" said and all attention was directed toward him. His aide stepped back towards the door but was immediately invited to have a seat at the table, which with a nod from Hank he took. Fortunately the double scotch arrived as Hank got seated. He took about half the glass in one gulp then reached in his Harris Tweed jacket pocket and retrieved a small envelope, a little larger than a dollar bill but somewhat thicker. He had it passed to Gary Martin. "As we agreed, with a little bonus. You gave us a full 18. I wasn't sure about you until I saw the expression on your face when Ed's first drive had stopped rolling." He cackled a laugh, or what sounded like what was supposed to be one.

Next he pointed at Ed. "You did what we wanted Ed. You played Morris Cornith's clubs as they were meant to be played. We want to see more and we will. Ben will take care of things." He then tried to smile and pointed his finger at Julia. "You, young lady, are in charge of taking care of Ed the person." Pointing at Willy he said, "You are in charge of Ed the player." He downed the remainder of the scotch and signaled his helper to take him home and they left the room.

Then for the second time in just 4 minutes Ben rose and said, "You have just met Hank. That was a long meeting for him. You should feel honored." They all, each for their own reason, did.

Chapter 34

The gathering lasted about a half an hour more and then the group dispersed. Willy talked to Ed for a few minutes and excused himself to head home to help out his wife with the foster kids. He told Ed he would carefully guard the clubs and Ed agreed that from now on the clubs would have to have more security because his results on the course would cast a light on not only him but on his equipment. Because of their odd look they would become the focus and neither of them was so naive as to think an attempt would not be made to get hold of them. They parted with a bond that was understood by both.

Ben took Julia aside and asked her to walk him to his car. Ed watched them leave the room and he had no doubts that these two would determine the course for the rest of his life. He would have to have some kind of understanding with them both that the relationship had to be secured. That he couldn't even think of going on, even one day, without that assurance. He had only known Julia nine days and he now thought he simply could not live without her. It was a ridiculous thought but it dominated his thinking. The golf only mattered if she was beside him.

As Ben walked Julia to the car he asked her a rather odd question. "Did you see what happened on the course today? What really happened?"

"Yes, Grandpa. Great golf and Ed Adams playing it. That was one part, wasn't it. The other, the important part, was that Ed Adams is on this earth to be my partner for the rest of my life. I have no answer as to why it has happened but I have no doubts about it at all," and she took Ben's hand and held it tightly until they reached his car. Julia saw a tear on his cheek and kissed it away. He hugged her, smiled and simply said, "See you at home."

Gary Martin went to his office in the pro shop and closed the door. He knew what he wanted for his future but did not know how he could get there. The golf was good enough but to walk onto the Senior tour would not be that easy. He had no family to care for so that would not be a problem but he didn't have enough capital which meant he would have to get a sponsor, or sponsors.

He pulled out the envelop to see if Hank had come through with the money. It was there, not only the $500 but a $1000. But more important than that was a wrinkled and somewhat soiled piece of notebook paper with some almost unreadable hand writing. It simply said, "Keep working on your game. It is good enough. I will work something out for you next year. If I don't last that long Ben will take care of it. Hank."

Gary leaned back in his chair, smiling. There was hope. It had been the best day he could remember. Then his phone rang. "This is Margret Benson. I am waiting for my private lesson on the practice tee. I don't see you," came over loud and clear. "I will be there in 5 minutes, Mrs. Benson," answered Gary in his smoothest professional voice. Even this could not dampen his spirits as he headed out to his appointment.

127

Ed waited for Julia on a bench overlooking the first hole. There was a foursome on the tee loudly discussing the wagers and who would be the partners. Ed thought it was probably a foursome that played every Wednesday afternoon with this tee time and had the same discussion each time. That was okay as every game of golf was different. Each shot was different from the last one. Each had a unique challenge and a unique solution. No two were exactly the same. Very few were made perfectly. This day it had been different. It was as close to perfect as he had ever come. Some day he might be able to pull it off. Ben Hogan once said, "You should be able to birdie every hole." That would be a perfect round of golf. He smiled. Morris's clubs could make that happen. A 54 on the card. Maybe. Another smile.

"So what are you smiling about? Is it about me or did you play the perfect game?" was Julia's greeting to Ed. Her walk and conversation with her grandfather had been quick and brief, had left her knowing what her future must be, but with a worry about his. Something was happening and she was now certain it had to do with his health. She was scared but didn't want to do anything that would spoil Ed's day. She needn't have had that worry as Ed already concluded the same thing and wanted to talk to her about it.

Chapter 35

They drove back and as Ed parked the Porsche in the basement garage Julia suggested they go upstairs to his apartment before walking back to Ben's.

"It's not what you think. I want to talk about us, me, you, Ben, our future. Even golf. I need to talk right now and I think here will be better than at home."

Ed took her in his arms for a gentle hug, kissed her cheek and told that he thought that is exactly what they should do. "I have some things I need to talk to you about. Now is the right time and in my apartment is the right place."

They entered and went immediately to the bed, laying down facing each other fully clothed. Ed didn't pause, looking into Julia's eyes he started with a single sentence.

"Julia, I love you and I can't imagine living, even a day, the rest of mine without you." He waited but not long enough for her to answer. "Married or not, legal or not. Just together for as long as I live. I want you to know this with out any question. That is the only thing that matters to me right now, and that your happiness is my only concern."

She was ready for this and wanted him to know that she felt the same about him. The only hesitance she had was her increasing concern about her grandfather's health.

"Ed, this is my first at being in love. I want it to be my only time and I want it to last forever. I give myself to you and trust you will keep your promise to me. Let's understand what this means and keep our relationship as it is for now. I think the next year is going to be very complex and maybe even difficult for us. How we come through it hopefully will bond us even closer than we are now. I am good with this. Are you okay with it?"

"Yes," was Ed's answer and then a silence prevailed as they held each close.

"It is Ben, isn't it? His health?" Ed said the words and Julia started crying.

She recovered a little then started. "About a year ago he had some tests done. He didn't tell me much. I was in my first year in graduate school. He said something about a watch and wait having to do with the prostate. Talking to my friends at school one of them said her grandfather had gone through that and was still being monitored. It was for occurrence of prostate cancer and whether it was growing."

They laid together, comfortable, holding each other but making no movements. Ed then leaned back just enough to be able to focus on Julia's face. He thought her the most beautiful person in the world. Certainly in his world. He didn't want to move but gently whispered "Let's go see Ben and find out what has happened. We can also tell him that we plan to be together the rest of our lives."

Julia gave Ed the smile he wanted and they collected themselves and started their walk towards home.

They entered and went back to the kitchen where Ben was seated at the small table. In front of him on the table was a manila folder. It looked old and was soiled with the edges worn. Like it had just been pulled from a rusted steel cabinet in some one's garage. He motioned for them to sit opposite him.

He looked at them both and gave them a weak smile. Both Julia and Ed were thinking that this was not what they had expected nor what they had wanted to talk about. It was a tense moment. Then Ben's smile grew bigger and he opened the file.

On the top of three sheets of paper were two new credit cards. Ben slid these off to the side. Next were the three letter size sheets of papers, the first headed PGA SPONSORS EXEMPTION and underneath the heading a bunch of text and near the bottom was ED ADAMS in bold print. Motorola Western Open June30 – July 3, 1994. The second sheet was similarly headed and had Anheuser-Busch Golf Classic July 7 – July 10, 1994 with ED ADAMS at the bottom. The third was New England Classic July 21 – July 24, 1994 again with ED ADAMS.

Ben looked at Ed and was still smiling. "Hank knows how to pull strings. On July 24, less than six weeks from now, you will know where your future might lie. At least as far as golf is concerned."

He then slid the credit cards toward them. One had Ed Adams name and the other Julia Renquest. "Each card has $100,000 behind it. These should cover all your expenses including $2,500 each tournament plus expenses for Willy. Willy is to receive that plus 10 per cent of any prize money. Twenty percent of any prize money will be donated to the Foster Care Center of Riverside County.

Fifty percent of winnings will be credited against your credit card draw downs, split evenly, and any remaining funds are yours to keep. It is a good deal."

Ed was speechless and Julia couldn't decide on whether to laugh or cry so did neither.

Finally, Julia broke the silence. "We came back here ready to talk about something else. We wanted to talk about what is happening with you, Grandpa. All this," waving at the papers and credit cards, "is great for us but not as important as what is going on in your life right now."

"After dinner we will talk about my life. It is not as bad as it may appear."

Chapter 36

Ben and Julia worked together preparing a cheese, ham and spinach omelet while Ed sat back and watched. A feeling of peace came over him he hadn't had in years. He had a family again. His eyes watered up and he wiped them hoping they wouldn't be noticed.

Dinner was served and eaten with a comfortable conversation about the days events and how fast things were moving. That Hank had done so much in advance it was obvious he had already predicted the outcome. It was no wonder he had been so successful. Ed thought it would have been nice to have known him in his prime. And then remembered Ben had, and he was of the same caliber. Ed thought, "I am among giants," and smiled.

Julia cleaned up the dishes and brought coffee and some cookies to the table. Ben took a sip and looked at his grandchildren. Ed was sure to be, in essence, his grandson-in-law and he already thought of him as one. He then told them what was about to happen and that they should not worry or let it interfere with their lives.

"I will be going into the hospital tomorrow afternoon and will have my prostate removed the next morning. The cancer has remained inside but has started to become more aggressive. It has been watched the last few years and my urologist says it would best to remove it

133

now and avoid more serious conditions later. I may not be the same quality ladies man afterwards but if you haven't noticed I don't really care about that much anymore. I am not worried about this and neither should either of you. I will need a week or two of recovery and will not be doing much for the next month. Ed, I expect to watch you on TV at the Western Open, especially over the week-end." Ben was looking at Ed and smiling at this last comment.

"Oh Grandpa, that so unfair. I can stay here and be your nurse. Ed can do without me. He and Willy can manage things." Julia could hardly get the words out fast enough.

"No it isn't, no you won't, no he can't and no they can't," was Ben's quick reply to her. "I will have a private nurse who will make regular visits and be on call 24 hours a day. By the time you two are ready to travel I should be almost fully recovered and if I have any problems the nurse will be called in. You and Ed must, and I mean must, carry on with your lives. Especially for the next few months," pausing then Ben added, "and that is final!"

Julia sat quiet, wiped away a few tears and agreed. "We won't let you down Grandpa. I will wave to you on TV on July third from the eighteenth green at Cog Hill."

"That's my girl," Ben said then turned to Ed, "You are the one that has to make it happen and I don't mean just the golf."

Ben stood up and excused himself for the night and headed to his office. He sat at his desk for about an hour. It was a good space, a good house and he hoped Julia and Ed would live here when the time came. He was sure he had five to ten years left and they should be quality years. He was planning on it and he was hoping his grandchildren would live with him for most of that time.

Julia and Ed had gone to sit by the pool and watch the colors change as the sun set. It had been a busy day, a fun day. They were tired but satisfied. Ed had played the best golf of his life and was confident he could do it again. He was at home, right here where he sat, and looking at Julia he knew this was whom he was meant to be with.

Ben's surgery was successful and the greeting to Julia and Ed, who had been waiting, by the surgeon was so enthusiastic about how it had gone that it left them thinking the same. He was able to come home a day early feeling better than expected. The nurse, a very attractive woman in her early fifties, seemed not only competent but friendly. She and Julia had immediately became close and Ed was glad to see that relationship form.

As Ben's first week home after his hospital stay drew to a close all the efforts in preparing for the Western Open had been completed. Plane tickets to Chicago, car rental, two motel rooms reserved, the Dubsdread course layout studied and the clubs selected to match the course. Ed liked the course's name, "Dubs" a plural of a slang name for a poor golfer and the "dread" was obvious.

Ed had advanced Willy his first paycheck so he and his wife could hire help at their house for her. They currently had five foster children in house and they required a lot of attention.

Gary Martin at Tamarisk had set up practice passes for the three of them and they had gate passes for both the Porsche and Willy's van. He also gave Ed a new bag which had double straps for carry and was much lighter than the big staff bags most players had on tour. It was about the same weight as Ed's carry bag but it of course had Tamarisk CC in big letters on both sides.

Julia had done some shopping for outfits for Ed. He had bought a second pair of golf shoes and wore them enough to make sure of the fit. The three of them met at Tamarisk for a last practice on the 27th and would fly out on the 28th. Ed would see the course for the first time the next day and he would be teeing off early in the morning on the 30th with two other sponsor's exemption golfers on the back nine. He would not be seen on TV until his last three holes on Friday.

Chapter 37

The flight had been good. There were no delays at Palm Springs and they arrived at O'Hare in Chicago ten minutes early. The luggage arrived as did the clubs in their travel case. The car was ready and the rental went smoothly. They were at the motel by 4:00 pm and quickly settled in. Both credit cards were getting plenty of use and they were working like magic. Dinner was at a nearby Kentucky Fried Chicken restaurant.

In their room Julia called Ben and passed the pleasantries. He was feeling fine and was glad to hear all was going good at their end. He asked her tell Ed to keep his eye on the ball but still enjoy the game. They would talk again tomorrow.

Julia came over to Ed, who was sitting in the only chair in the room, and sat in his lap wrapping her arms around his neck. "So far so good, don't you think? We can do this. At least for a while."

Ed thought it was a big question being asked in a round about way. He answered slowly.

"We can do this as long as we both want to. We will have to give it a try. If I can get into the top ten we will keep at it as long as it doesn't come between us. We have three tournaments to find out, either way. We have to get through them before we make a decision."

"I am good with that but there is more to life than just golf and I think we should work at that right now," was how Julia got his attention for what sometimes is much more important than all the other distractions in life.

They had reserved two adjacent rooms at the Red Roof Inn in Willowbrook and it would be a short drive to Cog Hill. The Continental breakfast was adequate and the motel was full. Ed had an early practice round scheduled and got off on time after about 30 minutes on the range. Willy was ready to go and Julia was in good spirits. Ed was paired with one of the regulars on tour and he helped Ed out on protocol and the way to use a practice round. His caddie and Willy hit it off so they had a good time and learned a lot. Two other players were supposed to join them but didn't show up and it made Ed's first trip around the course a good one. It was a big course and it was going to be set up tough.

That evening they went over each hole making notes of both shot making and green breaks. Willy had his book full and ready. After another fast food dinner he begged off for bed. Ed and Julia were also ready to turn in early. A long phone call with Ben was a nice nightcap for them both. Things were fine and he was feeling good and had taken several walks. As he put it he was still wearing diapers but thought he would out grow them soon. He told Ed to have a good day tomorrow and enjoy the fact that he was out there. Morris had a dream and Ed had to chase it for him. That sounded good to Ed and he was planning on doing it.

Ed was called to the 10th tee at 7:35 am. Two other golfers were also called and Ed couldn't remember their names after he struck his first ball. The 10th is 383 yard par four and right where a drive would end up were a row seven small bunkers. He started his first PGA tournament with a 5 metal wood. It was perfectly struck down the left side of the fairway and left him 153 yards to the middle of the green. Willy gave him the distance and the location and he hit a soft 7 iron to 4 feet. He birdied the first hole. The course then started to bare it's teeth. The next hole, the 11th was a 607 yard par five, the second handicap. He made his par.

At the turn he was still one under par having one more birdie and one bogey. Ed was feeling a little disappointed and as they approached the first hole tee box Willy came close and said, "That was some good golf you played. You are one shot out of the lead. Pars are a good score on this course today. We don't need to press here. You understand?"

"You're kidding! I wasn't paying any attention to the scoreboard. Thanks Willy. Let's keep the ball rolling."

Julia was following outside the ropes and joined them before they entered back onto the player's course. She gave Ed a hug and kiss and gave Willy a good squeeze. She was happy and her face showed it.

"It's just two of you the rest of the way. The guy with the floppy hat was seven over and said his back was hurting so bad that he couldn't play another hole." Julia laughed at that. Ed hadn't paid much attention to the guy other than respect his order of play. The other member of the threesome had his card and now Ed had his.

Number 1 is a test at 458 yards with bunkers every where around the landing area and requires a big drive, which you have to try. Willy lined Ed up and advised, "Just your regular shot. That will be plenty," as he backed away. Ed hit the shot and parred the hole with two putts. The last hole for today was the 9th. Ed parred the brutal number 1 handicap hole and his card showed a 70 for two under. It placed him in he middle of the field and that's where he was as the first day ended. He was only three back of someone who shot a 5 under in the afternoon. Ed was one shot ahead of Nick Price.

Chapter 38

July had been a dry month by Illinois's standard and the course was running hard but fair. Dubsdread had many angles, bunkers and traps to consider and Willy and Ed were consulting on every shot. The other players had the same problems so play was slow. The weather was good and the temperature a little below normal so that was not a problem. It was the toughest golf course Ed had ever played.

After the first round Ed, Julia and Willy were all tired. Back at the motel they ate from lunch boxes provided at the course and then each tried to rest. Willy went to his room and did get a good nap. Ed and Julia tried but only managed to lay back and talk over the day. The combined stress of preparation, travel and the long days on the golf course had worn them down.

"I don't know how they can do it. Week after week," Julia speaking of the full time tour players.

Ed looked at her and smiled. "We are going to see if we have what it takes. I am not so sure we do but it is our first tournament and by Sunday evening we will probably have a better idea. One thing is for sure, I will not do it unless you are with me."

After breakfast the next morning they had time to kill. This was another problem they had not anticipated although they knew the schedule. With the big field playing the first two days in morning and afternoon games meant for Ed the 7:35 am start yesterday and a 12:00 pm start today. Even the big name pros had the same time differences to contend with.

Ed's Friday play was almost identical to Thursday but as he got to hole number 16, the start of his last three holes for the day, several cameramen and a course announcer had joined them inside the ropes. He was now 4 under par and in the top twenty on the big scoreboard. He was an unknown, was using strange looking clubs, good looking, had a beautiful girl friend, and a big and very black older man for a caddie. In other words, made for TV.

He parred 16, birdied 17, and parred the long par four 18th. As he left the the eighteenth green he had his first TV interview with Julia at his side and Willy in the frame. It was short and just a few questions and answers with a quick pan of Willy with the bag showing off the driver. Willy mentioned Morris Cornith design and the word was out.

Back in Palm Desert Ben was watching the Golf Channel's coverage of the second day's late pairings with his visiting nurse, who was there on a personal visit, and there was Julia, Ed and Willy. He smiled and told his new friend, "That's my family."

Just a few miles away Gary Martin was sitting in his office, alone, watching the broadcast as the interview started. He focused on Willy and as the microphone was pointed toward Willy he turned and the side of the golf bag with the Tamarisk CC logo got full coverage. "Yes!" and Gary's day had gone from boring to one of his best.

Dinner was at a nearby sit down restaurant and

the meal was better than they had expected. The three of them felt good but were again tired. Ed had not only made the cut, he was in the top ten, would be paired with a recognized pro and would be getting a lot of attention and TV time tomorrow. Nick Price, one of the favorites as he had already won two tournaments this year, was 4 strokes behind Ed Adams, still in contention but a long ways back. Ed was in the big time. Julia was starting to get nervous but Willy was too tired to worry. Ed felt great. He didn't understand why but he wasn't going to question anything now. Every time he gripped the club today, even his trusted Wilson Winsum, he was confident he could make the shot. He could hardly wait until tomorrow at 1:36 pm to start his third round.

He was paired with Greg Parry, a seasoned pro from Australia two years younger than him, shorter by 6 inches and just a bit on the stocky side. A fun guy and they immediately struck up a good relationship. It was a grind. The play was slow and the course played tough. Ed shot even par and Parry played to one under par. Behind them Nick Price finished with the tournaments best round of 67 and and moved to 6 under and take the lead.

Sunday pairings would have Parry paired with Price and Ed in the following pair tied for second. That afternoon's interview was much longer and by the time they got back to the motel Ed was the new player to watch in the final round.

Again, Ed did not seemed bothered by this which confounded Julia who was having a hard time coping with all the attention and activity that was going on around them. Willy was tired, as he had been the night before, and begged off to his room as soon as they came back from dinner.

"How can you be so calm? I am about to fall apart and you act like it is just another day playing golf with your friends," Julia said with tears starting to fall.

"I don't know. But know this, you are the only thing that matters to me," Ed told her this and collected her in his arms. They readied for bed and said their good nights. Sleep came for Julia first and Ed laid awake for several hours. He was replaying the holes and each shot was as clear as when he had hit them. It had been a good round even if he had only just stayed even. He knew he would play better tomorrow and had a chance to win. His last thoughts, before finally falling asleep, was of an old man in a wheel chair pouring over technical drawings on a work bench in a garage with a strange looking golf club in his lap.

Chapter 39

Julia awakened first. Ed would be in the second pairing on the final day of the Motorola Western Open. She smiled and it was a confident smile. She had met him exactly four weeks ago today while trying to fill a boring day helping a friend of her grandfather keep his golf museum open. She started to laugh out loud and woke up Ed.

"What so funny, funny face," was Ed's ribbing as he too felt extraordinarily good having Julia happy and beside him.

She didn't wait and started kissing his face and tickling his ribs. The kissing slowed down and the tickling stopped.

"Ed, I am good this morning. I am ready to spend the day watching you play. I'm not nervous at all. Not like I was yesterday. We met four weeks ago today and you have changed my life completely and I can hardly wait to see what comes next. And today is a good one to see what it might be."

"I like that. Let's go out there and bring that course to it's knees. Then see what comes next," was Ed's good morning to someone he thought he had known forever. They met Willy for breakfast at the motel dining area and he was in good humor too. He had a nice telephone call with his wife last night and she said that

145

when the kids saw him on TV at the golf course interview, and heard him speak, they all cheered and started marching around the room chanting "Willy, Willy, Willy."

"She is good with me being here now and that makes it better for me," was said with the best smile Ed and Julia had seen since they had been here. They knew it was tough on him to leave his wife with the kids and were hoping that would resolve itself so he could continue being part of the team.

They were at the course by 10:00 am and on the practice range was a space between two markers with a sign having "Adams" in big letters. There was a pyramid of new Titleist balls waiting. He and Willy spent an hour hitting shots and then made use of the practice pitching area and sand traps. They were followed by a collection of photographers and interviewed by several reporters. A TV crew was there and for about 15 minutes Ed spent time with one of the announcers that would cover the golf starting about an hour before his tee time. Ed had arrived at the big time for sure.

Nick Price and Greg Parry were nearby and getting the same treatment. Several other big names were also about and giving similar time to the press and TV crews. Parry came over to say "Hi" and wish him well and not to hit into Nick and him on the long holes. He then asked about Julia and how she was doing.

"Pretty good. She was a little down last night but was back in good spirits this morning. You might think she is just one beautiful woman but keep this a secret, she has a three handicap. And if you could see her swing a golf club you would want to give up golf," was Ed's answer.

Ed Adams Chases a Dream

Greg took out his fancy flip phone, dialed a number and asked someone to send the head of something Ed couldn't hear out to the driving range. A few minutes later a nicely dressed official showed up, introduced herself to Ed and gave him an official looking badge on a neck cord and a clip board with a pen attached by a string.

"Give these to your wife, or girl friend, and she can walk inside the ropes with you today. Doesn't need to do anything but the clip board will make it look official. The crowds are going to be enormous today. I think it is going to be a record," and she turned and walked away.

Ed looked for Greg and saw he was involved in another interview but acknowledged Ed's wave and the mouthing of "Thank you."

They had lunch at the clubhouse and Ed gave Julia the badge and clip board.

"I will write a love note to Greg Parry. This will be so good. It is going to be a mad house out there, especially at the end, and I was just going to watch it on the TV in here. How nice of him."

With thirty minutes left Ed did some putting, loosened up with some swings on the range and then he and Willy were standing next to the first tee waiting for the announcement.

"Ed Adams from Palm Desert, California. You have the tee. Please hit away."

At 458 yards it requires a big drive to clear the bunkers on the left side of the fairway. As Ed gripped his driver he could feel the confidence building. He went through his routine and then hit the ball exactly the way he wanted. His second shot was just as good and an easy two putt gave him his first par of the final round.

147

Again it was slow play. A very long and difficult course, tremendous galleries with cheers, applause and groans seeming to converge from all directions. Julia was happy to be inside the ropes and she sheltered herself by walking among the officials that were supposed to be there. They understood and accepted her presence without any complaint.

The real contest was in the last pairing. Ed made an appearance on the leader board twice when he birdied the second and third holes and was tied for the lead until both Price and Parry birdied right behind him. He birdied the tough ninth and the easy tenth and had the lead alone. It then became Parry and Price. Ed finished with a par on 18 to finish 9 under. Parry closed at 10 under and Price finish first with a second 67 at 11 under. It had been a great afternoon of professional golf and Ed had third place to himself. No other Sponsor's Exemption, not having professional status, had ever placed that high in a PGA tournament and it was not lost on the crowd or the media.

There was the presentation to the winner and run-ner up and then more interviews in which Ed was included. By 6 o'clock he excused himself, had a few words more with Greg Parry and thanked him again for taking care of Julia's situation. Julia also did and he was delighted with her hug and kiss on the cheek. Willy was ready and they hustled to get to O'Hare in time to catch their 9:15 pm flight back to Palm Springs. All three of them were exhausted. Julia repeated her, "I don't know how they can do it," but then added, "It's worth it!"

They landed in Palm Springs just a little over an hour after they left Chicago as far as the clock was concerned. Ed was ready to hail a taxi when a gray 1958

Lincoln Continental pulled up and the driver jumped out and opened up the massive trunk.

"Hank sent me to pick you all up and conveys his congratulations. Give me the directions."

Willy was first and Julia and Ed were home 15 minutes later.

Chapter 40

As Julia and Ed entered the house Ben was waiting to great them. He was in a bathrobe and looked surprisingly good. His face had gotten it's tan back and he was standing straight. It had been just over two weeks since his operation and they had been gone just six days. It was good to see him up and about and happy. The happiness they would meet tomorrow when Jennifer, the visiting nurse, made her next official visit.

After the hugs and a handshake, congratulations and kind words, Julia begged to retire from the conscious world and headed to their bedroom. Ed stayed up with Ben for a few minutes longer. Ben's first serious question to Ed was how Julia had done on the trip and the tournament.

"By this morning she was into the whole experience. It wore her down at first and I was afraid she might want to give up on the project. I couldn't blame her. I was tired and Willy looked beaten down as well. I think making it to the final four and realizing it could be done was what got her thoughts turning positive. It is really tough on you out there, tougher than I had imagined." As Ed was saying this Ben took his arm and lead him to his office. He sat in his chair and motioned Ed to take a seat.

"I wear down quickly and can't stand more than

ten minutes without a little discomfort. It has not been bad and I am feeling good. In fact, better than for some time. Watching you play on TV was a thrill and today's coverage was really great. I recorded both days for you and also the interview at the close of the second round. You will have something to show your grandchildren, if that happens. Hank has called me three times in the last two days. You have given him a new life, too," he paused and then added, "My visiting nurse, her name is Jennifer, will pay me a visit tomorrow afternoon and will stay and have dinner with us. I want you and Julia to meet her. Time for you to get some sleep and rest up for the next one." He had finished and stood up.

Ed rose and they shook hands again in a mutual understanding that their worlds were merging.

Ed prepared for bed. He needed a shower but was too tired to take one and didn't want to wake Julia as she seemed to be sound asleep. As he slipped in between the sheets she moved toward him and accepted his embrace. It overwhelmed him how good she felt and how comfortable he was with her. She kissed him softly and whispered "Tomorrow, first thing," and fell back to sleep.

He laid still for some time. The entire day was running through his mind and he was wide awake. Finishing third did not bother him in the least. To play at that caliber was such a high he didn't think he could come down. The grind was excruciating and the competition greater than he could have imagined. It had given him an all new perspective at what these players had to do to compete at that level. To finish as Nick Price had done with a five under round under those conditions. Greg Parry was right there to the end. And what a nice gesture he had made to get Julia inside the ropes.

He then started to think about his part in all this. Were Morris's clubs an unfair advantage for him? Was it cheating? It was he who was swinging the club and the club could care less who it was that was swinging it. Was having such confidence wrong and unfair? You had to have confidence to play the game. Every player out there had to have it to a level as to not let it even be thought about. It was when doubt entered the mind that the game would desert you.

He moved to get more comfortable and Julia reached her hand out to keep contact but did not wake. He looked at her and even in the darkened room could see enough to clear his mind of golf and dwell on what was important to him. Those thoughts let him finally relax and fall asleep.

Chapter 41

Today was July 4th and Julia's first words to Ed upon waking was something about fireworks happening and that was how they started their morning. Then a long shower together and Ed was beginning to think his life could get no better as he carefully washed her trying not to miss anything. It did get even better but after that it was time to dress and see about breakfast.

They found Ben in the kitchen and he was just putting the waffle batter in the waffle iron and the table had been set. Ed didn't ask how he knew when they would show up and Julia took it all in stride without even a questioning look. Ben told Julia about Jennifer making a visit that afternoon and that she would be staying for dinner that evening. He would need some help in the kitchen and it would be nice if they both could work together with him.

"Grandpa, what have you been up too while we were gone? Shame on you!" she said as she danced around the room happy with life and for her grandfather. Ben's worry about how the possibility of having another woman in his life might be troubling for her had been misplaced. He had steered her toward accepting Ed and hoped she would support him if he choose to go in that direction with Jennifer.

153

It was a fine breakfast and they had the rest of the day to relax. Jennifer showed up at four and spent 15 minutes doing her official tasks recording temperature, blood pressure and the answers to a questionnaire. That done, she put the records away and they exited to pool side deck chairs and whiled away the afternoon in good conversation. It quickly came out that Jennifer had been widowed fifteen years ago when her husband, a test pilot, had been killed in a crash while testing a top secret experimental plane being designed for the air force. They had no children and his life insurance plan was generous so she had no financial problems. She was an R.N. and chose doing visiting nursing as it gave her freedom and was something she enjoyed doing.

"You meet all kinds of interesting people. Some good and some not so good. Once in a while some one special," she told them looking at Ben.

Both Julia and Ed had liked her when they met right after Ben got back from the hospital, but it had been a brief acquaintance. As the evening went on it became more and more apparent that she and Ben were comfortable in their relationship and Julia and Ed were happy for them both.

The fireworks could be viewed from the pool area, following an excellent dinner prepared by the three cooks in the kitchen, and it provided a nice closing to the evening. It was Julia that posed that Jennifer could stay and use her old bedroom if she would like. Ben actually blushed, not much, but just enough to be caught if you had been watching. Ed had and it brought a smile to his face.

Ben told the happy group that he was tiring and thought it was time for him to go to bed. Jennifer went with him to his room and returned shortly to wish Julia and Ed good night. Ed walked her to the car.

"Your not going to grill me on taking advantage of a recovering patient are you?" she asked politely, but making the point.

"No, of course not. Ben is the most important man in Julia's life. Even I would come in second and that is how it should be. He is also the most intelligent and smartest man I have ever known. That is some statement for me to make as my parents were in that class. Julia truly likes you, she is a good person and I think the more you come into their lives the more welcomed you will become," was Ed's response to her.

"A pro golfer in the making. I don't think so, Ed. There will be something more in your future. I hope I will be around here to see what it is. Good night and thank you for walking me to my car." She smiled at Ed as he held the door, waved good night and drove away.

When Ed returned to the kitchen Julia was busying herself with putting things away. He could see she was troubled and Ed could guess what it was.

"She is a nice lady. I like her, Ben likes her and so do you. It will work out as it is meant to be and I think it will be good for all involved. Your Grandpa is one smart and wise man and he won't do anything foolish. I think you can count on that," was said in a gentle tone. Julia came to him before he finished and was in his arms when he stopped speaking.

"I am just worried right now about the two men in my life and don't want things to change. You can understand that, can't you?" she said asking for an answer.

"Of course I do. Look at what has changed in our

lives and how good it has been. Give Ben and Jennifer the
time they need and it too will turn out as it should. We
have a big day tomorrow so let's go get some sleep. Did I
tell you I love you today?"

It was a question Julia didn't have to answer.
Once in bed and the lights turned off sleep came quickly,
this time for both of them.

Chapter 42

The next day was the travel day for Ed's playing in the Anheuser-Busch Golf Classic on his Sponsor's exemption. It was being held at Kingsmill Resort in Williamsburg, Virginia. They had the morning to get ready for the afternoon flight to Dulles Airport in Washington DC. It was a direct flight and renting a car and making the two and a half hour drive south seemed the easiest way to get there. They planned to stop part way down at a motel along the way and had an early check in at the Red Roof Inn near Williamsburg for the tournament nights.

Breakfast was taken out to the pool area and consisted of fresh squeezed orange juice and cereal with fruit followed by coffee. It was a pleasant start for the day. Ben was feeling good and mentioned his liking Jennifer and hoped that he would be able to find a new friendship.

Julia concurred and Ed shared his thought that she seemed a very nice person. It was left at that but each knew the meanings of what had been said.

Willy picked them up in his van and they would park it at the airport. The flight was fortunately uneventful and by 10:30 pm that evening they were driving towards Williamsburg. A little after midnight they found a motel and pulled in for the night. They checked in at the Red Roof Inn by 11:00 am and Ed and Willy were shortly

157

taking their first look at the River Course at Kingsmill.

It was a good experience. Totally different than Cog Hill Dubsdread. Shorter with much more needed in strategy rather than length. Willy took notes while Ed hit shots. The greens were tricky and ball placement would be critical. It was a nice day but warm and a bit humid. They met Julia at the club house, which was geared for resort guests, and she had had a good time browsing about and meeting a few players wives to visit with. She confided with Ed that she probably would have enjoyed the walk with him and Willy more but it had still been okay.

Ed's first round tee time had been scheduled before the last tournament and they would play in traditional threesome format. His starting time was at 7:25 am. The only gallery there at that time were wives, relatives and a few friends of the players. Julia was able to walk the course outside the ropes but still had a view as if inside. Ed and Willy would often walk along the edge near her and then veer over to his ball. The first hole was a short par four and a well placed 5 metal-wood followed by a perfect wedge to 5 feet and he had his first birdie in hand. A par on hole two and his second birdie on the par 5 third got his day going.

In the threesome in front of their group was Bob Lohr. He was a little known professional but today he set a new course record of 61. Two 59's had been previously recorded on other courses, one by Al Geiberger in 1977 and the second by Chip Beck three years ago. When the word got out about Lohr's chance at a 59 the crowds started to form. Small at first then growing as his round reached it's final hole. Eleven birdies and one bogey. By the time the favorites had started their rounds Lohr already sat atop the leader board and stayed there until after the second round was well underway.

Ed finished with a respectable 67. It had been a good round on a unfamiliar course and he hoped to do better in round two. An afternoon thunderstorm storm came in after he had finished and caused a 3 hour delay. The last 24 players had to finish their rounds the next morning. Ed's position on the leader board fell as several of the better players finally finished their rounds.

The second day the weather was better but the soggy course had a dampening effect on scores. Ed had a disappointing 69 but at the end of the day found himself in a group including Marc McCumber, Mike Reid, Glen Day, and Justin Leonard. He would be in the next to last pairing on Saturday. Bob Lohr had fallen back but still had a chance. Saturday see-sawed back and forth but by Sunday it became obvious the 15 year professional, McCumber, was going to go the distance. Sunday was a battle but it was McCumber's tournament with him finishing 17 under with Glen Day 3 strokes back at 14 under. Ed was third at 13 under. The golf was good but the heat and humidly were brutal. Half way through the final round the temperature hit 99 degrees which by Palm Desert's heat isn't that bad but in Virginia in July is almost unbearable. Ed and Willy were soaking wet with perspiration and Julia wasn't much better off. They were glad they had decided to stay over Sunday night and had a late afternoon flight home from Dulles. In the morning they took a tourist style walk about Colonial Williamsburg which helped make their flight home a stress free trip. Willy dropped them off at Ben's house and home sweet home had never seemed better. It was becoming Ed's home.

Chapter 43

Ed lay awake and was thinking how nice it was to be so comfortable. Julia was still sleeping and the sight of her next to him was what he was enjoying the most at that moment. It had been a hard trip for them as with the travel, motel rooms and heat and humidity it had taken a toll. The Tour was a tough occupation. But he thought that playing a game you loved and getting paid for doing it made it seem understandable. The game itself was the most important in the equation. The competition came next and then of course the celebrity and the money. All that he could like but the rest was becoming questionable.

His thoughts drifted to more of whether he would want to pursue it as a profession. Still looking at Julia, her breathing gently moving the sheet that covered her, made him think she may not want to go down that road. He remembered Jennifer's comment the other night as she said goodnight "A pro golfer in the making. I don't think so."

Julia started moving and then opened her eyes and gave Ed a smile.

"What are you thinking now?" was in a sleepy, not quite awake voice.

"I was thinking about what Jennifer said to me the other night as I said good night to her."

"What!" was spoken in a very awake voice.

"She was doubting that I would become a professional golfer. Or words to that effect."

Julia moved over to him and wrapped him up in arms and legs. A few good kisses and then a few more. "We can talk about you and Jennifer later. I will make sure you don't think about her anymore. At least not until after breakfast. Or make that after lunch," Julia whispered in his ear. And that would be the case as Ed suddenly had more important matters to attend to.

After breakfast with Ben, Julia and Ed decided to have coffee out by the pool. Ben was off to his office and was in good spirits as his recovery had gone well and he had some new interests to occupy his time. Not surprisingly, Julia asked Ed to expand on his conversation with Jennifer. He repeated her questioning his becoming a professional golfer and that she hoped to be around to see what might come next. Ed thought this an interesting observation and shared it with her.

"I think I maybe very interested in that too," and reached out to touch Ed's shoulder. "What are these broad shoulders going to bear next?"

Ed took a long look at Julia. "I want you to be with me no matter what. Whatever it is we have to do it together. It has to be we."

"Let's go for a walk down to the civic center area. They have just installed a new memorial sculpture I want to see," was her suggestion and they headed there. It was a nice morning, and a good morning to be alive and well. Holding hands they entered the garden area and were the only ones there. The new memorial was named "Desert Holocaust Memorial" and had just been installed. Work

161

was still being done on the landscaping. The sculpture was done by Dee Clements from Colorado. There were a number of figures, bas-relief panels and scripted plaques. The centered sculpture was of a grouping of figures on a black granite Star of David base. It was engrossing and then a sadness came to them both. That such a thing could happen, could ever happen, left them both disheartened but as they left the memorial the realization of how fortunate they were to be alive and able to walk away into their own world revived their spirits. They walked around for another hour, not really paying attention to where they were or what they talked about, and then headed for home.

Ed's next tournament was the New England Classic being played at the Pleasant Valley Country Club in Sutton, Massachusetts. It would start on July 21st with the practice round the day before. They planned to fly into Boston the day before that on July 19th, a week from today. It was less than 40 miles from Boston and Julia was trying to reserve a motel room some where near the country club. She spent the rest of the morning on the telephone and using this new thing called the internet to find lodging. By noon the flights were booked and a motel secured for the three of them.

Ben was taking Jennifer out to dinner that night so they were to make plans for them selves that evening. Julia looked at Ed, and he at her, and together they said "Pedro's." At 5:30 pm they parked the Porsche in front of the window and Pedro excitedly seated them at the table with the view of the parking lot. It was a fun time. A good dinner, the margaritas tasted so good they had two, and the beer was ice cold. When they got back to Palm Desert and parked the car in the garage at Ed's apartment another quick look at each other and they spent the night there. Nothing like the guest bedroom at Ben's house, but it did have it's charm.

Chapter 44

Ed had Willy bring his clubs over to Tamarisk on Wednesday as he and Julia had set up a game that afternoon. Gary Martin was delighted they had taken his invitation to not only practice there but to play whenever they liked. The exposure the club was getting from Willy carrying the Tamarisk bag had already produced three new family memberships. TV's messaging power could never be underestimated and Gary appreciated it's value for the club.

Willy didn't stay as Ed wanted to have a full practice day on Thursday and probably one more before they headed to Pleasant Valley. They would walk but chose pull carts for the clubs. Gary hadn't let it be known Ed would be playing and the course was open until around 2:00 pm when the "doctors" arrived for their mid-week golf. They played the white tees and would play even, no handicap. Ed thought this would be unfair but Julia insisted. She had two things in her favor. When ever she took her address and swung, Ed's mind would lose it's focus on golf. Each time he would think, "No one should look that good and have a swing that was that good. It wasn't fair to the rest." The other thing was that she was really good. As the afternoon progressed he kept thinking she should be taking more strokes but at the turn she was

2 under to his 4 under.

Ed was trying some new ball flights with the Cornith clubs but what ever little tweaks he tried it made no difference. The ball flight was always the same. Gary had come out at the turn and asked he could join them for a few holes. The three played four holes together before he had the first telephone call that required him to return to the club house. Ed ventured that his game seemed a little more solid and relaxed. Gary told him he had decided to try for the Senior Tour in 1996 and having a goal to pursue had helped his game. He asked that they not spread it around as he needed time to get some sponsors and his game in place.

"That is nice. What Gary is going to try. Having a goal to look forward to is so important. I think I almost like him again," Julia then added, "What is your goal Ed?"

"To beat you by 8," he answered in jest.

"Double or nothing," was shot back. Then, "Did we bet anything?"

Ed ended ahead by 3. Julia knew how to play the game. He couldn't have been happier.

Dinner that evening was for four. Ben would accept no help in the kitchen as he had prepared lasagna ahead of time and a big tossed salad and sliced Italian bread would be the simple menu. The lasagna was beyond compare. Red wine was served and they ate out by the pool. Ben and Jennifer were totally at ease with each other, and with Julia and Ed. There was no doubt a family was forming. The conversation flowed between them as each asked and had answered questions. Ed's discovery was that Jennifer was one intelligent lady. Julia liked her honesty and that there didn't appear to be the slightest pressure being put on her grandfather. She found her back and forth with Ed interesting. Julia knew Ed was both smart and intelligent, but was beginning to think Jennifer saw something she didn't, or at least hadn't found out yet. It then dawned on her that Ben also recognized that in Ed and she would have to do some closer examining of what they were seeing that she hadn't.

As the evening shadows descended and darkness came it was time to call it an evening. Again Ben excused himself first, still being a bit tired from his condition. Jennifer went with him to his bedroom but this time she didn't return. Julia took Ed's hand and gently gave it a squeeze. She was smiling when she said how happy she was for her grandfather. And how happy she was for herself.

Chapter 45

The next few days flew by in a blizzard of activity. Three practices, two at Tamarisk and a short one at the College Golf Center. Ed and Julia had a rematch round at Tamarisk with a tie with Ed using his old set of clubs. He learned two things in that round. First, playing golf with Julia was fun. And second, Morris Cornith's clubs didn't mind him using other clubs. His practice on the range the next day had him hitting the best shots of his life.

On Tuesday afternoon, July 19th, Ed, Julia and Willy were flying into Boston, Massachusetts to start Ed's entry into the big time spotlight. The flight went well and a nice bed & breakfast near Sutton was to be their home for a few days. Another player, along with his wife and his brother, were staying there. They were all young people, about Julia's age, from Wisconsin: Steve, Nicki and Jerry Stevens. The six of them filled the four rooms and it was a nice change from the Red Roof Inns. By the end of the week they were all close friends. Even Willy, although reluctant at first, became family.

The course at Pleasant Valley was very much like Tamarisk. Relatively flat, adjacent fairways and enough doglegs, bunkers, sand traps and water hazards to keep the golfers honest. It was not a long course but as the golf equipment and golf ball were being improved at an alarming rate, the just over 7,000 yards was becoming too short to make par a good score.

Wednesday's practice round went especially well for Ed and his confidence that this might be his week was growing. He and Willy decided to put the two 5 metal woods with the draw and fade ball flights in the bag and took out the straight 3 iron. One could see seven dogleg holes but for three of those a long straight drive would clear the approach around the corner. The other four could be handled with the 5's. Even Ed's putting was running true and the old Wilson Winsum was his best friend again.

Nicki Stevens had been Steve's caddie his first 3 years on tour but was now well into her first pregnancy and therefore his brother would be carrying the bag. Julia and Nicki bonded immediately and it made their week such a pleasure that the golf took second place. It was only a 10 minute drive to the venue so they could go back and forth easily. It turned out to be a good thing as it was going to be record setting heat for the entire tournament. Friday it hit 100 degrees.

Ed and Steve had almost identical starting times but Steve's was on the front nine and Ed's on the back. Both are long par fours, hole number 1 being the number one handicap while 10 is the number 4. They both had pars. The front nine has three par fives and par is 37 while the back nine has only one and par is 35. Ed had a very good day and had a 4 under score of 68. Steve was one more at 69. Both finished in the top 10 and were very satisfied with their play. Kenny Perry was atop of the leader board with a 67.

Pleasant Valley had some very long holes, such as 1, 7, 10 and 17 requiring long, carefully placed drives followed with long irons to narrow greens. Seven was a three shot par 5 which no one reached in two. The fairways were narrow in some places and where wide there was always some trees to contend with or water lurking. You could post good scores and it would be close to the end. Kenny Perry's final round 66 bested all others at 16 under and Ed had to be satisfied being tied with David Fererty for second one stroke back. Steve was two more back but still had a good payday.

Ed, Julia and Willy stayed one more night but the Stevens party had packed up and started by car to the next tournament in Tennessee. Nicki had wished she could stay but that was not the life of a professional golfer, at least not until winnings hit the big time. Julia had a hard time saying good bye and Ed could tell that life on the road may not be for her. He was also thinking it may not be for him either and definitely not if Julia would not be with him.

Chapter 46

It was quiet at breakfast the next morning. The three of them were tired and missing the Stevens's company. Then Willy, reluctantly, told Ed he thought his days as a caddie were over. Age, health and wanting to be with his wife and the kids were enough to keep him happy at home. It had been a great experience to be inside the ropes and involved in golf at this level. That if he didn't have his other life to pursue he would be begging to keep on being his caddie.

Ed wasn't surprised and he could see from Julia's expression she was sympathizing with Willy's thinking. He told Willy that he understood and they had had a great run together. Also that if things in his future developed that he needed help he would try to get him back on the bag, so to speak. Willy looked relieved and showed his first big smile of the morning. Julia looked at Ed and wanted to know just what was going on in his mind as for the future. She decided he would tell her when the time was right and she would wait. Ed had no idea of what was to be in his future but knew he wouldn't let golf dominate it or let Julia not be a part of it.

They had an easy day. Made a mid-day tourist visit to downtown Boston and then were at the airport early and their flight was on time. About half way back Ed leaned against Julia and spoke to what she was thinking. "Professional golf isn't it. Am I right?

"Oh Ed, I'm not sure. The excitement is there. The competition. The beautiful places and courses you get to visit and play on. The people. The glamour. How can it not be enough. But I am not sure it is," she responded with a forlorn look he hadn't seen before.

"I tell you what. I have an invite to play in the PGA Championship at Southern Hills Country Club in Tulsa. We have a little over a week to prepare and you could caddie for me. After that we can decide what to do with the rest of our lives. I would like to give a major tournament a shot and maybe win a big one for Morris, Hank, Ben and Harriet. One more try and that should be enough, unless we change our minds."

Julia took his hand and leaned her head against his shoulder.

"Sounds like a good plan to me. I want ten percent plus expenses," and she let out a sigh of relief.

Willy dropped them off at Ben's and parked in front in the driveway was the silver 1958 Lincoln Continental with Hank's driver leaning against the big spare tire cover.

"Hi you two. Hank sent me over with some stuff we carted back from Harriet's place this morning. He says you are to get it out of his car today!" was said with a I don't care what you do with it attitude.

"We can put it in Ben's garage," ventured Ed.

"Ben already says no but that you got an apartment you could store it in just a few blocks from here."

Ben came out and greeted them both, especially Julia. He looked like the happiest man alive. He suggested

171

to Ed that he get the stuff unloaded at his place and hurry back for dinner. Jennifer would be over in a half hour, was bringing take out Chinese and was planning on them being here.

Ed suggested the garage and Ben countered with describing how big the trunk was, pointing at the Continental. "It is full and there is more in the back seat. Julia can stay here but come right back after you unload," Ben instructed as he and Julia went into the house.

As they drove the few blocks to Ed's apartment he took a peek into the back seat. There were four Banker Boxes, looking a bit the worse for age and wear, stacked up two by two. His next thought was how big the trunk was and it then dawned on him what would be in them. "Oh God, it has to be Morris's files," he said out loud. "You better believe they are heavy, man!" was the driver's comment. He had to load them all at Harriet's place himself and wasn't to excited on having to help Ed.

It took half an hour. They were heavy and the stairs were steep. There were fourteen boxes. The oldest ones looked to be ready to come apart but they all made into the apartment intact. Stacked against the wall it didn't look too bad but every one, except the newest looking box, was full. Ed opened it and on top was the photograph of Julia, her mother and father, and her maternal grandparents. In a ragged handwriting was a note for Julia to save all this for the right time to show Ben. That she would know when it is time. It was simply signed, Harriet.

Ed locked up the apartment and turning to thank Hank's driver for the help he saw the big car make the first turn and disappear from sight.

Chapter 47

Dinner was served on the pool side table. The Chinese takeout was very good with two entrees and the restaurant's special fried rice. Those that could used the provided chop sticks but Ed enjoyed his meal using a fork. It was a warm evening and they were all dressed in light summer wear. Not bathing suits but close. Ed was looking at Jennifer surprised at what an attractive woman she was. It was not lust and the smile she gave him back, when she noticed his gaze, acknowledged that she knew it wasn't.

Ed was beginning to understand that she had an intellect that was a match for Ben. What he didn't realize, however, was that he had one that matched theirs. Jennifer and Ben knew this even if he hadn't ever given it a thought. When his parents were killed he dropped out of that world. He was at Stanford on a golf scholarship but was majoring in mathematics. He had started in engineering but migrated into mathematics and was a straight A student. Several of his professors were cultivating him to be their star protege. It was a world he walked away from and hadn't given a second thought to in the last ten years. He had been living day to day until Julia entered his life. Hank knew, Ben knew and now Jennifer knew. They were waiting for Ed to find out there should be more for him than just golf. There was, but Ed had carefully not let it come back into his life. It was too painful to pursue as it was so involved with his mother's hope for him at the time she was taken from him that he couldn't go there.

Ben and Jennifer picked up the dinner plates and took them into the kitchen. Julia and Ed could see them from where they were sitting and were watching them when Jennifer said something that made Ben smile. She leaned forward and kissed him. Not just a peck, a kiss that meant something much more. They were smiling as they came back holding hands.

"We are going to take a walk. You two have had a long day and if you choose to head to bed we will see you in the morning," Ben said this giving instructions, telling them something and saying goodnight.

As they left, Julia came over to Ed and sat close. "She is so good for him. I haven't seen him so happy in years," and then followed with questions: "Do you think she is too young? She is good looking, don't you think? More than pretty, beautiful in a way. Should she be falling in love with someone Grandpa's age?"

Ed took Julia's hands in his and looked her in the eyes. "He has found his intellectual soul mate and she has found hers. When this happens, nothing else matters. Don't worry about them. Just be happy it has happened."

Julia looked at Ed and then asked "Have you found your soul mate?"

"Yes. I think right now Ben and I are the luckiest two men on earth. Some things are meant to be and that describes us. And tomorrow we will start the hunt for our future," and Ed left it at that and waited.

"What are you talking about? Hunting for our future? Finding it tomorrow?" Julia was pulling on his arm and laughing.

"Okay, here's what I am thinking. There are fourteen boxes that Hank picked up from Harriet who must have stored them as a favor to Maureen. One of the boxes is actually for you, from Harriet, and the others have got to be Morris's files on his golf clubs. I will bet you there is something for us in one of those thirteen. Just like Ben and Hank waited for me, or someone like me, to show up there is something for that person hidden in Morris's files. What do you want to bet on my being right?" Ed let the question hang in the air.

"Let's get to bed, stare at the ceiling, and try to imagine what it could be," Julia announced and suddenly had another thought.

"If you know one box was for me you must have opened it. What was in it?"

"On top was the photograph of your mother and father with you and your grandparents. There is a note from Harriet saying you will know when it is time for you to show what's in the box to Ben," Ed said this as gently as possible.

"Something is happening with Harriet and we need to visit her. Soon!" Julia was near tears and Ed said that they would make the visit. He thought it was also time to visit with Hank, if that was possible, and Carolyn and Harold Finegold. Golf was not that important. They could do all three but first things first.

Once in bed they on lay their backs looking at the ceiling. There was one small lamp in the room that was still on that gave off just enough light to make out the patterns in the plaster. Julia moved slightly and put her hand on Ed's shoulder.

"Do you see our future?" she whispered.

'I am still searching. It has got to be there some-where. How about you?" Ed answered.

Julia then moved closer and told Ed what he wanted to hear. "My future is right here next to me. Don't you go anywhere without me." Soon Ed could hear her breathing steady and see her eyes had closed. A faint smile was on her face and he knew that she was his future. Tomorrow was going to be the beginning of something. They only had to make sure they recognized it when they saw it.

Chapter 48

After a nice breakfast with Ben and Jennifer Ed told them of their plan to spend some time seeing what the boxes contained and then drive over to La Jolla and take Harriet to lunch. On the way back they would stop to see the Finegolds and would be back for dinner. Ben surprised them with the news that he and Jennifer were having dinner with Hank at his home.

Julia was quick with "You have to be kidding me, Hank Morgan hasn't invited anyone to his house in years."

Ben laughed and answered "He found out about Jennifer and said he wanted to meet her, or any woman that would spend more than one hour with me. I have warned Jennifer of what it will be like."

"Nothing like a challenge to make life interesting. I think Hank and I are going to have a lot in common and we will become friends in ten minutes," Jennifer voicing her opinion with humor.

Julia smiled at that. "Let us know how it turns out. You win the medal if you're right about a friendship. Tell Hank 'Hi' for us and that Ed and I would like to have a visit this week." They made their excuses and walked the two blocks to Ed's apartment. Once inside Ed placed Julia's box on the floor where there was some space and she settled in to see what it contained. It was mostly photos, both loose and in albums. School year books and scrap books. It was divided almost equally with her mother's and her grandmother's memories. It was going to take a long time to go through and she started to sort them into piles. The framed photograph of her mother and father was propped up on the side of the box and she repeatedly picked it up and looked closely at them and her grandparents. She had missed a very important part of her life and she hoped that some of the things missed would be there.

Ed opened the first box on the top of the stack at the left end and pulled out a manila file which was stuffed with letter size white papers with all sorts of mathematical equations, numerous notes and small sketches. It had to be the 5-iron as a 5 was in the upper left hand corner with a page number, or at least it looked to be that. The top page in this file was 5-3b65x. "This isn't going to be easy," he said aloud as he closed the file putting it back and pulling the next one out. It's first page had 5-3c65x. This went on for an hour. Each box was filled but in the very back was a smaller box containing multiple golf club heads having a great variety of shapes with nothing in common except the face angle.

After another hour Ed told Julia that it was time to head to La Jolla. She was ready as she knew she couldn't rush through her family history that was secreted in all the things now on the floor.

"I just started to get it sorted out and already need a break. Going to visit Harriet will be perfect. The drive over will be just what I need."

Ed responded with just, "Me too."

The drive over was just what they needed. It was

a nice day and the temperature was starting to climb. The Porsche's windows were both open and provided enough breeze to keep them cool. They talked about what had been discovered and agreed nothing yet had been found. Ed posed he would have to learn what Morris's codes meant if he wanted to search through all his records and find anything of value. Julia remarked she would need Ben to help her find what she now desperately wanted to know. What her mother's and grandmother's lives had been like and where she had belonged in theirs. By the time they parked near the park in La Jolla they agreed that it may take some time to discover their future. Ed, at least, was still sure it was in one of the boxes.

Chapter 49

Jimmy opened the door and they were invited in. It was quiet in Harriet's condo. Ed immediately noticed that more than half the framed photos were missing from the hallway wall. He took Julia's hand and whispered "Be ready, she may be sick."

Harriet sat in a wheel chair at the table looking over the Pacific. Her skin was gray and even with her hair nicely combed and a touch of make up there was no doubt she wasn't well. A hug from Julia and a gentle hand from Ed and their greetings were taken care of.

"Don't ask and don't tell me any lies," were her first words. Before Julia, or Ed, could speak she continued, "They want me in the hospital but this is where I want to be. Right here looking out the window. Jimmy has been fabulous. I have a nurse from two till two to care for me. We will lunch here. Talk about things and you are to leave just before two. That's the plan," and she seemed to wilt in front of their eyes from the effort.

Jimmy had set the table while they talked and again served a very nice lunch. Harriet recovered a bit but the fire in her eyes was no longer there. They talked about the box of things for Julia and she repeated to show them to Ben when the time was right. Julia told her about Jennifer and her being there with Ben. She smiled her first

180

genuine smile. Ed commented on all the boxes of Morris's files and Harriet almost got out one of her signature laughs. She did offer Ed good luck. Nobody else had been able to make any sense of them.

Then Harriet surprised them both asking Ed. "Are you playing in the PGA Championship?" He answered yes and she said, "Good. I will hang around to see if you can win it. Doesn't matter if you do or not. That will be enough for Morris and he can rest easy from then on."

Harriet then closed her eyes and drifted off to sleep. Jimmy was at her side and told Julia and Ed she would sleep for several hours. He wiped his eyes. "I don't think she will make until after the PGA but she is one tough little lady and I wouldn't be surprised if she does."

They said their goodbyes to the sleeping lady in the wheel chair, thanked Jimmy and headed back to the park. There was no ticket on the windshield and Ed put two more quarters in the meter. They needed a walk and some time on a bench overlooking the ocean.

Julia couldn't let go of Ed's hand and as they drove back to Palm Desert she rested her hand on his thigh. She was quiet, as was he, and it wasn't until they started down on Highway 74 into the valley that their spirits began to come back. Pulling into the Finegold's driveway they were greeted with such smiles of welcome they were able to set aside their visit with Harriet and be good company for Harold and Carolyn.

Entering their home the first thing noticed was the long banquet table with a computer monitor, keyboard, scanner and printer. The computer was on the floor and there were cables running every where. Two office chairs were placed in front of the table. Papers were scattered about. More than half the living room was taken up.

Ed started to laugh. "I thought you told me you two were computer illiterate. What's going on here?"

Carolyn started and they reverted to each other finishing the others thought. What had happened was that Ben and Hank had hired them to keep track of all printed articles about Ed's progress in professional golf. One of their neighbor's son was a computer geek, got them set up and taught them how to search on this new thing called the Web. He was almost a full time employee because as fast as they learned one thing they would forget another one.

They quickly sat down and gave a demonstration. Typing in Ed Adams in a box on the screen, then Enter on the keyboard there was the sound of a telephone dial tones and in a minute there was a list of items with Ed's name in the title. With a mouse they put the cursor on the top one, hit Enter and a newspaper article came up on the screen. Carolyn reached over Harold's shoulder and touched the print key and the printer came alive and printed out what was on the screen. Carolyn picked up the copy and handed it to Ed. It was about last Sunday's finish at the New England Classic. An article published in a Connecticut newspaper from yesterday's edition.

"Wow, can you believe that?" Ed was surprised and he handed the copy to Julia. She read the first few paragraphs and smiled.

"So you two are now computer wizards. How about that," and Julia's smile lit up the room. Carolyn and Harold were almost bursting with pride and told Ed and Julia that the last two months were the most exciting they had ever had. They pulled out a big note book off the shelf that had page after page of articles, all referring to Ed's play. Many had photographs, a number of which feature Julia and Willy.

"We buy all the local papers, some of the national ones, and the golf magazines that are just starting to catch up. If you are mentioned we get them too. We can scan them and print a copy to put in the notebooks," saying this in their usual duet.

It had been a good visit. On the short drive to the apartment Julia thought out loud, "Is this our future?"

Ed responded, but slowly, "I don't think so but I think it is a part of finding out what it is to be."

Chapter 50

Ed drove by the apartment, and as he did, he asked Julia if Pedro's sounded good to her. She didn't hesitate saying that it was exactly what she needed. Pedro didn't disappoint and insisted they have one of his new recipe Chilles Rellenos. It was agreed it was the best they had ever eaten and he would become world famous. Ed offered they would no longer be able to get a table again once the word got out.

It was quiet driving back. The last two days had been long with a lot going on and the previous week with travel and tournament play had taken their toll. Ed parked the car at the apartment and they walked backed to Ben's holding hands. There was a slight detour to share an ice cream cone and then it was time for bed.

Sleep came quickly and morning came at the usual hour. Julia looked at Ed and smiled. "I think maybe this afternoon. What do you think?" was said and she was off to the bathroom before he could answer. She didn't need an answer and knew what it would be in any case.

Breakfast was fun and Ben and Jennifer seemed particular happy. They asked Julia, almost together, what she would think about Jennifer moving in with them. Ed wasn't included in the question and was neither surprised or offended.

"What should I call you?" addressing Jennifer in the affirmative and a smile of acceptance.

"How about just Jen. I think Ben and Jen sounds good," was Ben's suggested.

"I think that sounds just fine. Ed, what do you think?" Julia asked Ed for his opinion.

"I think Ben is one very lucky man. That is what I think," and he meant it.

Julia was happy, ready for the day to start. Ed had been mulling over how he should combine getting ready for the PGA Championship and searching through the boxes. He had been invited to play based on his finishes in the three events he had played in and only for that reason. He was an unknown five weeks ago and adding to the mystic were the strange clubs in his bag which made for a good story. He needed to perform and earn the invitation.

He and Julia talked it over as they walked to the apartment. She was still coming down from the high of seeing her grandfather in love again. Ed's suggestion of spending the morning at Tamarisk practicing was deemed a fine start to the day so that is what they did. Ed took the clubs out of the bag and placed them and the bag across the small back seat in the Porsche. A smile came to his face as he remembered one day he and three friends stuffed themselves into the little car and going downhill on a long deserted stretch of highway made it to 110 miles per hour. It was another time but was worth a smile.

The practice went well. The shots were crisp and on target. One after another. He felt good and Julia took interest. About half way through she started calling out ball flights just as started his back swing. Draw, fade, low, high. She kept delaying the calls and made them as he started the downswing. It was amazing how it worked. His mind had complete control of his swing without him actually thinking. It was almost scary the amount of control he had with the Morris Cornith clubs.

Gary came out to the range just about the time they were finishing up and the pleasantries were exchanged. He had heard Ed had been invited to play in the PGA Championship and wanted him to know Tamarisk was his for practice. He could have the tee and play almost any time he wanted.

Ed then asked if he and Julia could have a few Tamarisk caps and hats to go along with the bag as she would be his caddie. Gary almost lost his cool at this.

"You are kidding me. I will put together a nice selection. Lot's of colors, you know green and gold lettering. Some towels and other stuff. Need another bag?" he said with laughter in his voice. "You are some nice guy, Ed. Has Julia found that out yet?" and he took off to get the supplies.

As they were packing up the Porsche Gary made it back with a two large bundles and they were stuffed in the back on top of the clubs. The pile went to the ceiling and fortunately the car had side view mirrors on both sides. As they left the parking lot Julia looked puzzled.

"Why all the excitement about golf caps and hats?" and as soon as she asked the question she answered it. "You just gave Tamarisk thousands of dollars in publicity, didn't you?"

She reached over and squeezed his thigh and planted a kiss on his cheek. "You are a nice man. I think that is a good thing for me to know."

Chapter 51

Dinner was taken out to the pool area and the new family adjusted to their places. It wasn't a difficult adjustment. Seating came without thought. It was comfortable, more like the very close and old friendship between two couples. The conversation covered a variety of topics. Ed and Julia with their plans for the next week and a half getting ready for the PGA Championship and the search of the Morris Cornith golf club files. But most interesting was Jennifer's account of her marriage and the accidental death of her husband.

She causally mentioned that her husband, Allan Mercer, had graduated from the Naval Academy in 1964. He was sent to the Navy Fighter Weapons School in San Diego that was newly being formed at the nearby Miramar Naval Air Base. This would later become known as the TOPGUN School. After training he was assigned to the carrier Forestall and ended up flying 32 missions into North Vietnam.

Ben interrupted her by asking if that was when John McCain, the senator from Arizona, was on the Forestall, involved in the missile explosion on board and later was shot down. She said that Allan arrived a few months before the explosion and it was 3 months later that McCain got shot down. She offered that Allan, and many of the other pilots, didn't like him.

She quickly tried to shorten her story with that he returned state side in 1974 and left the navy as being a flight instructor was not what he wanted to do. He had a good offer as a test pilot in Fallon, Nevada and four years later there was a crash of a prototype fighter he was flying and he was killed.

Jennifer had abruptly finished and Julia asked her "What was it like to be married to a TOPGUN?"

"You cannot imagine how exciting it was. How many people you would meet, the places you would go. The separations were terrible, the reunions fantastic. I wouldn't trade those years for anything but I wouldn't want to live them again. I want to be here now. With you," she said saying this with some tears, but still with a smile.

Ben had been quiet. His thoughts had returned to his personal losses. Of his daughter and then his wife. It had been a long time, and until Jennifer had come into his life he had resisted letting anything come between his memories and himself. He suddenly knew the time had come and he felt as if a burden had been lifted from his shoulders. He didn't know how to express what he was feeling at the moment but he could live with the memories and with a new person in his life. Jennifer was what could ease his pain and give him a future. Julia now had her life to live, and he could enjoy sharing part of it with her, but he now had his to live and he was looking forward to it.

Ed had been watching and listening. He could see Ben's demeanor changing just by his expression and how he looked at Jennifer, and then looked at Julia. Something had happened in the past few minutes that was life chang-ing for Ben. Ed knew because Julia had lifted from him the pain of the memory of losing his parents.

Later in bed Julia reached out for Ed and laid her head on his chest. She didn't say anything at first and he waited. Finally the conversation started.

"That was nice seeing Grandpa looking that way at Jen. He had a different look tonight. He is happy. Not just satisfied but happy. Did you see that?" Julia was whispering as if she was telling him a secret.

"It was the sun braking through a cloudy day. No mistaking he is happy right now and that is how life should be. Now I will tell you a secret and don't you tell anyone else. I am happy for the first time in years. It is for the same reason that Ben is happy." Ed was whispering too and ran his hand over her head and down to rest on her shoulder. Julia snuggled closer and fell asleep. Ed didn't move until she moved to a more comfortable position, still touching, but with her head on the pillow. Sleep for Ed did come but he was in no hurry to get there.

Chapter 52

When Ed woke, Julia was still laying next to him asleep and he didn't want to move. Today was the last Thursday of July and in two weeks he would be readying to tee up his first ball in the 1994 PGA Championship. Two months ago he had wakened in his small apartment, alone, with absolutely nothing to look forward to. He looked at Julia, then around the room, and then back at her. He wondered if Ben could even approach having the feelings he had at that moment. He hoped so.

"Hey big fella, what is that look on your face. Did you just win it all?" Julia's happy voice made Ed's perfect morning come into focus.

After a long kiss good morning he managed to tell her some of what he had been thinking.

"Two weeks from right about now you should be handing me the driver, telling me just to relax and hit it straight just left of center three hundred yards. Then give me a smile and watch me do it," Ed said but not sounding convincing.

"I don't think that was what you were thinking and I can feel what it is," and then quickly added "We better not miss our starting time," and pulled him closer.

At breakfast they were joined by Ben and Jennifer and Ed thought that it may have been that they almost missed breakfast, too. It appeared that all were in very good moods this morning.

Ed and Julia were going to spend the morning working through the boxes in the apartment with no plans for the afternoon. Ben and Jennifer were off to Newport Beach and would have lunch there and be back for dinner. Julia offered to cook and would make it a surprise.

At the apartment they first just stood and looked at boxes stacked along the wall. Ed had a plan which was more along the line of at least doing something and hoping an idea would come along that made sense. He arranged the boxes singly instead of stacked and positioned them so they were open side by side. The manila file folders were identified by 1,2,3, etc. front to back on the left tab corner and by club numbers of the box 3, 5, 7 and 9, W1-W6, P, D and FW on the right side. Each folder in a box was therefore identified as to which box it should be filed and it's order. The right hand tab numbers were on the left corner of the boxes. Simple, but they should be able to keep the papers in the right places.

"Well, what box should we start with?" Ed asked Julia.

"Why do you always ask me to make the really tough decisions?" then, "Seven, that is were it all began."

Ed pulled out the last two folders from the 7 box and handed 16 to Julia and kept 17 for himself. "Let browse through each page and see if anything rings a bell."

They sat on the two small chairs at the table and started with a cursory look at each page. Fortunately Morris had very good hand writing and only wrote on one side of each page. Unfortunately it was mostly mathe-

191

matical formulas and notations. Ed had enough high level math in college that he could occasionally spot something he could recognize but Julia didn't have a clue what all the mumbo jumbo meant.

"You can't expect me to understand any of this do you?" she complained, smiling.

"No. Just if anything looks out of place or is written in plain English. Like a note that says see such and such. Or a use this or measure that. I haven't seen a single thing I understand. There are a few familiar equations I recognize but not in any usable context." Ed's answer was said in a discouraged voice.

He got up and went over to the 7 box and pulled out the small box in the back of the files. Taking it to the table he set out the half dozen club heads on the table and he and Julia examined them and passed them back and forth.

Julia spoke first as she was turning one rather beaten up head over in her hands. "This is one of the early Ping irons, maybe over twenty five years ago. A lot of the perimeter weighting is gone but has been added back on the heel and toe. The scoring on the face has been changed. It is really ugly but similar to a seven iron."

"You're right. Look at this one. It has that crazy number 7-5c65x in black ink on the sole. That references a page, or pages, in the files so let's see if we can find it, or them."

Ed was now getting excited. In folder number 8 they found the pages with 7-5c65x. There were 12 pages in all. On one of the pages was a drawing of the club head and arrows to various places with designations of A, B, C and D. He found A and it was another undecipherable equation.

He looked at Julia. "It's a starting point but I don't have any idea in which direction we are going."

Chapter 53

They had a nice evening together. That afternoon Julia had spent an hour at the grocery store with Ed pushing the cart but not paying much attention. He carried the several bags from the car into the house to the kitchen and was then instructed by Julia to leave her alone. She looked so happy he didn't want to but after a little fooling around he was escorted out and she got to work. The entree was Coquilles Saint Jacques which was served in large shells with a tossed greens salad and diagonally sliced baguette. Chilled white wine was served in large crystal glasses. The dining room table was beautifully set and the meal tasted even better.

Dessert was Creme Brulee, caramelized perfectly, and served topped with a single large raspberry. Ed had never in his life tasted anything as good as what Julia had just put together. He couldn't stop looking at her in amazement and pride. As they toasted the cook with the last of the wine Ben spoke to Julia in almost a whisper.

"Your mother could cook like that. She would see a recipe, or just a photograph of a menu, and put it all together and it would come out like this. Just like this and she would have the same expression on her face that you have now knowing she pulled it off as good as it could be done."

"Thank you Grandpa. I like hearing you talking about her. I have a photograph that Harriet gave me of you and Grandma and my mother and father with me. Would you like to see it," Julia offered hoping this was the right time.

It was and she brought out a small box of special photos she had selected from the collection Harriet had given her. The four of them sat close together and went through the collection. Ben talked without any hesitation and it was the first time Julia had heard the stories he told. Ed and Jennifer just listened and watched as a grandfather told his granddaughter the things about the two most important women of his past. The things she needed to know about them.

That night as they lay together in bed Julia let out a long sigh and snuggled up even closer to Ed. "That was nice tonight. Harriet was there in my head telling me it was the right time. She is a wise old woman. We have to visit her before we leave for Tulsa."

"Let's go Monday. It won't be too crowded at the park and we should be back here before the traffic gets bad. Call Jimmy in the morning and set it up. Why don't you call Nikki and see if we can get a place together with them for the Championship." Ed said hoping he was not being too pushy.

Julia sat up and gave him a curious look. "I was already going to call Nikki, and you don't have to ask me. At least most of the time." She then gave him a smile, a different look and told him what he should do. Ed thought that was a very good idea and complied without another word being said.

The next morning was to be a practice session and

Willy was going to come over to Tamarisk and work with them. They were meeting at 8:00 am as summer was here and by noon the temperature was reaching the low hundreds. If you were going to be outside, the earlier the better.

It was a good practice and Ed felt that his swing was right and the ball flights showed that to be the case. The golfer calls it grooved. Swing after swing, each the same to the point you don't have to think about it. All the concentration is then on making the decisions on lie, target, alignment and weather. Go through your routine, address the ball and start your swing. Then watch the ball and if your decision was correct the ball will end up where you wanted it to be.

Willy had a good time just watching. He missed the interaction with Ed and Julia but needed his time at home. He suggested they play 18 with Julia on the bag, in a competition style, to get any problems sorted out. He would walk with them and help out when questions came up. They decided on Tuesday, August 2nd, which would be one week before they would fly to Tulsa.

They had sandwiches at the snack bar, enjoying the shade and Willy's stories of handling five foster kids, ages four to twelve, three boys and two girls. Occasionally one would be adopted but this group had been together for three years and were family. They had started the legal proceedings to adopt them.

Ed and Julia headed for the apartment. The air conditioning was running, it was cool inside and the boxes were waiting with their hidden secret.

Chapter 54

Julia was the first to find a clue and it was in the box that had the family photos and albums. It was a photo of an older man in a wheel chair. Standing on either side of him was Ben and a man who was a younger looking Hank. Something had caused them all to be laughing.

She handed the photo to Ed and he took a look and smiled. Ben was the handsome one of the three. He started to hand it back to Julia and then took a second look more closely.

"That's it! You may have just solved the problem for us. Look here, in Morris's lap. It's a putter. It is the putter that he never finished," Ed said excitedly.

Julia looked and said, "You can just make it out. The shaft is under his arm and the head you can just make out. It is a putter. Which box has putter on it?"

"There isn't one but there is a box that has P on it. I just thought pitching wedge since everyone said he never made a putter. There isn't one in the clubs we have but that sure looks like one in his lap," Ed was saying this as he headed for the boxes. It was there and held a number of files and a smaller box in the back. He pulled several files out and started to thumb through them. Julia came over and did the same. They were like all the other files, filled with equations and mathematical symbols.

Ed pulled out the small box and headed for the table. It was closed with some type of tape that was stronger than normal packaging tape and wouldn't pull loose even after all those years. Ed found the sharpest knife in his kitchen drawer and started sawing away. Julia was standing beside him hardly able to restrain herself from reaching out to help. The box was finally open and inside was a cloth wrapping something the size of a club head. They looked at it and then at each other.

Julia spoke first but said simply asked, "Is this it?"

"I don't know," was all Ed could answer.

"Well, let's see what it is."

They both sat down and Ed placed it on the table. There was nothing else in the box. At first he was afraid to unwrap it but then grasped an edge of the cloth and slowly lifted it part way. Julia was starting to squirm about in her chair but didn't say anything. One more pull on the edge and out fell what had to the strangest looking putter head you could imagine. Almost square in shape with a flat bottom, rounded sides, angled back and the only good looking side was a face with a myriad of various shaped grooves. It had been polished but now looked somewhat like tarnished silver.

Ed picked it up and turned it around in his hand. He handed it to Julia and she did the same, examining it from all angles. She then set it down on the table. There was no hosel but there was a hole for the shaft to be inserted. It was at an odd angle and when Ed stuck a pencil in the angle seemed to be in the wrong direction. Julia picked up the photograph with Morris and the putter and laid it on the table next to the putter head. They moved the putter head to match the position of the one Morris was holding and could just make out it was the same. Ed could tell the shaft had to have been bent in at least two directions to achieve the angle shown in the photo.

"Ben will know. He knows a lot more about these clubs than he has let on. Hank will know even more. It is time they quit playing with us. That is why they are laughing in the photo." Julia was excited with the revelation and then started laughing. Ed caught the spirit and joined in.

They brought the file box over to the table and started going through each file examining each page. Ed pulled one sheet out and there was a single line drawn with odd bends at it's end. It also had several arrows with letter designations. He knew what they meant and also knew he had no way to find out what that was.

Ed packed up the Bankers Box with the P and they headed home. Ben and Jennifer were out by the pool and when he set the box on the table Ben smiled.

"You found it. Good. Now all you have to do is fit the right shaft and see if it will work for you like the other clubs."

"You knew about this all along. None of the other clubs worked for you or anyone else. Then I came along and they did for me. So the only club left that could possibly be made to be sold to the public is the putter. All this is for Morris. It was a game you three played, wasn't it?" Ed got it out before he started to laugh.

Ben was still smiling. "No, it was not like that. Not a game. You have to understand we three were best friends. When Morris and Hank first moved here Morris was already in a wheel chair and wanting something to do set about creating golf clubs using computing technology. He never let anyone, not even Hank or me, swing them. Occasionally when he wasn't paying attention, or left the garage to attend to something in the house, we would grip one but never swung it. We both thought him a bit crazy about this but he seemed to love the challenge much more than the results. Just before he died he asked the two of us to see if his putter design would work. To actually test it on a green. After his funeral Maureen had all the clubs put in the big bag and his files put in the Banker Boxes and they were taken and stored with Harriet when she moved into her place. His shop equipment was sold as a package deal and we lost contact with it." Ben took a break and his face showed he was having trouble with what he needed to say next.

"Harriet called Hank about a year ago and asked him to come get Morris things as she needed to prepare for her own exit. Hank called me and that is when we decided to finally try to fulfill Morris's request about his putter. Once we saw all those clubs and boxes of files we thought we were in no position to get that done so we concocted the plan to find a younger man to carry the burden. One big problem, there was no putter in the bag," and looking at Ed added "And that is why you are here."

Chapter 55

Ben could see the expressions on Julia and Ed's faces and quickly said "I think I didn't say that quite right." He hesitated and then continued, "Ed, you would have been welcomed here as Julia's friend and in the future as you are now. Your meeting her had nothing to do with Hank's and my plans. Understand my knowing so much about you from his investigation made me comfortable with Julia falling in love with you. You are family now and I couldn't be happier for myself and you both."

Julia smiled and walked over and kissed Ben on the check and then asked, "So now that our family problems are all solved what about this putter?"

Jennifer started laughing. "What kind of family have I joined. Brought together by a putter, designed by a computer genius who never played golf and is deceased, handed down by his widow to old friends who promised years ago to find it a place in golfing history."

"Speaking of which, let me see it," was Ben's request. Julia brought it over to Ben and unwrapped the towel. It truly looked ugly and it was Ben's turn to start laughing. He picked up his phone and punched a speed dial. They all could hear the raspy voice of Hank Morgan ask "Is it there?" and Ben's saying it was. "Be there in fifteen minutes," and then the dial tone.

The doorbell rang fifteen minutes later and Ben went to the door. Hank's first words once he got out to the pool area were "Christ Ben, couldn't we take a look at the damn club in your office. You may have to carry me back to the car."

Hank had been a tall man, just under 6 foot 6 inches but was now bent over with his head about chest high to Ben. Ed was surprised at his firm handshake even though the hand was a gnarled bunch of bony fingers. The fragrance of scotch and tobacco was there, but a bow to the ladies was made and then it was to the putter.

"That's the ugliest putter I have ever seen. Ed, it's up to you to see if you can do anything with it." Then pausing and trying to look heavenward continued, "I have seen and held it Morris. I am done with your damn clubs. Just kidding, we will make it work," and Hank turned to leave but Julia came over and took his hand.

"You go over there and sit next to Jennifer. She told us about your dinner together and what a fun guy you are. So be nice," Julia saying this through some laughter. Hank looked at her with such love you could see he would do anything for her and did just what she asked. The next hour was fun for all. When Hank saw the photograph of Morris with the putter, and he and Ben on either side, he got very quiet.

"Maureen took that picture. Remember Ben? You had come out to visit and see if you wanted to move out here. That was the day you made the decision to do it. You found this house and the Realtor had taken you over to where Julia would go to school. It had been a good day and Morris was still feeling okay. I miss those days. I miss Morris."

Jennifer took his hand, gave it a squeeze and then continued holding it. Conversation then turned to more happy subjects and Hank lasted another half hour. He then made his good afternoons and Ed walked him to the door where his driver was waiting next to the big Lincoln.

"Make it work for us Ed. The PGA was important but the putter will be the Gold Medal. You can trust me on that."

They shook hands for the second time that day but this one had some meaning that was more than just good afternoon.

Chapter 56

Saturday was going to be a fun day for Ed and Julia. The task was now to get a shaft to fit the putter and see if it held any magic. They spent the morning going through the files. Sitting at the small table near the pool they had all 14 folders out and were going one page at at time. Nothing gave even a hint at how to proceed after they had looked over half of the pile.

Ben came out, took a seat and picked up a few pages. "Oh yes, that looks familiar. That brings back some memories," he explained and then, "Too bad."

"What do you mean by that?" asked Ed and Julia in unison.

"The coding on each page. That identified his program and gave him access to the mainframe. The mainframe is long gone with all of the memory. Morris could understand what the numbers and equations mean but unless you are a mathematical genius you won't learn anything from what's here." Ben said this as if none of it mattered. Ed and Julia looked at each other and began to put the papers back into their folders.

Ed then asked Ben if there was a thrift shop that had golf equipment. They could pick up some old putters and use the shafts to experiment with. He smiled and asked for a couple of minutes.

"Hank, it's Ben."

"I know who it is. What do you want now?" was the unmistakable voice they could hear clearly.

Ben continued as if he hadn't been interrupted. "Do you still have that box of putter shafts of Morris's? Didn't think we would be needing them so soon. Can your man bring them over?"

"Give me ten minutes!" and Hank hung up.

Ben smiled. Julia smiled. Ed was speechless. He was beginning to understand what forty plus years of a close friendship was all about.

It was twelve minutes before the big Lincoln was out front. Ed and Julia jumped in and they rode up to the apartment to unload their new treasure. Ed was able to pick-up the weathered box in which, it turned out, held close to a hundred putter shafts with an assortment of grips. By the time they got to the top of the stairs the Lincoln was out of sight.

They laid out the shafts on the floor. It was quite a collection. Ed picked up one at random and fit to the putter head. It was tight enough to hold but would need epoxy glue to secure it for play. He took his stance and slowly made his putting stroke. It felt awful and the look on his face showed Julia what he was thinking.

All the shaft tips had angles that had been formed to fit the putter in the correct lie position but each would be different for the address of an individual golfer. Ed was standing in the middle of a sea of shafts not knowing which way to turn.

Julia started with a giggle and then real laughter. "One truly ugly putter head which requires each to be fitted to the golfer. That would be a marketing nightmare.

Do you think that was what they were laughing at in the photograph?"

"Maybe, maybe not. I won't give up on this yet. Why don't you get the photo and we will see if we can figure out which shaft was being used then. There maybe more to the joke than meets the eye." Ed was hopeful but not sure.

Julia tripped off to the house and Ed started to examine each shaft without the head. He aligned it in his stance and grip and could see the subtle differences. He started to sort them into groups trying to combine similarities. He was about half way through when Julia returned with the photograph.

She gave him a special look coming to him placing her arms around his neck. Leaning back she smiled. "That is the longest we have been apart since you moved into my house. I don't like it!" and kissed him. Ed hadn't noticed but suddenly he realized he never wanted to be away from her, not even for a few minutes, and kissed her back.

Once they got that settled the work, or play was more accurate, began. Ed had Julia sit in Morris's position in the photographs and started to position the putter with one style of shaft after another. He finally narrowed it to three. Trying each with his putting stroke he found one that felt good but not with the confidence he sensed with the other clubs. He had Julia try each of the three and she picked the same shaft that he liked.

"Maybe we are close. I am going to glue this one into the head and we will do some putting drills and see if some minor tweaks will set it up to our liking. If we both like it that means we will be close to finding one that could be marketed." Ed sounded relieved as was Julia.

"Let's go watch the end of the third round of the Federal Express St Jude Classic. Steve missed the cut. That's two in a row," Julia said in a sad voice. "It has to be really tough to lose your game."

Chapter 57

It was hard to watch others play golf, especially if they weren't the well known stars of the game. A 24 year old rookie named Dicky Pride was having a good third round and would have the lead going into Sunday. Gene Sauers and Hal Sutton were in the mix and Nick Price was close behind. Ben and Jennifer had plans for the evening and Ed and Julia decided to have breakfast cereal and fruit for dinner. By nine they were ready for bed and by ten they had fallen asleep.

Sunday morning was special. Ben was up early and as Jennifer, Ed and Julia made their appearance he started preparing breakfast. This morning Eggs Benedict, with his own special hollandaise sauce, fresh squeezed orange juice and coffee served poolside. It was the most pleasant time of the day in the the desert. This day couldn't start any better as watching Ben and Jennifer together made Julia about as happy as she could be. Ed thanked his lucky stars.

Just before noon Ed and Julia, with the putter and a dozen balls, made a quick trip to Tamarisk. It was beginning to get too hot to be out and there was almost no one about. The practice green was vacant and Ed rolled the balls out on the green. He pulled a few into a line and stepped up to the first one, took one look at the nearest hole and stroked the club. Clunk, into the very center of the cup. Clunk, Clunk, Clunk. He looked at Julia. She wasn't smiling. In fact she looked scared.

"Your turn." Ed handed her the putter and waited.

Julia hesitated, then pulled six balls over and took aim at a hole fifteen feet away. Three of four found the cup. The fourth stopped one inch short but on line.

She picked up the remaining two balls, then the four she had putted. Turning to Ed she said "Pick up yours and take me home," and started for the car.

Ed knew what had just happened. They had the proverbial tiger by the tail. The putter was dynamite. If you had the line you would make the putt, or a putt so close you couldn't miss the next one. It didn't feel good in his hands as did the clubs. It was different. The clubs gave him confidence. He had to make the swing. This thing seemed to have something very different. What it was he couldn't describe.

Julia sat in the car without speaking until they were almost back to the house.

"Let's go up to the apartment," she said in a voice Ed didn't recognize.

"Okay. Are you alright? Julia what's happened? Tell me," Ed begged.

The apartment was a mess. Clubs were every where, leaned up against the wall, a few on the floor, putter shafts in piles, the boxes of files. And the big staff bag was still in the center of the room.

Julia looked worried and Ed could see was scared about something. He held her and could feel she was trembling. "I didn't care, or even try, to make a putt. Just looked at the hole, then the ball and made my stroke. I knew the minute I hit the ball that it would go in. I froze on the last one and it stopped short but was on a perfect line. It wasn't me putting. It was like it was some one else."

"Julia, that's not possible. You choose the perfect line, made a perfect stroke. The sweet spot is most of the entire face. It is a great putter. It just looks awful."

She started to relax and then asked Ed, "Prove to me it's not the putter, not some kind of magic."

Ed let her go, moved a away and picked up the putter. He gripped it and swung it back and forth in a putting motion. Looking up at Julia he spoke softly. "It is just a golf club. I don't feel anything special about it. It is not like the other ones that give me a sense of confidence that I will always hit a good shot. It seems to be the only club that I don't get that feeling of confidence with. It is just as ugly but the other clubs feel different in my hands. This one doesn't."

Julia was silent but nodded her head in understanding what Ed was trying to tell her. She knew the clubs had nothing for her and she didn't even want to swing them. The putter had no special feeling either. She had a good putting stroke and the putter did have a good balance. She didn't even notice that fact when she putted with it and this opened her mind to maybe there was something in the design that made her stroke smoother and even better.

"Okay. I will accept that the balance is there. I didn't even think about it when I made the strokes but how can each contact be that good to get the ball to roll perfect?" was her next question.

Ed held the putter up vertically about a third of

the way up the shaft with his thumb and index finger. Just tightly enough to keep it from slipping from his grasp and with a ball in his other hand rapped the putter face with it in the center of the face. The club swung away from the strike but didn't twist in either direction. He then repeated this striking either side of the center and the club didn't twist until he was an inch to either side of the center. Most clubs would twist when struck within a fraction of an inch off center.

Julia looked with disbelief. "How can that be Ed. Let me try that," and took the club from him. She had the same result as he did. She was now smiling as one of the many things that has a putt go astray was not hitting the sweet spot on the face and with this club you could not miss it.

She handed it back to Ed. "It is so ugly but with a sweet spot that big a lot can be over looked. The perfect roll must also be in the face angle and surface. I think there is something here after all and I think I will give this misjudged piece of art a second chance."

Ed knew at that exact moment that Cornith Golf would be next.

Chapter 58

The afternoon continued being a pleasant time for the new family. Ben and Jennifer acted like they had been around each other for years. Ed thought how strange it was that two couples could form a bond in such a short time and be so comfortable with each other in one house. He could only marvel that he was part of this and that it was Julia who was his partner. Only in one's dreams could such things happen and this was no dream. He was now looking forward to living each day and could barely wait to find out what would be next.

They were all in the living room watching the golf tournament as the afternoon shadows lengthened and the outside temperature started to slowly drop. Dicky Pride, looking even younger than 24 with his big eyeglasses, had just rolled in a birdie put on the first playoff hole against Gene Sauers and Hal Sutton to win. He had just won $225,000 and Julia let out a little cough and looked at Ed.

Ed smiled at her. "It pays to be first. But that's just the money," and before he could elaborate the announcer started listing all the other benefits that winning a PGA event bestowed on the victor.

"Don't even talk about the PGA Championship," he said to all in the room.

Julia's phone rang and she answered in an excited "Nicki, Where are you guys?"

Smiling at Ed she took her leave. Ed told Ben and Jennifer about Steve Stevens and his wife and brother. Also that Steve was going through a rough patch and had missed two cuts. Mostly caused by poor putting. Just as he was about to continue on how Julia was trying to see if they could work out some housing arrangements together at the Championship she rushed into the room.

"Guess what, we have a place to stay. Steve befriended his pro-am partner at the Bing Crosby in Pebble Beach and he said if you ever come to Tulsa stay with us. Bring your friends too. We have a room with a private bathroom and guess who else is going to be there. Phil Michelson and his caddie, Jim Mackay. It's going to be so much fun!"

Julia then went on to say that Nicki was worried about Steve. His putting stroke had deserted him and they were playing in next week's tournament in Michigan. He needed a break but had committed so they were packing up the car and driving part way tonight.

Julia was saddened by, this and said she wished there was something they could do to help them out.

Ed offered "There is something we might be able to do. What do you think?"

"You don't mean . . . .?" and Julia let it hang there.

"Yes," is all Ed said.

This conversation meant nothing to Jennifer but Ben quietly smiled but said nothing. Ed and Julia didn't even notice.

The next morning the family met again at breakfast and the days plans were discussed. Ed and Julia were off to visit Harriet in La Jolla and Ed had made an appointment to meet with TaylorMade in Carlsbad on the way home. Ben was meeting with Hank in the morning and would take Jennifer to lunch afterward. They would spend the rest of the day doing nothing which they thought they were starting to get good at doing. A rather subtle smile passed between them on his mentioning that.

Ed and Julia found Harriet in declining health. She remembered seeing them not too long ago but that was about all even though it had been less than a week. Jimmy was showing the signs of a care giver and companion who knew his ward was passing away. The only time Harriet showed interest was when Julia talked to her about Ben and Jennifer and that she had shown him the photograph. She reached out for Julia's hand and got out "It was the right time. Good. You thank Jennifer, honey. You thank her, now," and smiling closed her eyes.

"She will be asleep for a while. No way to wake her," Jimmy saying this in such a way Julia, nor Ed, knew who to feel sorrier for.

As they left Ed asked Jimmy to keep his calendar open when the time came to look for another position. He had something that would be totally different that he may be interested in doing but it was still in the early planning stages. Just a possibility to keep in mind.

The next stop would be more interesting and on the way to Carlsbad Julia asked "Now what is this thing Jimmy might be doing and is it what I think you are talking about?"

Chapter 59

Ed was just about to answer Julia when he saw the turn off to Torrey Pines Golf Course. "Do you want to make a quick stop here and putt a few before we get to Carlsbad?" he asked and then wished he hadn't.

"Yes. I need to find out more about that thing. I am going to call it 'Thing' for now," was her quick and surprising answer.

Torrey Pines Golf Course is a big place with a small practice green. Fortunately there were only two others golfers on it and Julia and Ed had a few minutes to do some putting. Julia was first and this time concentrated on each putt. Four for four from ten feet. She looked at Ed and he motioned her to try from twenty feet and the result was the same. Just then two foursomes crowded into the small area talking loudly and making nutty sounding bets. Ed picked up their balls, covered up the putter and they headed back to the car.

"Not such a good idea I guess. What did you think this time?"

Julia didn't hesitate. "It is fantastic! It putts so straight. That is a flat surface, no breaks, so aim at the hole and putt. It starts the ball rolling with no bounce or back spin. I take it back. It is my stroke and if I have the line the ball goes in."

215

"Good. What I want at TaylorMade is to have them pour a half dozen replica heads in their foundry. I can make the mold, pour the waxes and we can then modify several to try to make them have a better look. We leave the face and socket hole angle alone. They can ready and cast them in the same metal they pour their heads. We have an appointment with Jason Poland who is the foundry foreman. I used my name and new fame to get into their office and they may make a push to sponsor me. Hopefully we can get by that quickly and be out of there in a few minutes."

By the time Ed finished explaining his plans they were back on the freeway heading north.

"And Jimmy? What are you planning now, Ed? You better tell me," Julia said this with some impatience.

"The putter is the club to run with. If we want to get into the golf business and promote the Morris Cornith brand this is our ticket. We have to figure out how to make it first." Ed paused, then continued. "I should have talked this over with you when I first started to think doing something like this might be a good move. If it develops as a business there maybe a position for someone like Jimmy. He is a good person and deserves a good break. Ben and Hank have set this up some how and I am just to carry it out. They make it seem like it is your idea and they get what they want."

"Oh Ed, I can agree with that! Go on. Tell me more," Julia said rather calmly but with a slight edge in her voice.

"When I saw you putt at Tamarisk I could tell the putter could be used by others, not like the clubs that no one else has a feel for. All along I have been thinking of

216

how we could do something with Morris's clubs that would be satisfactory. The putter might work but first we have to see if it can be produced." Ed again paused and then couldn't think of what more to say.

"And Steve, how does he figure in this?" Julia asked already knowing the answer. "He uses the putter and overnight it cures his putting woes telling the story on national TV. You mean something like that?" she finished her thought.

Ed responded with "You never miss a thing," just as Julia exclaimed, "Your are about to miss your turn for TaylorMade!"

It was a much bigger place than Ed had imagined. And just around the corner was an equal size building housing Callaway Golf. At the front desk Ed was welcomed by a nice looking woman who efficiently handled his introduction and in less than five minutes they were being escorted by Jason Poland to the foundry area.

Jason took a quick look at the putter, almost hid his grin, and said nothing about it's looks.

"No problem. Bring us the waxes and we will add them to one of our casting trees and you can pick them up in a week. Have you picked out the finish you want. You get VIP treatment and that comes from the top." Jason didn't mince words but was polite.

Ed held out the putter and asked Jason if he recognized the metal. He wasn't sure but thought it might be a hardened pewter that had been silver plated. "Odd." was his only comment. As for the color Ed suggested whatever they were using at the time.

Ed and Julia said their thank yous and Ed told Jason he would try to get the waxes back next Monday, but if they weren't ready it would be a week or two later. Julia started to comment on the PGA Championship but caught herself just in time.

They thanked the receptionist, headed to the little silver Porsche and were home two hours later.

Chapter 60

On the drive back from TaylorMade Julia learned a little more about Ed's life that he hadn't at the time felt was of any importance for her to know about. It was about the year he spent working in a bronze art foundry. He had spent most of that time doing metal chasing. It was hard, dirty work done in a small booth wearing a dust mask, face shield, heavy clothing and gloves. Ear plugs softened the noise of the pneumatic tools. For a couple of months he was in the mold making department and found that more to his liking.

One of the local sculptors he had met in his time as a gallery manager did most of his own mold making and wax pouring. Ed had already contacted him to use his studio and supplies to make the mold. He could pour and modify the waxes in the apartment. Julia could help him do the work on the waxes.

"When do we start?" was Julia's response.

"If we aren't too tired after our practice round tomorrow we can get started then. Otherwise we can start on Wednesday. During the down time between the various steps I, and we, need to focus on getting ready for the Championship. I want to finish in the top ten or better." Ed answered.

Julia smiled. "You are indeed making my life

interesting. Don't make it too interesting. I need some time to just be alone with you. And with Grandpa and Jen."

Dinner was whatever was in the refrigerator. They ate out by the pool. It had become almost a sanctuary for the four of them. Ed was almost overcome by having a place to belong again, to have found Julia and in turn Ben and Jennifer. He had a family again and was meeting new people he could consider friends. It must have shone on his face.

Julia nudged him in the ribs. "Hey big fella, are you hiding something from me. You look like like you are floating around on a cloud. Got room for me there?" she asked as she climbed onto his stretched out body on the chaise lounge.

Ed saw that Ben and Jennifer had left and he put his arms around Julia and held her tightly against him. "I am floating on a cloud and you may join me. It is a very nice place to be and you feel so very good right where you are so let's stay here a while longer."

"Okay, but it's almost time to go to bed and I may feel so very good to you there. Let me know when it's time," and Julia started kissing him.

At 8:00 am the next morning they stood together on the first tee at Tamarisk. Ed was dressed in slacks and golf shirt, Julia in medium length shorts and collarless T-shirt with a Tamarisk caddie bib holding Ed's golf bag upright on the grass. Gary had come from his office and was standing next to Willy who had come out to walk the course with them. Several other club members had shown up and Gary announced that Ed Adams had the honor and to play away.

Ed's first drive was about as good as could be played. Julia hoisted the bag and they started down the first fairway. As they walked Ed handed the driver to her which she stowed and they gave each other a smile. Arriving at his ball they briefly discussed the distance and where he should land the ball. Ed choose the club and Julia agreed. The next shot was taken and was a good one. The first nine was played in less than two hours and the back and fourth between Ed and Julia was good. As they finished 9 another twenty members had collected into a small gallery and the number grew as they played. By the time they reached the 18th green there were over 300 surrounding it. Two photographers were busy scurrying about trying to get pictures.

Ed had a putt for a birdie to give him a 7 under round and made it look easy. Julia came over, still holding the flag stick, and gave him a kiss. The photo that was on the front page of the Desert Times the next morning was taken. Gary was beside himself seeing it. A handsome pro golfer and a strikingly beautiful young woman as his caddie. Both wearing Tamarisk caps and just behind them, but strategically placed, a green Tamarisk golf bag.

Chapter 61

The practice round had gone well. Julia had made the carry and felt confident she could handle the five days of the tournament. She was tired but not overly. She enjoyed it. The conversations, shared experiences and the effort. Even as a good player she had no sense she wanted to be the player and Ed be the caddie. Even Willy had worried about that but could see that Ed and Julia were a team. He only stepped in a couple of times to guide Julia, the rest she already knew.

They had lunch at the club and didn't get back home until mid-afternoon. Showers, a change of clothes and some off time around the pool had them rested. Ben and Jennifer were back and Jennifer was going to do hamburgers and a tossed green salad for dinner. The putter project would wait until tomorrow. One week from today at about this time they should be in Tulsa, Oklahoma.

It was an easy mold to make. The shaft was removed from the putter head and it was supported by three screws driven into a Formica topped plywood board. The screw heads were topped with epoxy glue and the head set on them top up. The pouring sprue was centered to the middle of the bottom of the head. Four small four inch boards formed the sides and sealed on the Formica with a molten bead of wax. There were no undercuts on the putter head so the two part rubber molding material could be poured having at least a half inch thickness. It was a simple operation.

The next morning early they were at the Tom Lawson studio just south of Coachella, which was a short drive from Palm Desert. Tom had several pieces in the Patricia Collins Gallery when it closed, got them back and was one of the lucky ones that was owed no money. He had developed a stylized wildlife series of bird and small mammal sculptures with exotic patinas that made them both universally attractive and fine art. They were also at a good price point so they sold quickly. His fortune was on the rise and he was also a very nice young man.

He mixed the two part rubber molding material and with a good sized bell jar vacuum system was able to remove most of the bubbles from the mix. It was carefully poured into the mold as it was slowly tipped side to side. As the last of the compound was poured in Ed could tell he had mixed the right amount and they would have a good mold to work with.

"Come down tomorrow and I will have it ready to pour waxes. I'll loan you a few wax chasing tools and enough wax to pour a dozen heads. You need a hot plate, or you can use your stove top burner if you are careful, and it should be an easy pour. It will take a couple of hours for the wax to harden so don't rush that. If you get coordinated you can get the chasing done on one just in time to take the last pour out of the mold," Tom patiently explained.

Ed settled up with him in cash and with many thanks he and Julia headed to the next stop. The challenge now was how to bend the shafts and Ed had contacted a small machine shop near Tom's studio. The owner was a crusty character, well into his sixties, and taking a look said "Another crazy putter inventor. I have done a dozen different shafts with bends like this."

He took a closer look at Ed's and a look of recognition came to him which he didn't try to hide. "I did this one. A guy in a wheel chair had me do fifty, or more. He would come down here and say try this, try that. If he hadn't been such a nice guy I wouldn't have done it. How many do you want?"

As they left Julia took Ed's hand as they walked to the car. "Ed Adams, do you ever think you lead a charmed life? How can this be happening? Where is this taking us?"

"Yes, I have no idea why, and I don't know that either," were his answers.

Chapter 62

The next five days were filled with activity for Ed and Julia, They picked up the mold from Tom Lawson. He had poured the first wax and they pulled it at his studio. It came out in excellent shape and would need little wax chasing to prepare it for the casting process.

Dropping off ten shafts at the machine shop they got more good news. Mack, the machinist, had found the drilling jig he had made for Morris and told them he could drill the shaft holes to some incredible accuracy in the new heads.

Ed was trying to practice his golf each morning and Julia was with him every step of the way. One good thing coming from the practice was that Ed's Wilson Winsum was performing especially well and Ed had no qualms in letting Steve Stevens try out the now named Cornith Putter to see if his putting would improve. Before heading to practice a wax was pulled and another poured and soon they were able to have six ready to take to TaylorMade on Monday. Four of those had been modified to a better look. Julia had done one which actually looked good and was the same weight and balance as the original waxes. The face was left untouched on all six.

Sunday afternoon was spent watching the last round of the Buick Open in Michigan. Fred Couples was the winner after a grueling 36 holes played on the final day due to a weather canceled first round. He had just come back after having back problems and then had to contend with the 36 holes in wet and cold conditions. He posted a 270, 18 under, for a two stoke victory. Very impressive golf and he would be in the field next week.

Monday came and the delivery was made to TaylorMade. Jason Poland didn't seem at all perplexed by the collection of the six waxes. He looked each over and pronounced they would make good castings and they would be ready in one week. He did ask about drilling the hole for the hosel and was surprised to learn they had a machinist that had the original jig.

By the time Ed and Julia were able to get to bed that night they were pretty much worn out from the busy week. Their flight out wasn't until after 2:00 pm tomorrow so they would pack what they needed to take in the morning. They laid on their backs, sides touching, staring at the ceiling. A light was on casting shadows on the surface of the plaster and it had become a game to imagine what certain patterns, or lines might mean. This night they were having trouble relaxing and talking seem the appropriate thing to do.

They reviewed the last week and how things seemed to still be working so well for them. Julia liked Tom and his sculpture. Liked Mack, thinking of him as another Hank in the making. Ed offered that he thought the way they were treated at TaylorMade was somehow connected with Ben and Hank and not by his early success on the PGA tour. That Gary had managed to orchestrate the last hole reception of their practice round last week and probably hired the photographers. The front page photo, in color, in the the Desert News was a win for him and the club. And Julia photographed drop dead gorgeous. Ed was just a prop.

There was a pause in the conversation and Julia reached over to touch Ed's shoulder. The light touch was such that his thoughts turned to thinking how much he wanted this relationship to be ever lasting. That he could not bear to ever lose her. His thoughts suddenly were of Harriet and that she was losing her battle with living. She never spoke of her own family and he didn't even know if she had one. Jimmy was there. Ben and Hank had kept in touch. She was part of his life, he felt, as he remembered their first meeting in front of the almost empty garage.

"I was just thinking of Harriet and that she didn't have much time left. I hope she is here long enough to watch the PGA Championship a little. If what happens with Steve and the putter is what I expect, it could be the Cornith Putter will get a mention. You may not think it possible but I think Hank, maybe even Ben, will see that it happens," Ed said and realized he had touched Julia with his thought.

Julia raised herself on her elbow and the sheet slipped off her shoulder. Ed turned toward her and was, as always, struck by how beautiful she was. She had a sad look on her face and said how much she would miss her.

"I don't want to be alone when I get there. Will you be with me then? Can we still be together?" Julia was quiet and waited for Ed to answer.

"I will be there. One way or another I will be next to you. I promise you that," Ed whispered barely able to get the words out.

Chapter 63

The three hour flight to Tulsa was on time and easy. Ben had taken them to the airport and Steve and Nicki Stevens were there to meet them in Tulsa. Hugs and handshakes were made and you would have thought they were long lost friends rather than two golf professionals, and their spouses, who had just recently been house mates for a few days at a previous event.

The golf club case, suitcases and hanger bag were tossed in the back. Ed was in the passenger seat and Julia in the back seat with Nicki. She was describing the big house and Ed and Steve just listened to the women. Steve did get in that there was a large putting green behind the house and it was built to have the same grass and roll as at Southern Hills.

As they entered the gated community Ed was duly impressed. It was one big house and on the porch was an attractive lady waving a welcome.

"That is Mrs. Margaret Mayfield, Margie M. Wait til you meet her. Get ready for some southern charm Tulsa style," Nicki warned Julia and Ed.

And meet Margie M they did. Hugs and kisses, perfume and lipstick shared and then bustled into the house for the grand tour. Ed and Julia's room was big and had an even bigger bathroom. There was room for a family of four. Steve and Nicki's room was the same size. Phil Michelson hadn't arrived yet but his room was almost as big and Jerry and Jim Mackay each had nice single rooms but would share a bathroom. The Mayfield's master was the size of a small house and the two walk in closets were not only huge, but fully stocked. There were more clothes and shoes than most stores would carry. There were two big living rooms, one having a entrance pool into the main swimming pool that connected under the picture windows. The tour went on and the rest was the same. The biggest and the best.

But Marge was just a friendly southern girl who might have been a high school friend. You soon realized that none of this was that important to her, it was just what happens when some unexpected thing changes your life. Such as your husband's parents having a 5,000 acre ranch, where they had scratched out a living for themselves and five children, become a prime oil field.

A helper, who just appeared and disappeared as needed, brought in their luggage and wished them a good stay. Mr. Mayfield wouldn't be back until late tonight as he was in charge of the volunteers for the tournament. Mrs. Mayfield had planned dinner for them at six and would appreciate their presence at that time. Ed looked at Julia and she at him. Both smiled and laughter came after the unnamed helper had made his exit.

Phil Michelson and Jim Mackay missed an excellent meal and a fun time at the dinner table as they arrived about 8:30 pm. Marge was a great host and was fast becoming a good friend. This was working out so well that all worries about accommodations and transportation were gone. Ed and Steve could concentrate on their golf.

Almost everything for their stay at the Mayfields was problem free, but for one minor problem Ed would take care of without any difficulty.

After dinner, Ed got the Cornith Putter from his bag, pocketed six golf balls and met Julia, Steve and Nicki on the putting green. He also brought his Wilson Winsum.

"How's the putting going?" was Ed's first words to Steve. He looked up from just missing his third try from about fifteen feet. The three balls were all to the left side of the cup by six inches almost touching each other.

"It's terrible. I can't seem to get the put on line. I have three putters and it makes no difference. The distance is good. I just can't start the ball on line." Steve's answer had a desperate tone.

Ed handed him the Cornith and took his putter in exchange. "Don't laugh, don't say a word. Pick your line and stroke the ball," Ed demanded.

He dropped three balls at Steve feet and backed away. Nicki had heard the exchange and walked over with Julia. The three stood around Steve so close he almost didn't have room to take his stance. The look on his face showed he was sure Ed was playing a joke on him. That they would all have a good laugh at his expense the minute he made the first putt.

Steve decided to play along and went through his entire routine. He then took his stance, took two more looks at his target and stroked the ball. It was a right breaking putt of about of eighteen feet with six inches of break. The ball tracked absolutely perfect and fell into the cup with maybe two inches of roll left. Steve froze. He couldn't move.

"Try it again," was Ed's comment.

He came to and stroked a second putt with the same result.

Ed walked up to Steve and put his arm around his shoulder. "Spend some time with this homely gem. Learn to love her, treat her nice and if you want you can put her in your bag this week. You only have two things to do. Pick the right line and when asked say it is the Cornith Putter."

Steve was at a loss for words. He just nodded his head in agreement and started an hour of putting not paying attention to anything else.

Ed was doing some practice too. It was a beautiful practice green, finer than most clubs and the best he had putted on in some time. Winsum was co-operating and he felt he could putt as good with it as with the Cornith. He knew this wasn't totally true but he had other plans for the future.

Michelson and Mackay arrived just at dusk and the outdoor lights had been turned on. Steve had met Phil several years ago and recognized, as almost every golf fan did, that he was an up and coming star on the PGA Tour. At 24, six foot three, single, handsome and with a winning smile the world was his oyster. It was when he was introduced to Julia that some of that would have to be tempered. Ed, watching their meeting, knew this immediately but Julia just let it pass as if she hadn't noticed.

Chapter 64

They met Roger Mayfield the next morning at breakfast. He was a big man. Tall, a bit taller than Ed, and big. Not fat, just big. His handshake was firm and his hand made Ed feel his was somewhat small. He had a pleasant voice and spoke softly with a slight southern accent exuding a friendliness that was authentic. Ed liked him immediately.

He explained that he would be busy throughout the tournament, would be in an out and couldn't be a proper host. That Marge would be both host and hostess and that Brent, the helper, would always be around and could take care of whatever needing taken care of. Their cook, Annie, could fix them up with anything they needed from the kitchen. Two tournament cars were out front for their use and they had the parking permits to park in the club's parking lot.

As soon as he had said this he excused his departure and wished them well. Depending on their starting times he might not see them again until the tournament was was over. They were invited to stay over a few days if they would like and he was off to organize the volunteers.

Marge stood by and received a real kiss from her big man and they said "see you later" with smiles. She turned to her guests at the table. "He is a better man than you will ever know. I thank my lucky stars for every minute he is with me. You should be so lucky." She then quickly went about seeing her guests had everything they needed.

The practice round went really well. The three of them were together and all were hitting good shots, taking a reasonable amount of time taking notes and conferring with their caddies. None were reluctant to point out subtle things they noted. Phil and Jim were already bonded as a player caddie team and Julia and Jerry picked up a number of hints on caddie protocol.

The one problem that arose was that Phil seemed to be walking a little too close to Julia and was not concentrating his attention on his game. It was bothering Ed and was also annoying Mackay. At the half way break Ed casually approached Phil away from the others and explained rather clearly that he and Julia were a couple. That he should look around elsewhere for his own soul mate and that Ed had no doubt that he would someday day find her. Phil flushed and gave Ed a bashful smile and apologized. "She is one special lady. You are one lucky guy. A friendship only then with you both, I hope."

The rest of the practice round went fine and a friendship then did begin to develop. Later that night, when Ed and Julia were in bed, she pulled him close and said, "You handled that so well out there. It was going to be a problem and I didn't want to say anything to him about it. Phil is a nice young man but I prefer an older one," and then went about to prove her point.

At 8:13 am the next morning "Ed Adams, from Palm Desert, California you have the tee. Please hit away," was announced and the first round of the 1994 PGA Championship was awaiting Ed's first shot. Number 1 was a long par 4 playing at 456 yards on the opening round. It required a good drive to get past the two fairway bunkers leaving a modest second of 160 yards. Ed did both shots well and two putted for his par. Steve was in the same threesome and did like wise, although his first putt was from 30 feet and he left it just 2 inches short. Still, he had a smile on his face and could hardly wait to get to the second tee.

It was a nice day in Tulsa and the crowds came early. Ed and Steve's gallery was small as only a few of those around the first tee left to follow the not so famous. Ed and Steve did have some fans, however. Steve had been on tour for three years and was thought to be an up and comer. The last few tournaments had lost him a few but he was still the popular player from Wisconsin.

Ed had gained some followers from his good finishes in the three events he had played in and there was some curiosity about the clubs he was using. And the underground had also spread the news that his caddie was worth watching even if his golf wasn't.

By the time they reached the ninth tee a sizable gallery had formed. Both Ed and Steve were under par, the buzz about not only Ed's clubs but Steve's putter was out, and just about everyone had heard about Julia. On the short par four they both had birdies. Ed's from 3 feet after a spectacular short iron approach and Steve's by a equally spectacular 34 foot putt.

They finished the round with Ed even par 70 and Steve one over. Both a little disappointed but still very much in contention. The best score of the day was Nick

Price at 3 under 67. Phil Michelson had a later starting time posting a 2 under 68 and was in second place.

Ed and Julia chose to head back to the Mayfields while Steve wanted to practice his short game a bit more. The Tournament had a shuttle service for the players so Ed took the car and Steve, Jerry and Nicki would take the shuttle. Marge was on the course as a volunteer so they had the big house to themselves. They enjoyed spending time browsing about the living space and in one of the hallways was a photo history of their hosts. From a hardscrabble youth as children of cattle ranchers to the luxury of their current home was a reminder of what life could offer. Julia asked Ed, "Would you ever want a place this big if you got rich?"

"No. I think your house is the perfect size and style," he answered.

"Do you only want me for the off hand chance it might be mine some day. Say 30 years from now?" Julia said giving him a rather strong punch in the ribs.

Ed pulled her down the hall and stopped in front of a photo of Roger and Marge standing in front of a barbed wire fence with a dusty Oklahoma prairie behind them. Their clothes were soiled from whatever work they had been doing but they were smiling and had their arms about each others waists.

"That would be just fine with me if that were us," he said with a meaning she understood.

Chapter 65

They had the early morning off as Ed and Steve had afternoon tee times. They were on the course's practice range by 10:30 am and were ready for their 1:07 pm starting time. Tulsa was having good weather, clear, not too hot and dry. The course was playing fast and fair. Julia was adjusting to her role as a caddie. Yesterday had been a strain for her, both mentally and physically. The excitement on the first few holes was soon replaced with the worry of not contributing enough. Half way through the back nine her confidence was building and by the finish of her first day she knew that she and Ed were now a team.

Ed had anticipated that Julia would go through the first round with some doubts and mood swings but wasn't surprised at the relationship they were having on the finishing holes. He was enjoying the moment and was playing great golf. The gallery towards the end of the round had started to see that the relationship between the handsome man and his beautiful caddie was much more than just golf. The smiles between them and the touching of a hand to arm or gentle shove wasn't missed. The TV cameramen had caught on early and several particularly nice exchanges had been recorded and played back when some fill was needed in the broadcast. Today started on the tenth tee as the time and starting hole are reversed for the first two rounds. Today they had a large gallery poplated with a surprising number of women.

Ed had a good day shooting a 2 under 68 placing him tied for third place at the end of the day's play. Steve also shot 2 under and he was in a large group tied at one under. Phil Michelson had a disappointing one over and fell into the same group as Steve. The stage was now set for the final two days of play. There was one problem for all the players: Nick Price. He had shot a unbelievable 5 under 65 and now was 8 under with Ed and two others 6 strokes behind. The rest of the field, including Ed, started thinking they were all playing for second place.

That evening a nice meal was provided at the Mayfields and by the time the host and hostess got back from the tournament grounds most of their guests had retired to their bedrooms. Phil and Jim didn't get back until much later, however.

Ed was tired and Julia near exhaustion but was still in good spirits. They watched a little of the late coverage on a local news channel and one of their exchanges was broadcast. Julia's smile was radiant and Ed was pleased, especially when she said, "That caddie is in love with her player. Did you see that?" referring to her gentle touch on his arm as they looked at the yardage book together. "No doubt about it. And he is in love with her," and he kissed her, more than once.

Saturday's round would be moving day as the players describe it. The cut had removed half the original competitors and the tee times were organized by score, the lowest last to tee off, all starting on the first tee. In the last group was Price, Ben Crenshaw, and Jay Haas. Before them was Ed, Cory Pavin, and John Cook. Steve and Phil were playing together, with Gil Morgan, and were four groups in front of the leaders.

It was another nice day and the crowds were enormous. Almost frightening to the players who hadn't played in this environment before. You had to go back at least twenty players to find any that hadn't been in this situation before except for one player and his caddie. Ed was calm and not bothered. Julia was terrified. It would be after the sixth hole had been played before she could relax. Ed made sure he was close to her at all times, kept her involved in every shot and had her help him line up every putt. Soon all the noise and movement from the crowds began to fade from her consciousness and she could concentrate on Ed's game and that alone.

By the end of the day Nick Price had carded an even par 70, Ed a respectable 1 under 69, Steve the same. Phil put together a brilliant 3 under 67, only one other player bettering that with a 66. The Sunday pairings were put on the board. Last to play would be Nick Price at 8 under, Jay Haas 5 under, and Corey Pavin 4 under. Just in front was Phil at 4 under, Ben Crenshaw and Ed each at 3 under. Before them was Greg Norman at 3 under, and Ernie Els and Steve at 2 under.

The pressure was becoming palpable and no one was joking or prancing about. Even the TV crew could feel it. Julia was sensing exactly what was now happening and couldn't decide if she should try to hide it or just accept that this was as it had to be. Ed didn't care. His life was so good at this moment nothing else mattered other than to wake up the next morning and live the day that to was to be.

Chapter 66

Sunday dawned perfect. Ed and Julia woke early and had no reason to get up so they decided to lay in bed and see if there was anything in the ceiling that they could see their future in. It was a perfectly smooth ceiling without a blemish. Ed decided to look for his future on another surface but Julia quipped that she thought he should concentrate his efforts on the game today. He agreed only if he could continue his search tomorrow morning.

They had a good breakfast and arrived at the golf course just after 10:00 am. The traffic was heavy and the crowds were already milling about trying to find vantage points. The area around the first tee was packed six deep and ran half way down the long fairway. Southern Hills was a tight course and the ropes allowing plenty of width for the players made the spectator traffic dense. Roger Mayfield's volunteers had their work cut out for them. Half of Tulsa's police force was there and in full uniform. Two policemen would walk with each group.

Ed's tee time had arrived and their group formed on the first tee. The three players shook hands, compared golf balls and how they were marked. The caddies stood back and each player had his driver in hand. Phil, a left handed golfer, was first on the tee. After his introduction and the applause had subsided his drive was long, perfectly placed and followed with more applause and cheers. Ben Crenshaw was next and stepping out between between 6 foot three Michelson and 6 foot two Ed his 5 foot nine looked very small. His reception was just as loud and long as was Michelson's and his drive just 10 yards shorter. Ed was next and his applause was robust but a bit shorter. Just as he started his routine a little boy's voice shouted out, "I love you Julia." Ed had to start again after the laughter had stopped and Julia had blown a kiss in the young admirer's direction. It didn't bother Ed in the least. His driver felt as it always did and his drive flew directly over Crenshaw's and 15 yards past Phil's. They were off and the final threesome was forming on the tee box behind them.

It was a long round stretching five and a half hours. Julia held up well and the smile she had on the first tee from the little boy's call lasted most of the day. Ed finished with a 1 under and would tie Phil who played to even par and a 4 under total for third place. Steve at 1 over would join Crenshaw who shot 2 over for a 1 under total and finished in a five way tie for ninth. In the last threesome Corey Pavin was 2 under and with a total of 5 under was alone in second place.

And then there was Nick Price. Even with a bogey on the last hole he shot a 3 under and finished 11 under par with a 269 total. No one else was even close. The next day in The Register-Guard, New York Times writer Larry Dorman summed up Price's performance. "Price, 37 years old, did exactly what it took Sunday. He shot a final round 67 and took his second major championship of the year, his third victory in his last four starts, his sixth 1994 tournament victory and his second PGA Championship." No one could have done it better. Not even someone who had clubs that gave him confidence that he could never make a bad shot.

After the award ceremony, shaking of hands, hugs and kisses the players, officials, gallery, workers and volunteers slowly went their way. For many of the players and their entourages it was to Colorado for the Sprint International at Castle Pines Golf Club just south of Denver.

In an apartment in La Jolla, overlooking the Pacific Ocean, an elderly lady had struggled to stay alert and watch the final round of the PGA Championship. Drifting in and out of consciousness she would exclaim, "That's Julia. Look, that's Julia, Jimmy!" and then lean back in her wheel chair and close her eyes. She was alert when Ed made his final putt on eighteen and garbled out "That's my boy Ed, Jimmy." She saw several of the TV close ups of Julia and Ed on the course and would say "What a handsome couple they are. You see them there? That's Julia and Ed." As the program ended she leaned back and smiled. Turning her head she focused on Jimmy and said slowly, struggling on each word, "I am going to leave you now." The sparkle in her once bright blue eyes had left and Jimmy Lee's tears began to fall.

Chapter 67

Ed and Julia were staying over until Monday, as were Steve, Nicki and Jerry. The Stevens were driving to the next tournament in Colorado and planned on a leisurely trip arriving in Castle Rock Wednesday morning. Steve had played Castle Pines Golf Club's course many times and this would be his third International. Phil and Jim Mackay had left right after the finish and were flying on a private plane back to San Diego.

Breakfast with the Mayfields turned into a high light as getting to know them turned out to be such a pleasure. They were genuinely nice people and unbelievably cheerful. They were both tired from a week of hard work organizing and herding the several hundred volunteers. They would be back to finish up later in the day but now had some time for their house guests. The breakfast was a ranch hand's feed with time taken for eating and good conversation.

One thing Ed always liked about people who had started life in hard circumstances was their appreciation for what they had at the present, regardless what that might be. Just glad to be alive was a good motto to live by and the Mayfields fit that to a T. And what a life they now had. It had not always been that way. Cattle ranching in Oklahoma was a tough business and the children on the ranch needed to be tough. They both had finished high school but went no further. It was not because of intelligence, as one quickly noted, but circumstance. The pick up trucks and riding bulls for Roger was over as was barrel racing and fending off cowboy advances was for Marge. They loved each other and life in general.

By the time it was time to leave you would thought their own children were leaving for good. The girls, Julia and Nicki were almost smothered with hugs and kisses and it would take half the day for Ed, Steve and Jerry to recover from Roger's handshakes and to get Marge's lipstick off their cheeks. They were always to come and stay anytime they were anywhere near Tulsa, "y'all hear", and this time their hosts would be home to properly take care of them.

The Stevens left first waving from the car and then Roger and Marge drove Ed and Julia to the airport. The hugs and kisses were repeated there and then Ed and Julia were suddenly on their own again and headed home.

Ben met them at the Palm Springs Airport and the clubs and luggage managed to be at the carousel as soon as they got there. It was about half way back to Palm Desert that Ben told them of Harriet's passing just after the end of the tournament. That Jimmy Lee had been there and she had seen them both on TV and made sure Jimmy knew who they were each time she spotted them. He said she died in peace and seemed not only ready to go but that it was time.

Julia took the news hard with some tears and mentioning that only Ben and Hank were now left of her ancestry and old friends. Ed felt he had lost his grandmother. Ben was silent for a few moments and then changed the subject. He and Hank were formulating a business strategy for Cornith Golf and were excited by the prospects of starting a new company. The amount of coverage the clubs and putter had gotten at the Championship made it a sure thing. They had taped the entire broadcast and had access to all the out takes. Steve had a three minute interview with the putter in hand extolling it's virtues and that it totally changed his game. He credited Ed for letting him use it and could hardly wait to buy the first one off the assembly line.

"That was a hundred thousand dollars worth of advertising. It couldn't have been any better," was Ben's enthused observation.

"Sounds good Ben. Julia and I will run over to Carlsbad tomorrow and pick up the castings. We should be able to tell if we can produce something close to the original in the next day or two." Ed answered.

Julia reached over from the back seat and rubbed Ed's neck.

"Take care of me Ed. Nothing can come between us. Remember that," and Ed understood what she had just said to him. Ben also knew what she was saying.

Chapter 68

That evening it was a pleasant change after the high pressure of tournament golf. Just the four of them sitting around the pool eating a cold dinner plate of ham, asparagus, hard boiled egg slices and torn pieces of baguette. A chilled glass of white wine added a nice touch. The conversation was mostly on the experience of being in the middle of top level competitive golf. Ben was interested but it was Jennifer who asked the most questions. Especially of Ed. She eventually let it be known that this was the level at which her husband had flown airplanes. That much of Ed's, and Julia's, descriptions had sounded very much like what her husband and fellow pilots talked about as to what it meant to place yourself in that environment.

It was nice to relax and feel perfectly at home. Ed was thinking of what Julia had said in the car and was planning to expand on that when they were alone. Ben scuttled that thought almost at the same time he was thinking it.

"Ed, you know where Hank and I stand in this idea of Cornith Golf. We need something like this in our lives right now. Hank knows he is running out of time and I am not worried about my time any more but need the excitement of a new business adventure." Ben paused and

245

looked at Jennifer. She smiled in a manner that let him know she understood.

Ed broke into the conversation. "You realize there may not be a Cornith Golf club that can be mass produced and perform like they do for me. The putter may work out and we will know that in a few days. The clubs may be a different story. I haven't found any one that likes them except me." He waited and then added, "And they are really ugly."

"That is where Hank and I want you to be right now. Put the putter on the table and we can run with it. Next, see if the two of you can build a wedge from Morris's designs. That would be all we would need to build a brand and a company. Unless you would like to carry on, we would sell the company and would have considered our time well spent." Ben said this like he was ordering a pizza with his favorite trimmings. Jennifer continued to smile.

"Tomorrow by this time we might know about the putter. The wedge, or wedges, will take a lot longer." Ed said and nodded toward Julia. She picked up the look and excused the two of them as it was time for bed.

When they were snuggled up in their favorite positions Julia began with telling Ed he had handled their position well.

"Do you want to do this now? How about the tour? Where are you going to take me next because where ever you go I am going to be there with you!" Julia said with an emphasis.

"I will know tomorrow about the golf business. Right now I don't think that is my future, not that I have any idea what my future should be. As for the tour, that was fun. The competition outweighs the getting there. I want you to be one hundred percent part of it if I go that way and if not we will find something else. What are you thinking?" Ed said feeling positive of her answer.

She pulled him closer and whispered in his ear "Right at this moment I am where I want to be and you will have my answer in the morning if you behave yourself."

As they approached TaylorMade the next morning she still hadn't answered but Ed wasn't going to do anything that would rock their boat. Jason met them in the lobby and hurried them back to the foundry. He was excited about how good the castings had come out and the putter heads actually didn't look that bad. When they reached the foundry floor they headed to his small office and on a dark blue velvet covered box lay the six heads. They did look pretty good. Especially the one Julia had modified. She picked it up and handed it to Ed. "I like this one best. How about you?"

Jason could tell from Julia's smile it was an inside joke but agreed with her.

"That is the one I would choose. Even the original ones don't look that bad and with the anodized gray finish you can look at them and not cringe," was Jason's rejoinder.

"They do look good, Jason. What do I owe you," Ed asked.

"All taken care of Ed. Hank settled with the boss so all is good at my end. You know Hank Morgan I trust?" Jason asked.

"Yes. He has been sponsoring me on the tour. Julia knows him better than I do."

"Ed, if you ever get invited to his place make sure he gives you a tour of his golf room. Don't take no for an answer because that is his life in there and it will make your life better for seeing it."

With that it was time to head back to Palm Desert and make a run down to the machine shop, get the heads drilled and pick up the bent shafts. It went like clock work. The jig that Mac said fit the heads did, even the modified ones, and the drilling took just minutes. The shafts were ready and they were back home by 4:00 pm for drinks by the pool before dinner. It was then, when Julia and Ben were in the kitchen, that Jennifer moved to sit next to Ed and said something he would carry with him the rest of his life.

Chapter 69

Jennifer moved even closer and put her hand on Ed's knee. He was unsure of how to react. It didn't seem to be a sexual move and as it turned out it wasn't. Looking directly into his eyes she spoke softly. "Ed, you need to understand something about both Ben and Hank. They are brilliant men. Nice men. Gentlemen of the old school. They are also bored and desperately in need some kind of project to work on to validate that they haven't lost the abilities they once had."

Jennifer paused and then continued "Hank was the lead engineer in some of IBM's most advanced computer technology at the time and Ben was a young and brash whiz kid in management of complex systems. They, with Morris, were instrumental in IBM's early success in commercial computers. Hank tried to loose himself out here after he retired and he thought golf could replace engineering. It didn't, but by the time he realized it the technology had passed him by. Ben losing his daughter, then his wife just drifted. He is getting over that now. You finding Julia, and he knowing the kind of person you are, has left him without that responsibility and I like to think that my finding Ben has brought more into his life, as it has mine."

Again she paused and then looked at him even

harder. "You are much more gifted than you think. That I am sure of and I am a good judge of people. Don't sell yourself short. I am not sure what should be your course in life but it is not just golf. Play some more tournaments. Go along with Cornith Golf and help our two boys out. But remember what I am telling you now. You are meant to do something much more meaningful in your life. You will recognize it when you see it Ed, but it hasn't been revealed to you yet. Julia will help you along the way, but it will be up to you to find it."

Jennifer stood up just as Ben and Julia came out with the evening's offerings for dinner. Julia couldn't resist a comment on what Ed and Jennifer had been up to while she was in the kitchen. She was met with smiles from both, but neither one would tell her. Ben pretended not to have noticed but he seldom missed anything and he put it in a special place he had for remembering details.

The evening ended after much good conversation, a good meal and fond good nights. Tomorrow was going to be an exciting day as the putters would be put together and tested. If they matched up with the original Cornith it would be a go to start the Cornith Golf business model.

"Well my love, what was going on between my grandfather's lover and mine?" Julia asked with good humor the moment they got into bed.

Ed was ready. "She told me something I am not sure how to take but it was not to under estimate myself. That golf was not what I should pursue but it would be alright until I found out what I should actually being doing with my life. Something about a pursuit that had a real meaning. She told me that I would recognize it when I saw it and that you should be with me to help me find it."

"Well, I can go along with that! You already had doubts about a PGA career. And so do I but that was fun after the first few days and I am ready for another go if you want. But, you know, I think she is right. You are hiding something from me, and maybe yourself, but let's find out what it is together," Julia said as she got closer and massaged his shoulders. "I think tomorrow will be an all new day and it is such a good feeling to have that I can hardly wait for it to start. How do you feel?"

"Good. Really good," Ed responded and he didn't think he could feel much better.

Chapter 70

They had the putter heads and shafts up to the apartment first thing in the morning. Julia was even more excited than Ed in getting them assembled. They would start with the standard length shaft of 35 inches, the same length as on the original. Ed was going to use the Lamkin Jumbo grip which was his favorite and Julia liked it as good as any. He quickly installed the grips on six of the shafts.

They first positioned a shaft in each putter head and the fit was tight enough to hold it's position such that the putters could be swung in a putting stroke. Lined up along the wall next to the original they looked almost acceptable. The two reproductions of the original didn't look that bad with their modern coloration. The one Julia had designed actually looked good.

"You first my lady," Ed offered and Julia quickly picked her design.

"It feels good to me," and she handed it to Ed. He had the same reaction.

Ed then went down the line. All six had the same feel as the original. Next was testing the sweet spot by gently holding the putter shaft a third of the way up and tapping a golf ball on the putter's face. Again, with just a minor difference, all had the big sweet spot they were looking for.

"Okay so far. It is now time for the real test. Let's load up the car and head over to Tamarisk. After which I will treat you to lunch." Ed was almost giddy with the excitement he felt.

"Sure, big spender. You know they will just put it on Hank's membership," was Julia response.

Almost before they had the Porsche parked Gary was standing there to open the door for Julia. He was smiling so hard Ed thought his face would come apart. He started babbling about all the phone calls he was getting about Tamarisk and memberships. The membership chairman had to be called in over the weekend and had already ordered more new membership packets to be printed and sent out. They were now in discussions on what the membership limit should be.

Gary finally calmed down and when he saw what Ed was unloading from the back seat he got it going again. Ed had to explain that the shafts were not glued yet and this was the first test of the reproductions. He mentioned that he and Julia needed some space and privacy. By the time they got to the practice green there was a temporarily closed sign posted.

A dozen new Titleist Professionals were dropped on the putting surface. Julia turned to Ed. "This is your show. I will try them later."

Ed picked the original and sighted a hole 15 feet away. Julia went over to it and pulled out the mini flag and stood back. It was a perfectly straight line, no break. He went though his entire putting routine then made his first stroke. The ball rolled true and into the hole. Two more were holed and Ed exchanged the original with one of the direct copies. Two out of three, the miss by less than an inch but of perfect length. The feel was almost the same and would not be noticed unless one had just putted with the original. The putter could be massed produced.

It was then to the modified heads. The first three were good but noticeably inferior to the copies. Then it was time for Julia's modified putter head. Ed took special care. Again he went through his entire routine. He spent just a moment longer as the look was so much better than the other clubs. He wanted, and needed, this one to putt as good as the original. He made the stroke. The roll was perfect. The feel better than the original and the result was dead center in the hole. Six in a row. Julia's turn. Six in a row. Gary showed up and Ed called him over to try one of the original replicas. Five for six. He didn't want to let go of the putter but did as Ed said they had more testing to do and it was going to be this one he needed to use.

Another hour was spent with both Ed and Julia putting long and short, small and big breaking putts, The result were incredible. They finally picked up the balls, collected the the clubs, picked up the closed sign and headed back to the car. They put the putters and balls in the Porsche and locked it up. What was inside had suddenly become very valuable.

Gary had been called back to his office before they started using Julia's design and hadn't seen the results that had taken place in the last hour. There had been one observer that had watched it all from a distance using binoculars. He bore a remarkable resemblance to Ben. When he lowered the glasses Ben was smiling as he exited his hiding place.

Chapter 71

They decided against lunch as they were too keyed up to eat. Gary wanted them to stay but neither could handle any more of his enthusiasm. They needed time alone. Almost the feeling they should go somewhere and hide. The apartment was the place. Once there Ed glued up all six shafts and an hour latter they could be used for years. Ed thought of his Wilson Winsum. Would he replace it after fifty years in the family. It would be a hard decision to make.

Around 4:00 pm they headed to Ben's house and took the Julia design with them. Ben and Jennifer were seated out by the pool and Ed and Julia joined them. There was a slight tension in the air. Ed could feel it but Julia hadn't.

"Dinner tonight is at Hank's house. We are all invited and he is wants to know how the putter's are working," was Ben's first real contribution to the chit chat that had proceeded his announcement. Ed and Julia were surprised and acknowledged that it would be fun. They had handed Ben the putter when they had arrived. He had not put it down and was still admiring it's look. Ed noticed this and he knew what was about to happen. Cornith Golf was underway.

When they drove into Hank's drive way the gates

opened automatically and Ed realized that Ben's car had a remote that activated the gate. It wasn't, at least from appearance, a big house but it was a big property. Ben parked in front and they walked up to the door which Ben opened without knocking or ringing the door bell. This was all natural to Julia and Jennifer but seemed a bit odd to Ed. But then this was his first visit and he had no idea what to expect.

When they reached the living room Hank was seated in a big chair but didn't get up. His aide stood nearby but merely nodded to the guests. Hank bellowed a good evening and asked what they would like to drink. He had what looked to be bigger than a double scotch. Ben, Jennifer and Julia asked for white wine and Ed decided to try for a Guinness Stout. Without hesitating Hank's aide was out of the room and back in one minute with the drinks. Ed's Stout was at room temperature.

Ben presented the putter to Hank. He took it in his big, gnarled finger tips and inspected it closely. Looking up he had tears in his eyes. "This will do Morris. This will do. Cornith Golf will become a reality by God. You did it!" was said in a voice that Ed had not heard before. It was a voice that Ben had not heard in years.

Dinner was excellent. Rack of Lamb with all the fixings. So good the cook was brought out to take a bow. Ed was overwhelmed that this crusty old curmudgeon lived like this. His house was spotless and everything was the finest money could buy. There was fine art on the walls and a number of excellent bronze sculptures displayed in style. The man had taste and if you could not see that you were missing some important lessons in life.

After dinner more drinks were offered but declined. Ed was unsure how to approach the request to see the golf room but decided just to ask.

"Hank, Jason Poland at TaylorMade told me not to leave your home without a visit to your Golf Room." It was quiet for a moment and Ed was not sure if he hadn't made a major blunder. Then Hank smiled and responded. "Yes! Let's take the party there. Ed, you do deserve a visit." He motioned to his aide, managed to get upright and, with a cane, hobbled down the hall.

It was a huge room. The entire back of the house with floor to ceiling glass walls looking out on a big pool with a waterfall feature and a golf hole stretching 100 yards behind it. The green at the far end was fronted by a sand trap and was raised just enough to frame the yard. When they walked in the outdoor lights had come on and the sight was surreal. The room's walls were covered with paintings, photographs and golf paraphernalia, all beautifully displayed.

Cabinets ran along one wall and more golf related items were displayed. It was a collection that rivaled the Golf Museum's. In the center of the room there was a piano. It was as if it alone was the reason for this space and didn't care a whit for all the other things around it. Ed walked over to the side of the piano with the curve and touched it. He looked at Hank and he said, "Go ahead, it's time."

Hank had sat in the only chair in the room and Julia, Ben and Jennifer were near him and had baffled expressions on their faces. No one said a word. Something was about to happen that they didn't understand. Hank knew and Ed knew. Ed didn't know if he could do it.

Sixteen years of piano lessons and able to play at

the concert level. His mother had been his teacher. She was a good pianist but soon had discovered it was her son that had the talent to go the distance. He hadn't touched a piano since she, with his father, died in the horrific automobile accident ten years ago.

"Go ahead Ed. Do it!" Hank's voice was a command and Ed pulled off the cover. It was a 1928 Model C Steinway, the Parlor Grand piano. Beautifully restored in concert black lacquer and had real ivory keys.

Ed pulled back the bench and sat down in front of the keyboard. He closed his eyes and tried to remember what he had played the last time he had touched a piano. Rachmaninoff number two. Yes, that was it. He was preparing for a concert at Stanford and had just finished the afternoon practicing golf at the driving range. His teammates never knew about his real love at the time and as it turned out they would never find it out. They thought it odd he seldom joined them after practice and only occasionally when on the road in tournament play. He had another passion and here he was now trying to decide if he should touch the keys again.

Another revelation came as he stared at the keys. This was his mother's piano. He looked even closer. It was hers. It had been restored and shown brighter than before but it was her piano. Hank had found out who had owned it, his mother's story and his. Now he knew why he was here.

"It's time Ed. Your mother is waiting to hear you play again." Hank's voice was a whisper.

It wasn't perfect. It had been a long time but as the memory came back his confidence grew and the keystrokes had the command they needed. It was almost as if it was yesterday that he was preparing for his first big concert. It was coming back and this is what he was meant to do.

Ben and, especially, Julia were stunned. Hank was pleased and Jennifer knew she had been right. Ed knew what path he should now take and hoped Julia would understand and go with him. It was where he had to go.

Chapter 72

It was a quiet drive home. In fact no one spoke. Each was deep in thought about what had just transpired. Ed was wondering how Hank had found his mother's piano and how he connected it to him. It brought back memories so clear he could not bear to think of them. She had been his teacher. A very good pianist in her own right but had realized it was her son that had the gift to become great. Her last few years were spent not only teaching him how to get there but why he should go there. Then she, and his father, were gone and not being able to cope with the loss he decided to erase all the memories. His father was all for his efforts in music but wanted him to have more and it was golf that was their bond. It was the escape that both of them needed to give relief to the pressures of every day life. Ed would use it as his private escape from the loss he had to endure. It had almost worked. Now he knew different and he would have to bring Julia along with him.

Ben mulled this unexpected event over in his mind. He had seen the piano in Hank's golf room two weeks ago and wondered what it was doing there. He knew Hank had once played piano but just a fraction above mediocrity. Hank had always been two steps in front of him so it was not really a surprise. Nothing could surprise him if Hank was involved. It had been that way since the first day they met at IBM. Morris used to comment on this repeatedly. Never underestimate Hank, he knows more than the both of us put together. It was then on to thinking of how this would affect Julia. He wanted nothing but happiness for her, and Ed had made her world up to now a delight. He wanted it to stay that way but knew they would have to find the path to take. Just when he felt she had all she needed with Ed for her future this major fork in the road had showed up. Then he thought, Jennifer knew. Somehow she knew there was something for Ed that was more than just playing a game.

Jennifer wasn't surprised that whatever it was she sensed about Ed, and his future, had shown up but music had never entered her mind. Maybe managing Cornith Golf or some other business executive venture demanding his talents with people. But not music. Not the life of a concert pianist. Maybe for the sake of happiness professional golf would be a better choice. Then she had a most unusual thought, could he do both. That was replaced immediately by maybe it was not what he chose to do but to what he was to those around him.

Julia couldn't think. A curtain had just been lifted on a secret part of the man she so dearly loved and she hadn't even a hint that music had been a part of his life. An extremely important part of it. Just a few minutes ago her life seemed as if it could get no better. Then a piano in a room full of Hank's memories of the life he had lived had turned the future of her life upside down. She didn't know who to turn to for help but the answer came to her before the thought had finished. She knew the one person that would know what to do was Ed. He had promised he would never break her heart. She believed him then and believed it now. They would handle what has to be and they would be together as it happened.

At the house they dispersed as couples after some observations on the evening events. Ben even mentioned that they would have to figure out how a Cornith putter and a Steinway Parlor Grand piano could be shared in their lives from now on brought some forced smiles, but smiles none the less. Jennifer gave Julia an embrace and whispered in her ear that things would work out. That she and Ed were meant to be together and they would be. Ben hugged his granddaughter and kissed her on the cheek. He gave Ed a pat on the shoulder and then he and Jennifer headed toward their room. As Ed and Julia entered theirs, he put his arms around her and told her this was his problem but they would solve it together. It would not change what they have and he would keep his promises, both said and implied.

Chapter 73

As they got ready for bed Ed could sense a tension between them that he had never felt before. When she came out of the bathroom wearing a long nightgown he knew it was time he told her what it was that he had been so carefully trying to avoid for the last ten years. Once in bed and close enough to touch he started.

"I had the most wonderful parents any boy could have. Intelligent, compassionate, loving, giving and beautiful human beings. They gave me the opportunities to experience all avenues to follow and at the same time guided me to where they thought I should go. Both professors at UCLA and my mother was also an accomplished pianist. My father, besides being a highly regarded mathematician, was an excellent golfer. They both shared their lives with me and I was never excluded from even a few minutes of theirs." Ed recited this summary with his voice starting to quiver.

Julia could feel his emotion and moved closer. "Tell me the rest. I want and need to know all of it, Ed. Every last detail."

"At the end of the fall quarter, which ended before Christmas of 1983, and the start of the winter quarter in the first full week of January 1984 our family plans were to have Christmas together in Manhattan Beach at home and then I would return to Palo Alto to wait the start of the second quarter of my junior year. I was on the golf team and we were, in an disorganized fashion, getting our games ready for a new season of competition. My parents went to Mammoth Mountain ski area for the week. They were driving back on Sunday, January first, so they could go to the Rose Bowl game the next day. UCLA was playing Illinois and they had faculty tickets. Also my father had Rick Neuheisel, the quarterback, in one of his under graduate math classes, liked him and kept up a casual friendship." Ed stopped and tried to gather enough courage to tell Julia what happened next, not only about the accident but to himself afterward.

"They had left Mammoth early and reached Cajon Pass just before noon. Traffic was light and the roads were dry. There were no eye witnesses but later it was established a big tractor trailer hauling bags of cement was having braking problems and was swerving back and forth across the two lanes heading down into the Los Angeles basin. On a steep incline my parents 1972 Mercedes sedan left the road and crashed head on into one of the big boulders that lined the highway. Half a dozen bags of cement had fallen off the truck and exploded just short of where they left the road. The indication was that the cement covered their car, some of which was found inside, and blinded my father who was driving. After the crash the gas tank exploded but later the coroner stated that they died on impact before the fire consumed the wreckage." Ed had to stop and Julia could only say, "Oh no Ed, how awful."

"I was told by my counselor that afternoon. Just that they both had died in a car accident. Nothing more. I packed my things an headed home. I was using the Porsche as my car by then and was in Manhattan Beach by two in the morning. I won't tell you what it was like to be in the house alone for the next week. My parent's lawyer was my savior and took care of everything. Their ashes were interred in a small cemetery near Forest Lawn in Glendale and I have never been back. I packed a few things, had my golf clubs in the passenger seat and my skis on the ski rack mounted on the rear engine hood. I went to Aspen and spent the season skiing every day. I didn't talk much and after a while no one tried to talk to me. They thought there was something terribly wrong with the expert skier that seldom spoke." The pain was coming back again and they laid in silence for a few minutes as Ed tried to regroup.

"The lawyer had me sign a power of attorney and he prepared the house for selling. He moved what he thought I might want someday to a storage unit near the house. He sold most of the furniture and my mother's piano. The house was sold. All the proceeds and the insurance pay outs, less his fees and expenses, were put into a trust for me. I have never touched it. I have never gone to the storage unit and the rent is still being paid by the trust and is current." Again Ed had to stop. Julia now had her arms around him holding him close. Her cheeks were damp with tears.

"When the lifts closed the second Sunday of April I headed back west. I really can't tell you much about the time from then until I arrived in Palm Desert. It's a blur, but managing the art gallery helped bring me back and even that is not too clear. But when I first saw you putting behind the display case in the Golf Museum nine weeks ago things have been different. I can describe ever minute to you. Each and every minute." Ed was able to say this before he choked up and could say nothing more.

Chapter 74

Waking the next morning took longer than usual to get started. Both Ed and Julia were tired. Last night had been an emotional experience for both of them. For Ed finally telling someone of what had happened and for Julia to have listened to what he had gone through. Julia still needed to know about the music in his life. He hadn't discussed that yet.

"You have to tell me about the piano and how you learned to play. Why is it now in Hank's golf room?" was Julia's good morning.

"Are you sure you want to know? You have to know so I will tell you," Ed said, pausing. He had re-hearsed this in his head before he fell asleep last night. She had to know and how it might affect their lives. He wasn't even sure he wanted to go there and knew what would happen if he did.

"I told you last night that my mother was an accomplished pianist. Almost at the concert level. At two years I would sit on the bench, watch and listen to her play. It was mesmerizing and soon I was pushing on the keys with my index fingers. She would show me a series of keys to press to make a melody. Simple little five note melodies. By the time I was four I was playing entire songs that my small fingers could reach. She knew early that I had a good ear and quickly could learn and remember more complex combinations. By six I was learning many difficult pieces and my lessons became more serious. By ten she felt that this should be my future. At the same time my father was teaching me golf, taking me on his club's course to play and I was playing from the men's tees. Neither of them ever discouraged me from trying to be good at both." Ed paused again. Julia looked puzzled and he could understand why.

"By the time I reached the end of high school I was playing classical masterpieces and had a 4 handicap from the championship tees. The golf got me a full ride scholarship to Stanford and the piano into a special advanced music class. The golf was as you might expect. The music class was the use of one of the piano rooms for two hours a day as scheduling permitted. I also had access to the best teachers in the department. I was taking advantage of both and also working towards a Bachelors of Science in mathematics. I was a very busy young man and I was happy. Then my world collapsed when my parents were taken. Golf was the only thing that saved me. That was until you came into my life." Ed managed to get it said and waited for the expected question.

"What do you want to do?"

"I am not sure," Ed providing the answer Julia thought she would get.

"That's not good enough, Ed!" she was quick to come back.

"Okay, let's do it all. We will get Cornith Golf off the ground and we will play in the Greater Milwaukee Open in a week and a half. It's in Milwaukee just a few miles from where the Stevens live. And after that we will consider how to approach the beautiful lady that has just come back into my life. As to the last item, meaning the piano, that will take some serious thought." Ed was able to offer this with some happiness in his voice.

It was what Julia wanted to hear and she gave him a long embrace and suggested they get some breakfast, after they took care of some more important things.

Breakfast was served poolside. Ben and Jennifer had already left early on some venture and Ed and Julia had righted their ship. She had been worried last night as he played the piano. He had made a number of mistakes but in between was some of the best music she had ever heard. And the piano itself was as Ed described, a beautiful lady. She was afraid she might loose Ed to her. This morning she felt confident that wouldn't happen. He, and she, could do both.

The house phone rang and Julia answered. It was for Ed and was the CEO of TaylorMade wanting to talk about the Cornith Putter. Ed begged off for right now saying he was talking to the people that had the rights, and yes he would tell them of their interest. Then the phone rang again. It was was Jimmy Lee saying he was organizing a small service for Harriet on Saturday in La Jolla and would have more details by days end. Next was from Carolyn Finegold, Harold didn't like using the telephone, and that they were swamped by news items about the Cornith Putter and they wanted to show him some of the articles and photos. Also they had a photo story about a good looking pro and his caddie they must see.

Julia started to laugh and Ed was sporting a smile that told her things were going to be okay in their world.

Chapter 75

Just as Ed and Julia were thinking of what they should do next Ben and Jennifer came back from their morning outing. They had been at a meeting with Hank. Willy was also there and the four of them had set up the framework for Cornith Golf, the company. However Hank had done it, he had already hired a small group of College of the Desert business majors to man a phone bank to receive calls for information about the Cornith Putters. The youngsters had set up a website with a domain name, Cornithgolf@aol.com, and the five new phone lines he had installed yesterday were buzzing. The golf room had been re-arranged with the piano moved aside and two long tables occupied the center space. It was what was known as a bucket shop.

A copy machine was also busy printing out order cards and envelops and they were filled out in a frantic race to keep up. Promised sales were stacking up and Jennifer said Hank and Ben had been running about like two little boys with a new toy. How the clubs could be made and at what price they should be sold didn't seem to bother them. They were going to fix lunch for the troops and then hurry back. They needed Ed and Julia to help out.

When they got to Hank's they quickly distributed

the sandwiches and soft drinks. Hank had slowed down a bit but the activity hadn't. "I may have underestimated the response to a website Ben," was Hank's gross under-statement of the day. Finally the website crashed and the kids had a chance to catch up. Five hundred orders for a total of two thousand four hundred putters had been taken.

Ed started to laugh but quickly saw that the others weren't. He then told Hank and Ben about the interest that the CEO of TaylorMade had indicated in the phone call that morning.

"Maybe we should explore that Ben. I don't think I understood what this internet thing is all about," was Hank's lament. Ben agreed. Then the website cleared and it started up again.

It would take the rest of the afternoon and most of the next day to lay the ground work for Cornith Golf to be bought out by TaylorMade. The order of over twenty five thousand putters in one day, until the website failed for good, was a good selling point.

While the mad house was going on around them Ed and Julia wandered over to the piano. Ed pulled off the cover, lifted the lid and placed the prop. Julia looked down onto the gold colored frame and strings and walked along the curved side running her hand along the rim. "She is a beautiful lady Ed. I can see why you would want to play her. It is irresistible," were Julia's soft words. Ed smiled as he thought maybe this will all work out.

Saturday, August 20th , 1994 Harriet's ashes were secretively placed in a special spot on the cliff side of the area of the park called Whale Point View. Jimmy had fashioned a crypt in the rocks that would allow the small metal box containing her ashes to be placed and sealed with a fitted stone epoxy glued in place. At 1:30 pm, with Ben, Jennifer, Julia, Ed, Harold and Carolyn Finegold and Willy standing just above, Jimmy quickly inserted the box with Harriet's remains and glued the stone cover in place. It was directly below the big picture window in her apartment where she had spent much of her time looking out over the incredible view of the Pacific Ocean, always watching for the migrating whales.

Jimmy had a buffet ready in the apartment and all agreed the site he had picked out was a fitting place. Each had at least one story to tell about her and the best was Ed's describing when she played the part of Maureen Cornith and sold him the golf clubs. It was eleven weeks ago to the day. She had stayed around long enough to do her part in the promise to Morris that Hank and Ben had made and that her sister had hoped would happen.

The two putters that were going to be produced were the original "Morris" and the new "Julia." Ed would have liked to put the "Julia" in his bag but would have to wait until the first production models came out. Steve had agreed on using one of two "Morris" replica putters now available. In fact he begged to use it. He and Nikki also offered a room in their home for the Greater Milwaukee Open dates.

Things were moving very fast and it appeared the idea of Ed being the CEO of Cornith Golf was no longer in play and he was relieved.

"I think it best that Hank and Ben let younger people take on the task of marketing the putters. I am glad it isn't going to be offered to me as I think I would have had to refuse. You are not disappointed in that are you?" he asked Julia.

She reached over and patted his thigh. "Not in the least. I want you where I can see you and touch you," and then squeezed his thigh hard enough to force an, "Ouch!"

"Okay, we are left with golf and the music. Can we do both and do you want to do both?" Julia inquired not to subtlety.

"Let us start there and see which one, or both, will work best for us. Music lasts forever. That is worth thinking about," was Ed's answer.

Chapter 76

Sunday was to be a rest day. It had been a very busy week and although nothing had been signed yet the purchase of Cornith Golf by TaylorMade was going to be a pretty big deal. Hank had lost none of his business acumen and with Ben at his side they had made a good deal for Morris's memory, the Foster Care of Coachella Valley charity, a distribution for Ed and Julia's efforts and a little for themselves. The deal was just for the putters and would not include the clubs. Big money was possible on the royalties based on the sales numbers and this was to go to Ed, Julia and the charity.

By Sunday afternoon sitting around the pool was deemed boring so they went inside. The 115 degree temperature made the air conditioning a little nicer than the shade outdoors. The Sprint International was finishing up in Castle Pines, south of Denver, and it was a spectacular day in Colorado. Steve Lowery would win but finishing five groups ahead was another Steve that would card two more birdies to get to fourth place and win some real money. Steve Stevens looked mighty happy and in the interview, with Nicki and Jerry standing near by, he noted he had missed a couple of birdie putts that would have bumped him up a couple more spots on the leader board. He was looking forward to next week in Milwaukee and added, "See you there, Ed!"

Julia punched Ed in the ribs. "Did you hear that?" and smiled the smile that Ed wanted to always see on her face.

Most of the next week was practice. Golf practice. A break was taken on Wednesday for a trip to Manhattan Beach. Julia convinced Ed it was time to see what was in the store room where the lawyer had placed his inheritance. Ed had the key but didn't know the name of the storage facility. Julia went on the trail of the lawyer and finally made contact. Ed talked to him, pleasantries were exchanged and the lawyer posed that the content might now not be worth the rental fees but wished him luck. He had the unit number and would call the manager and tell him Ed would be showing up and to let him have access.

It was a fine day for a drive and once near enough to the ocean to get the sea breeze it was comfortable. At the storage unit the fun began. The key fit the lock but the lock was rusted closed. The manager brought out the bolt cutters and made short work of the lock and sold Ed a new one before he left them alone to sort through the boxes and things inside.

Ten years in a southern California sea side storage unit is not kind to cardboard so they had to be careful opening each box. The packing tape wasn't a problem as it had all loosened and fell away. There were several of interest, more to Julia than Ed. Lots of family photos and mementos. Looking through a few of them she could see Ed was right, his mother was a beautiful woman and his father a handsome man. His yearbooks were there and all sorts of newspaper clippings of his golf wins and other achievements in high school. There was one 8 x 10 black

275

and white photo of him in a concert setting at a grand piano with the orchestra in the background.

Several other boxes had collections of quality dinner and cook wear. There were now outdated computers, cameras and projectors. Most held little interest and would have to be gone through later. There were two small lock boxes, the kind that hold business size letters and documents. Ed didn't have the keys so he set them aside to take back to Palm Desert. There was a fine chess set with beautiful pieces of carved ivory and ebony. A full size filing cabinet which was half full, mostly with college papers, none of which had much meaning to Ed so they could wait.

His mother and father's golf clubs were there. Tennis rackets and two 10 speed bicycles having flat tires. On a metal set of shelves were some nice hand tools and several tool boxes.

And then there were the books. Both his parents loved books and there was at least twenty boxes of them carefully loaded on a pallet and wrapped in plastic which was securely taped. The lawyer had thought that regardless how long they would be in storage they should be protected and did just that. Ed silently thanked him. In one would be his mothers collection of sheet music for the piano that she was so proud of. He could remember her showing him one or another and telling how and where she had obtained it. Some were signed, one in particular was Rachmaninoff Concerto Number 2 and had his signature.

"We will have to rent a truck, have Willy come with us, and haul this stuff back home. I think I will be keeping the apartment for some time, or rent another storage unit." Julia took that in stride and they loaded up what they had set aside in the Porsche, locked up the unit and headed home.

Chapter 77

The rest of the week was busy. Ed was concentrating on his golf and Julia was with him every step of the way. A trip was made to TaylorMade to deliver the replica of the original Morris design and Julia's modified version. They had agreed to keep the names "Morris" and "Julia" and they also would use Mac for bending the shafts. They could have made their own dies but some loyalty had to be given to those that had been there in the beginning. Mac did sell them the jig for drilling the holes which they would copy to accurately drill the heads. Mac was happy.

By Sunday afternoon it was time for a rest. The NEC World Series of Golf was on TV and it was relaxing to just watch. The young Spaniard Jose Maria Olazabal was the winner. Steve was not eligible so he was home watching it, too.

Tuesday they flew to Milwaukee, picked up by Jerry Stevens and were soon at the Stevens's home. They had a comfortable bedroom and a new family to enjoy for the week. Julia and Ed were immediately adopted by both Steve and Nicki's parents. Ed came away from the experience, as did Julia, knowing that the family bonds of the mid-westerners were something special. These were truly good people.

Nicki told Julia Steve was sleeping with his new

putter and wouldn't let it out of his sight. Wednesday was Ed's first look at Brown Deer Park's golf course. It was not a long course by PGA standards and was a municipal track. The fairways were mostly tree lined but fair in width. However, if you went astray it would be bogey time or worse. Steve had made a copy of his yardage book for him and they played together in the practice round. Both Ed and Julia received a good schooling as Steve had played the course many times. Also, this was the first time the event was played at Brown Deer and many of the players were also seeing it for the first time.

Ed felt comfortable here and the weather would cooperate. It was the mid-seventies with the final day just a little cooler. A few rain showers didn't slow the play. It was the beginning of fall and several of the many trees were showing some color early. It was a very pretty place.

Steve and Ed weren't paired together in the first two rounds, and were just separated by two groups in the third. They were tied starting the final round, and that was fine for Steve and Nicki's family and friends who also wanted to watch Ed play. They ended up tied for third behind the winner, Mike Springer, who closed at 16 under, 3 shots better. Steve won the putting contest between them by 4 putts less, but Ed won the tee to green total. If they could have combined Ed's tee to green play and Steve's putting they would have won the tournament.

That evening was the family dinner, plus a few close friends, at Nicki's parents home. At least 25 people were there and Julia and Ed were treated as family favorites. They were staying over to Monday and that night when they finally retired and closed the bedroom door Julia snuggled up to Ed and told him two things. She

279

couldn't ever remember having as good a time as she had today, both that nights party and the golf tournament, and she wanted to do it some more. She rolled over towards him and asked.

"What do you, Ed Adams, want to do with your life? I have to be included but what is your dream?"

Ed knew. He had tried to ignore it but it was back. When he played the piano his world seemed complete. He liked the competition of golf and liked the game. Even liked most of the people. But for himself, and just himself, it was the music he needed. Could he do both? Julia had to be a part of his life and pursuing his music would probably be a selfish undertaking.

"I like the golf. The competition and most of the people. It is fun. The travel, the places where we play. But deep down I want to try the music again. I want to see if I can get back to where I once was," Ed said hoping he had said it right.

"Let's see if we can do both. See if it works out the way we would like. I am good with that," Julia said and yawned. "Let's sleep on it."

The flight home was uneventful. Steve took them to the Milwaukee Airport, their plane was on time, they had an empty seat between them, all their luggage made it to the carousel and Ben and Jennifer were there to pick them up. Arriving at the house they got the car unloaded and when entering Ed could sense something was up between Jennifer and Ben. They steered them toward the living room and there in the perfect place was the piano. The lid was up, the bench in place and on the music rack was a placard. On it in a ragged scroll was "Enjoy Your Piano, Hank".

Chapter 78

As you walked into the living room between the partially open kitchen to the left and the open dinning area to the right the living area was spread out in front of you. The floor to ceiling windows and glass french doors leading to the pool area, cabana and garden were the focus but now in the right hand corner was the beautiful Steinway Parlor Grand piano. The lighting had been altered to present it in a manner that took Ed's breath away. He couldn't move. Julia was also frozen in her position next to him. Both knew at that moment their future would be determined in the next few minutes. Ben and Jennifer were aware of what was happening and waited, hoping that their plan had been the correct thing to do.

The furniture had been moved and several additional chairs were in place. It was set up so a dozen or more people could be entertained in comfort. It was a music room. If one could set up a room to create a space for fine music to be performed it could be no better than this. Ed's total focus, however, was on the piano. He had tried to divorce himself from his music, and all the memories that were a part of it. He had almost succeeded but now it had all come back.

He forced himself to move, went to the piano and sat down on the bench. He gently touched the wood, sliding his finger tips along the smooth edges, and then did the same over the ivory keys. He could remember in detail his childhood with his mother at his side as she guided his hands with her long, shapely fingers. He could almost feel their softness and smell her fragrance. He could see her smile and the love in her eyes. Her encouragement and her voice he could remember as if it was happening at that moment. It was all coming back. All that he had tried to forget as it had been too painful to have the memories be so clear.

His first performances for his parent's friends in their home, and then bigger ones in high school. One at UCLA for the faculty and students with his mother and father in the front row beaming with pride. It was his vision of his father that brought him back to the present. He had told Ed to always find a place you could go to hide from reality. A place where the concentration was such that nothing else mattered but the task at hand. Don't stay there too long and don't think that you cannot share that place with another. It had been golf where he could hide but now that was not going to be enough. He had decided he wanted to play the piano again, but had been uncertain how he was going to be able to get there. Now it was right in front of him.

While Ed was sitting as if in a trance at the piano, Julia was recognizing that it was also her world that was about to change. First was the fear of losing Ed and the life that had just been laid out before them. The idea that both the music and golf could be the route to take was in jeopardy but then she thought that if it was approached in the right way it still may be possible. She did have some back ground in music, singing and acting in a number of musicals in high school and one in college. One way or another, she could still be a part of his life which she desperately wanted.

Julia walked over to Ed, placing her arms around his shoulders from behind, and whispered in his ear "You have to do it. It was meant to be. Chase your dream, Ed. You have to and I will go there with you."

Chapter 79

Ed sat frozen in position not knowing where to go next. The memories were cascading through his mind and then for some reason he placed his hands on the keyboard and his fingers started the playing the melody of the song of "The Way We Were." He was twelve or thirteen when his mother asked him to learn it so she could pretend to be Barbara Streisand and sing along. The movie was very popular about that time. She would walk about the room singing, with a very good voice, the lyrics with such feeling that now Ed was thinking there had to have been be more to it than her just liking the song.

Julia recognized it immediately. She had the roll of Katie Morosky in a college production and started to hum the score in Ed's ear. He matched her key and worked backed to the beginning and played with more force. Julia swung around to sit on the bench next to him facing the piano and sang the lyrics:

"Memories light the corners of my mind
  Misty water-colored memories of the way we were
  Scattered pictures of the smiles we left behind
  Smiles we gave to one another for the way we were
  Can it be that it was all so simple then
  Or has time rewritten every line
  If we had the chance to do it all again

Ed Adams Chases a Dream

Tell me, would we?
Could we?"

Ed and Julia continued through the entire song as if they were polished professionals. Neither missed a note, word or timing. The acoustics of the room were right and to Ben and Jennifer it was a love song so powerful they were spellbound. As it ended Jennifer was in tears and Ben was trying to hold his back. They rose and with arms around each other left the room. Ben was shaken and only able to say to Jennifer "It was the right thing to do."

Ed turned to Julia and could see her eyes were moist but that she was smiling.

"You never told me you could sing. Not like that. You have a beautiful voice. Everything about you is beautiful," he said and was now also smiling.

Julia took his hands in hers and responded. "You never told me you could play the piano, or even liked music. At least not until a few weeks ago. You never once mentioned it before then."

"I couldn't. I didn't want to remember how it was. How it was with my mother and father. I can do that now. It is because of you. You, Ben and Jennifer, Hank, Willy, and the others around you. I feel alive again and I think there is a path to a good place we can go to together that will work for us," Ed said rushing the words.

He turned back to the piano and started playing a medley of Broadway show favorites and Julia hummed along, occasionally singing a few parts. Ed then stopped and turned toward her and a told her about accompanying his mother, sometimes for hours, as she sang the songs. "She had a good voice, maybe even better than that, but never performed in public. Not even with my father present. I now think I understand what was happening. She could have been a star but was afraid to take the chance. Would you like to?"

Julia didn't answer. She had thought about it now and then but with all the things that were happening in her life never gave it a serious thought. Several times her music teachers would mention she should think about pursuing a career in music. Even Ben thought her voice and stage presence was such that it would be something she should consider doing but never pushed her in that direction.

Ed then continued. "You have the voice, the presence and the looks. If you have the desire I will be your accompanist until you don't need me any longer or don't wish to continue. I can get back into form quickly and I am good at it. This is something we can do together. I can also put in the effort for myself to get back to where I was before I gave it all up."

Julia stood and asked Ed "Give me a few minutes. I will be right back," and she went down the hall to her old bedroom. She pulled a large flat plastic bin out from under the bed, took off the lid and cast her gaze over the piles of sheet music and newspaper clippings. On the top was a full front page from the Pamona College newspaper, The College Life. The headline was "Freshman Julia Renquest Shines in The Way We Were." The tears came and she quickly looked away not wanting to get anymore stains on her keepsake.

"How could he have known?" she thought. It was the last time her mother would see her perform and the last performance she would make. In the next year she would lose first her mother and then her grandmother.

Chapter 80

Ben and Jennifer tried to comfort each other over what they had both experienced from Julia's rendition of "The Way We Were". They readied themselves for bed and were laying close together when the conversation started.

"It brought it all back for each of us. In fact for all four of us. Julia's in her old room crying her heart out. I can hear Ed playing pieces he hasn't played in over ten years. He is living his memories that way." Jennifer spoke with a quiver and sadness in her voice Ben hadn't heard before.

"Jen, you do see things clearly. You can see right through me so you know what I am feeling right now. How much I need you to be here. What it means to lose those who are closest to you too early in their lives," was the best Ben could come up with and then he added, "I will go talk to them both. They know which way things are going to go now and I want them to know how good they will be together. And that they can do it all."

Ben got up, put on his robe and as he passed the open door to Julia's room he could see her still sitting on the floor with her bin of memories, cradling her head on the mattress and quietly sobbing. He decided to talk with Ed first.

287

He was still playing show and movie scores apparently not realizing what he was doing. It was his memories that he was going through. Ben could only think what a sight it was to see this big man having the talent to express himself this way with his music. He gently sat down on the bench and watched Ed's hands move and the fingers touching the keys.

"You played those for your mother. Was she a singer, too?" was questioned just loud enough for Ed to hear.

"Yes. Every lesson she gave me ended with at least an hour of her singing the popular songs she loved while I accompanied her. She was a beautiful person, just like Julia. That's what we are going to do, Julia and I. You knew that already, didn't you?" Ed said this as he kept playing.

Ben put his hand on Ed's shoulder and answered "Yes," and then, "I will go talk to Julia and she will be out here in a few minutes. Ed, this will turn out much better than you may think right now. A number of doors will open for you both. Go through them together."

As Ben entered Julia's room she looked up and tried to smile. He sat next to her and stroked her head. "You are an exceptional young lady. You sang one song that left all four of us in separate places with our own memories. That is why that song was written and why it is still so popular. Jennifer was with her husband when things were as they were. You and I when it was the four us here together. And Ed is playing the music for his mother to sing her songs when she needed them. Memories are powerful, especially the good ones." He paused and could sense Julia recovering. "Take that newspaper to

Ed and tell him that is where you want to go. He already knows this and is ready to go there. You two can do it all and can do it together. I am looking forward to watching it happen."

Ben rose and left Julia to collect herself and she did as he suggested. Ed was still playing as she sat down next to him. He finished the last piece and then turned to her.

"Your grandfather said doors will open for us and that we should go through them together. He is a very smart man and I am thinking that is very good advice. That is exactly what we should do. It is time for bed and we can talk there." Ed said this as he picked her up and carried her to their room.

When Julia came out of the bathroom Ed was reading her keepsake newspaper and was smiling. "Julia Renquest, you really do shine. That is where we are going to start on this next adventure and we will see where it leads. I am ready, are you?" Ed asked even though he knew what the answer would be.

He did know part of the answer but was surprised by the other part. "Yes, yes, and yes but what is the next golf tournament we can play in?"

Chapter 81

Ed woke with Julia running her fingers through his hair just above his ear and to the back of his head. She then pulled him to her and gave him a proper kiss. "Good morning my best friend. It is a very good morning. How is your morning?" was her happy greeting.

"I think it is going to be a very good start for this next day of my life. It seems that what is important to me is that you are in a very good mood," and he kissed her back.

The sound of the coffee bean grinder filtered through to them and Julia jumped up and did a nice little dance toward the bathroom as Ed watched. He smiled, sat up and stretched. He was well rested, satisfied with his life and was glad to be alive.

Entering the kitchen they found Ben and Jennifer fixing breakfast and it was easy to see that the morning had also dawned nicely for them. Jennifer gave Julia a hug and offered that last night she had been given a gift. To come to grips with what had been the focus on her past life that was now onto her future life with her new family. She wanted her to know how much she appreciated having this new outlook. She smiled at Ed and said, "You too, of course."

All four had crossed a barrier that had been in the

way of reaching full contentment. Julia's singing of "The Way We Were" had somehow removed it and they were now a family. The past was a memory but no longer an impediment. It was a very good morning, as was breakfast of French toast poolside with a nice sunrise casting a soft pink glow in the desert around them.

Plans were made. The Buick Southern Open being played at Callaway Gardens, Pine Mountain, Georgia was selected as the best option. They would be flying three weeks from today, September 27th, to Quad Cities International Airport which was a short drive to the venue. Julia would try to arrange lodging with the Stevens again and as soon as Ed made his entry certain, she would make the plane reservations.

Tomorrow they would rent a small truck and empty the storage room that had Ed's inheritance, store them here in Palm Desert and sort them out as time permitted. Between these two efforts they would practice Ed's golf and their music with emphasis on Broadway musicals and movie track songs. Ed was to have some private time to spend getting him ready for playing more classical works.

Ben smiled and Jennifer looked aghast that they expected to get so much done in next few weeks. Ed calmed her fears with acknowledging that maybe they could get four to six songs for he and Julia to do and that for him it was just to get part way back in remembering how to play. The golf he would work on to be acceptable. Top ten would be just fine as a goal.

Today they would spend organizing the rental of a store room, a truck rental and collecting the sheet music they needed for Julia's songs. She had most of what was

needed in the storage box under her bed and Ed was
hoping he could find the box that had all his mother's
sheet music. It had to be in one of the boxes of books they
would be bringing back from Manhattan Beach.

Later this morning they would spend a couple of
hours on the driving range at Tamarisk. In the afternoon
some time at the piano and then have a relaxing late
afternoon and evening. This brought up another subject
that Ed was sure needed to be settled before it became a
problem in this happy family.

"We may have a problem I need to discuss and get
resolved before we go much further," was Ed's opening.
He then continued, "Working my way back on the piano
will take long hours and the sounds are not always pleasant. Likewise working with Julia will take some time and
only when we are together as we were last night will you
enjoy what we are doing. The sounds will carry and there
sits our future," Ed said gesturing toward the piano.

Ben looked at Jennifer and she returned his gaze
with a smile and a nod. Ben then posed that they had been
thinking about some extensive traveling over the next few
years. In fact they were about to make reservations for a
four week tour to Europe starting next week. This brought
a smile to Ed's face as he thought he should have known
that Ben knew what would be involved when the piano
was placed and his living room converted into a music
room.

"I should have known you would have planned for
that Ben," Ed said expressing his thought and then turning
to Jennifer, "He is the smart one, don't you think?"

The two hour practice at Tamarisk went well. Gary
Martin helped Ed get his entry to the Southern Open se-

cured. Julia had remained home and by the time Ed returned she had contacted Nicki and they had rented one of the 3 bedroom Villas at Callaway Gardens. It was walking distance to the Mountain View golf course they would be playing and right in the center of all the activities. The plane reservations had been made and Julia was one happy lady.

After lunch they found and rented a storage unit about the same size of the one in Manhattan Beach and arranged to pick up the rental truck in the morning. Willy wasn't going to be able to go with them but the truck had a hydraulic lift and they rented a dolly. It wouldn't be that bad. Ben and Jennifer were leaving on Friday, first stop New York City and then on to Paris, Venice, Florence and Rome.

Chapter 82

The round trip to Manhattan Beach had gone well. The boxes of books were loaded first and once that was done the rest was easy. They sorted things in groups of that which to save, that to send to a thrift store after offering them to Willy, and a few items were deposited in the storage area dumpster. Ed's father's chair would go over to the apartment. They had decided to keep the apartment for a few more months to use as a work shop and a hide away when necessary.

Returning to Palm Desert the unloading was done quickly. Going through the book boxes didn't go so fast. In about box number 12 the sheet music was found and set aside. They appraised the book collection and decided it was too good to leave in a store room so they would see if Ben would mind them buying some nice bookcases to go against the wall near the piano.

Returning the truck they made it back home and took a long shower together and then made it out to the chaise lounges by the pool by five o'clock. At six Ben and Jennifer were back with several impressive clothes bags, and better yet Chinese take out. Dinner was served and the new family of four were comfortable together watching the sun go down.

Julia brought her plastic storage bin into their bedroom and sitting on the bed she and Ed started sorting through the contents. Ed was surprised that there were some forty odd sheets of music, more than enough to get them started. There were also the year books, a scrap book and photo albums. Everything stopped a little over five years ago just after Julia's 20th birthday.

"We will go through the photos and scrap book later. She pulled out her high school annual and showed off her senior picture. A beautiful girl in a professional setting and pose. It was next to the music section and on stage in 'South Pacific' she was washing her hair and obviously singing the signature song as the lead. To Ed she looked even better in the sports section showing the girl's golf team, both the team photo and one of her swing. He fell in love with the high school girl in the photographs.

"Enough of this for now. Let's pick out 6 songs to work on this week." She looked up as she said this and then asked, "Why are you looking at me like that?"

"I just fell in love with the high school girl in that year book that looks just like you. I had thoughts about making love to her and almost could imagine what it would be like. What a lecher I am," Ed said, only half in jest.

Julia put everything back in the bin, secured the top and slid it under the bed.

"We can pick out the songs in the morning."

When they went out to breakfast the next morning Ben and Jennifer were still in their room and Julia started the coffee bean grinder. Jennifer was out first dressed in a nice fall outfit and did a little modeling walk about.

"Outfit number one," she announced and before

any comments could be made she headed back to her room and closet.

"I don't think they plan to travel light," Ed said giving his opinion. As Ben came out in his bathrobe, with a rather mischievous grin on his face, he decided not to pursue any more thoughts on traveling light.

Jennifer soon was back in her Palm Desert outfit and they fixed their own breakfast bowls of cereal and fresh fruit in the kitchen. It was then outside to the table by the pool and ate with minimal conversation.

"One suitcase and one carry on bag each. Ben gets an extra camera bag. That's it," was Jennifer's declaration as she and Julia started picking up the dishes.

Ed then asked Ben about having a bookcase installed on the wall next to the piano and he agreed as long as it matched the quality and style in the house. The next question Ed asked was how he should pay for it and if he should use the credit card they were using on the Cornith golf project. Also as he wasn't putting his full effort into trying for a PGA win should he make some other arrangements.

Ben smiled at this. "You haven't seen the books. Hank keeps them and he will be making you and Julia itemized spreadsheets. You haven't been paying any attention to what is coming in, have you?"

"Well, you know what, I haven't. I assume we are not over drawn or we would have heard about it by now." Ed answered although he had assumed enough was coming in to cover most of their expenses.

"Let me put it this way. There is more in both accounts than when we started. And enough more will be coming in from the deal Hank is making with TaylorMade to set you both up for a long time. Keep using the cards and Hank will take care of everything. Just don't buy a Lear Jet just yet," Ben said trying not to laugh.

Chapter 83

Julia and Ed spent most of the day sorting through the songs they wanted to do. It seemed like deja vu to Ed as each one picked by Julia was one his mother had liked. He was surprised, then thought he maybe shouldn't have been, as most were popular between 1960 and 1980.

Julia started to laugh and held out the score for "Show Me" from My Fair Lady. "Do you know this one?" Ed took a quick look and headed for the piano with the score. He placed it on the music rack, positioned himself on the bench and played the first few bars. Then giving her the cue with the first notes for "Words! Words! Words! I'm so sick of words" and they were off. Both worked from memory and pulled it off in a spectacular fashion. Julia bobbed about as Eliza on stage opposite an imaginary Freddy.

Ben and Jennifer came in from the pool area and were treated to a nice collection of songs which included "I'm Gonna Wash That Man Right Outa My Hair" from South Pacific followed by "Raindrops Keep Falling On My Head" from the movie Butch Cassidy and the Sundance Kid. Then some romance with "You've Lost That Loving Feeling" with the beautiful first line "You never close your eyes anymore when I kiss your lips." And then "Woman in Love", the first three lines being

"Life is a moment in space, When the dream is gone, It's a lonelier place." They finished up with Ed playing the first bars of Carly Simon's "Nobody Does It Better" and Julia launched right in with, "Nobody does it better, makes me feel sad for the rest, nobody does it half as good as you, baby you're the best," while running her hand through Ed's hair and across his shoulders in an provocative way.

When they finished Ben and Jennifer applauded them and Julia, and then Ed, followed with their own applause. Julia almost knocked Ed over as she jumped into his arms and kissed him. "We can do this. We can do it! I love it! You make it so easy, Ed. How do you do that?"

Jennifer was suddenly quiet. She knew why but Ed still didn't have a clue. She had sensed it the moment she first met him. He had a gift that very few people have of being able to make the lives of those around him better than they otherwise would have been. It would probably be best if he found out, if he ever did, when the time was right. For now she would just watch as it unfolded around her.

Ed and Julia spent the afternoon finding a cabinet shop that could build and install the bookcase. They met a young cabinet maker that had a number of very nice examples of his work in his show room in the front of his shop. He came over to the house and took the measurements, photographed all the built ins and took copious notes. He had time and should have them built and in place in two weeks. That would work out and Ed gave him a down payment.

The next morning Ed and Julia took Ben and Jennifer to the Palm Springs Airport for their flight to New York City where they would spend three days and then fly to Paris. They had booked a room for the week at Hotel du Champs de Mars. Ben guaranteed Jennifer he could walk directly from the hotel to the bakery where he met Julia's grandmother. Providing it was still there.

The next two and a half weeks were busy as Ed and Julia prepared for an event that would turn out to shape their future. Ed was trying to bring his skills as a pianist back to where they had once been and his golf game good enough to be competitive. In addition he was working with Julia to polish her skills as a singer and they as entertainers. He had set aside two hours each day for his classical piano playing and it was coming back better than he had expected, but not as fast as he had hoped. Every other day, half was spent on golf practice. They worked in playing four rounds of golf at Tamarisk.

Ed and Julia were making good progress with their musical vignettes. It was becoming more than a singer and her accompanist, more like an integrated show. Her vocals were getting so good that sometimes Ed would lose his place as he listened to her interpretations. He was able to work in a number of solo introductions to Julia's songs with a skill that matched his classical efforts. Their confidence was to the point that they were ready to take it public.

They had been bringing over boxes of books and by the time the book cases were installed there were rows on the floor on the opposite side of the room ready to be placed. The cabinets were properly done and looked as if they had been in place since the house was built. When filled it made an impressive display of the hundreds of fine books Ed's parents had collected over the years.

September 27th arrived and Willy had them at the

airport in time for their flight to Quad Cities and Callaway Gardens. It was there that the events would occur that would shape theirs lives for years to come.

Art Myers

Chapter 84

Jerry Stevens picked them up at the airport. The club case and luggage came to the carousel promptly although this time there was an extra hangar bag. Julia had gone shopping with Jennifer as she insisted that Julia have at least one outfit that would be appropriate for a songstress. Also in the bag was Ed's "Gallery outfit."

Julia was also carrying a small case loaded with sheet music. Ed had noticed but had said nothing, especially after his comments on traveling light. It was only a thirty minute drive to Callaway Gardens and when they stopped in front of the rented villa both Steve and Nicki were waiting on the porch to greet them. They were family now and Julia and Nicki immediately went inside to talk of the things that women talk about.

Steve apologized about not coming to the airport as he had been taking a nap trying to recover from too much golf and too much traveling. He had taken only one week off in the last five and his game was being affected. Also Nicki was getting closer to the delivery date and this would be her last trip with him for a while. Ed said "No problem," with a good handshake.

The Villa was perfect. Ed and Julia were given the master suite and the Stevens would share the other bathroom but both had nice bedrooms. It was a ground floor unit with no stairs, the large living area open having a good kitchen and dinning space. It was a five minute drive to the golf course and you could walk if you wanted to but probably wouldn't if carrying clubs.

Nicki had the dinner menu planed and provisioned, along with everything for breakfasts and snacks. They sat around and talked having soft drinks with some chips and dip. When it was time to prepare dinner the ladies asked that the boys take a hike and be back in forty five minutes. Julia took time to tell Nicki all that was going on in their lives. Especially about the music and how happy she was to be doing something with Ed that they both seemed to not only to enjoy but were surprisingly good at.

Ed wasn't so open to Steve and Jerry but did let it be known that he was back with piano playing and that he and Julia were doing some numbers together. He did re-mark that Julia had a terrific voice, stage presence and liked to perform. The conversation then turned to golf, golf clubs, and Steve wishing that some of the putter's magic could be shared with his driver.

Dinner was excellent and after another short walk all retired for the evening. Julia snuggled up to Ed and after telling him how nice it was having Nicki to talk to softly said, "I don't think I have ever been as happy, or content, as I am right now. Are you?"

"Yes. I sense that something is just about to happen that will be good for us and that we will remember this moment as it's beginning."

Practice day was excellent. Steve and Ed were paired up with another Steve, Steve Elkington and a fel-low Aussie of his, a third Steve, Steve Rintoul. That was a lot of Steves but to Ed they were all fine fellows and they had a good time and worked together to get the most out of the round. Elkington had the most experience having played the course many times and also thought it one of the best on the tour. It suited his game as a straight ball hitter and a good putter. Ed was glad to hear that and paid attention to the advice given.

Day one dawned pleasant, play was fast, and the scores low. None in Ed's practice round were together and the three Steves never saw each other until after almost all the play had finished. Steve Elkington was the only standout of the group carding a terrific 66 and was atop the leader board. Steve Rintoul was only two shots behind and the third Steve who shot even par and would have to do better the next day if he was to make the cut. Ed shot two under and had a lot of company there. Julia had a good time and did her duty for Ed. She was probably the happiest person on the course and was getting a gallery all of her own, which had little to do with golf.

Ed spotted Steve and Jerry on the practice area and with Julia, who let him carry the bag, walked over to join them. Steve was still having problems with his driver. The straight drives were fine when he hit them. It was just that the same swing would then be left, then right, then high with a fade or low with a draw. Ed pulled his driver out and asked Steve to hit a few with it.

"It feels awful. How can you swing this thing?" was his first comment.

"Just give it a try. You won't be able to hit a decent drive but it might make you think that your driver is so much better that it will start working for you."

He gave it a try. Going through his entire routine and address. He hit a ground ball off to the right. Ed was watching closely and only said "Hit another one."

The result was just at bad and Steve handed Ed's club back. As Steve gripped his own driver he muttered something about how good it felt compared with that log Ed was swinging and hit a perfect drive, long and straight. Then another. And another.

"Don't waste them all out here," Ed told him as he shouldered his bag and he and Julia headed back to the Villa.

Chapter 85

Day two was similar to the first day as Steve Elkington shot another 66, but more important Steve Stevens shot 2 under and made the cut. Ed had a 3 under and now at 5 under was 7 strokes behind Elkington. He would have been in second place except for the last Steve, also shooting 3 under, placing him six shots behind and pushing Ed down to third.

Saturday was to be the big day for the golf but it turned out to be Sunday for Ed and Julia. Elkington wouldn't be denied with a 68 ending the day at 16 under. Steve Rintoul had one of the best rounds of the day with a 67 and moved to 11 under and in second place. Steve Stevens had his best round in a month with the other 67 and ended up 7 under tied for fifth with three other players. Ed carded a 68, was now 9 under and in a tie for third place.

That night was the big party for players, wives, caddies, friends and volunteers. It was held under a huge tent with a big stage at one end with a sound system and would host two local bands. There were large round tables and seating for 350. On either side were serving tables offering bar-b-que, coleslaw, corn on the cob, beans and breads. Large coolers offered cold soft drinks and water. Wine was available and iced cans of beer were in tubs scattered about. It was well attended but not crowded, the food good and the entertainment adequate. Ed and Julia, along with the Stevens, had dinner and listened to the first band then headed back to the Villa.

The weather report was not looking good for Sunday and shortly after the fourth group had teed off the predicted rain came. It was heavy rain from a big tropical storm and after 90 minutes the tournament was called as the heavy rain was to last most of the day. Ed being in the next to last group hadn't even left the Villa. Julia was disappointed as she really enjoyed the big scene and being part of the play. They decided to walk up to see what was going on and under Ed's golf umbrella they headed up towards the clubhouse.

There was a lot of activity going on in the big tent so they detoured and walked in under it's shelter. The tables had been removed and folding chairs were being place in rows. The stage was being set up for a major orchestra and out front was a huge covered Concert Grand piano. Ed and Julia went up on the stage and just as Ed was about to lift up the cover on the piano to see what make it was a rather harried man came running up and called out, "Don't touch that!" He had a cell phone in one hand and what appeared to be a fresh plaster cast on the other. He was in his sixties, wearing dark rimmed glasses and was talking excitedly on his phone.

Turning his back to Ed he spotted Julia, gave her a nod and continued talking to whomever was listening. "It just happened this morning. I stumbled on a step and fell flat on my face." He paused, and then continued. "No I can't play. For Christ's sake my left hand is in a cast. My fingers are swollen and I can't move them. I don't know.

Call everyone you know and I will see what I can do," and closed the phone.

Julia smiled at him and politely said "Sounds like you have a problem."

He took a long look at Julia and then turned toward Ed and sized him up. "Why are you up here?"

"I like pianos and this looked like a Steinway Model D. Just wanted to look at it up close."

"Do you play the piano?" was asked.

"Yes I do. I was thinking that since the golf tournament has been called all us golfers have nothing to do and most have to hang around until their transportation arrives to head home. Many, if not most, of the fans have the same problem. Julia and I could provide some entertainment for them. She is a talented singer and we are developing a nice repertoire. We could put on a show for a few hours." Ed was able to say all this with a perfectly straight face.

He took another look at Julia and she gave him another smile. He was a man and Julia was Julia. "My name is Lalo Schifrin and I somehow ended up being in charge of this concert featuring members of the Quad Cities Symphony Orchestra and the special Youth Symphony Orchestra. My good friend James Dixon is the music director and this is a fund raiser for the youngster's program. I was supposed to be the pianist for tonight's performance." Waving his cast in the air he finished with, "Guess what?"

Ed smiled and introduced himself and Julia. "How about you let Julia sing you a song as I accompany her on this big box."

Lalo Schifrin gave them a second look grumbling

something about having nothing to lose and said, "Go ahead, I have to sit down. I don't feel that good."

Julia brought over a chair from the orchestra section and Lalo took a seat.

Ed pulled off the big cover and folded it up as best he could. He lifted the lid and positioned the prop, pulled back the bench and got seated. He looked at Julia and said, "Let's do 'Rain Drops' and follow that with 'The Way We Were." Ed played the introduction and Julia walked to the side of the piano and turned towards Lalo just as she voiced the first words. The piano was in excellent tune and had a great tone. Julia sounded better than ever, confident and poised.

The color returned to Lalo's face. He watched them both carefully and when the last of "The Way We Were" faded to silence he asked, almost in a whisper, "Have you ever played parts of experiments in modern music?" and Ed immediately played the first twelve bars of "Rhapsody in Blue."

"I think I need to talk to you both." Then looking at Ed he asked, "Have you ever played Rach Number 2?"

Ed smiled and answered "A few times."

About fifty golfers and caddies had entered the tent and several were on their cell phones excitedly telling who ever they had called that Julia was singing and Ed was on the piano. "Get over here!" Fans were also starting to file in from all directions around the tent.

All this activity was not lost on Lalo as the small crowd was quickly growing and pushing up to the stage. He looked at Ed and then at the eager audience forming. "Go ahead. Have a good time and when Julia needs a break a little Rachmaninoff would be nice."

Art Myers

Chapter 86

By the time Julia had gone through the six songs they had practiced the crowd had grown to over a thousand and more still were coming. The crew putting the chairs in place had finished and seating was to be for two thousand. At the same time the sound crew had placed all the microphones on the stage and were busily trying to test the hook ups. One of the crew had a live microphone and asked everyone to be seated and they should have the system working in fifteen minutes.

Lalo Schifrin was on his phone, pacing about the stage talking rapidly about this walk on that could play the piano. "Maybe. Yes, you heard me. He and his lady just walked up and started doing Broadway show and movie pieces. Hey, I let them! What else can happen! You should hear the girl sing. And not only that he knows Bernstein. No! I mean he can play "Rhapsody." I will call you back."

Schifrin came over to the piano and sat down on the bench on Ed's right. With his right hand he fingered a few notes of the first part of "Rhapsody in Blue". "Want to try this?" he asked Ed.

"Sure. My mother and I did this for hours. We would even trade places sometimes." Ed answered as he matched Schifrin's notes.

The sound crew had just lit up their equipment and

310

the initial adjustments were made quickly. The two pianist gave the large crowd a show. Fifteen minutes of great music and showmanship. Julia moved around the piano in an almost surreal way that complimented the mood. As the two pianist finished and congratulated themselves they heard an ovation from the over two thousand people filling the tent and about as many that were outside under a sea of golf umbrellas.

"Play me the third movement of Number Two," asked Lalo standing and backing away leaving Ed alone. Ed did not disappoint. It was flawless and Lalo was back on his phone "It has come from heaven James, from heaven. Listen," holding his phone out.

When Ed finished Rachmaninoff he immediately went to "Take My Breath Away" from the movie "Top Gun" and Julia stepped forward with microphone in hand. She had to wait for the applause and cheering to subside and then caught Ed's key and sang the opening "Watching every motion, In my foolish lover's game," and again they had to wait for the cheering to die down.

Forty five minutes later they brought down the house with "Nobody Does It Better" with Julia's final antics of running her hand through Ed's hair. The call for more did not stop until they went through three more songs, repeated but that didn't matter.

Lalo then took the microphone and announced that they had to clear the tent to make the final preparations for tonight's concert which was to start at 8:00 pm. They had 500 tickets that could be purchased after 7:00 pm. As a subtle reminder he mentioned that this was a fund raising event and the Quad Cities patrons would be dressed to impress. He was relieved that there was no grumbling or booing at this and it was actually received with more applause.

He then stepped over to Ed and asked, "You will do it, won't you?"

"Yes," was Ed's answer.

It took an escort by six policemen to get Ed and Julia out of the tent and to a waiting courtesy car to take them back to the Villa. Steve and Nicki were packing and hadn't realized what had been going on at the tent. Jerry got back and when he came into the room he almost lost control talking about what Ed and Julia had just done.

"No way are we going to miss this tonight! Get your winning the tournament clothes out. I'll get the tickets." was said in a rush of words and he was ready to go back and stand in line.

"Hold on Jerry. Let me make a call. That okay with you?" Ed offered looking at Nicki and Steve. They nodded yes but still didn't understand what was happening.

Ed was able to make contact with Lalo and the seats were reserved. Also he had another request. Could Julia sing a medley of several songs, with him accompanying, as the last guests were seated before the conductor made his entrance.

That being taken care of what to wear became the focus. It was an easy choice for Ed and Steve. Ed would wear his Gallery outfit and Steve had a dark blue blazer and dress shirt to wear over khaki pants. Jerry would have to be content wearing an extra dress shirt Steve had packed. Julia had two outfits and the one that was almost too revealing was the unanimous choice. They then set about to try to fit her other dress to Nicki. That wasn't going to work so a quick trip to the resort's high end dress shop solved the problem. A good portion of Steve's winnings were spent.

While this was going on the weather had cleared. The Symphony's truck had arrived and all the large instruments unloaded and placed on the stage. By 6:30 pm most of the golf fans had left the and many of the players left to make the drive to Florida for the next tournament.

Ed and Julia were greeted by Lalo when they arrived and he was visibly moved by Julia's appearance.

"You two will become famous. Mark my words. Take your time on getting there. This is a cut throat business and the sharks will be circling." He paused, took a deep breath, then started the introductions, first to James Dixon the Music Director and the conductor for tonight's performance. Then to their wives.

Dixon hustled Ed to the side and after the thanks for being there said he would try to cue him each time he was to enter and wait for his exit phrases to bring the orchestra back in. Ed told him of the hundreds of times he had played along with recordings and thought he could hit most of the transitions. He didn't tell him it had been over ten years since he had done this.

They then arranged how Julia and Ed were to have fifteen minutes starting at 7:45 pm and trusted the patrons would quickly quiet, find their seats and sit down. James would make his entrance and introduce Julia and Ed and then explain that Lalo had had an accident and that Edward Adams would be playing in his stead. When they finished Lalo, showing off his cast, would come on stage and escort Julia to her seat.

There were lots of nervous people in the group but for what ever reason two were not. Ed was confident and

Julia's confidence fed from his. At 7:45 pm the members of the Quad Cities Symphony with the Youth Symphony were in position and Ed and Julia crossed the stage to the piano. Ed positioned himself on the bench and they exchanged smiles. With a nod Ed started the theme of "Take My Breath Away." The sound crew had the volume just right and the surprised audience suddenly quieted. Julia's clear and beautiful voice filled the tent just as the lights were slightly dimmed. Later it would be written that two thousand people were mesmerized in one second.

They went through their songs without breaks not allowing any applause. As Julia finished with "Nobody Does It Better" and mussing Ed's hair, James Dixon strode out to stage center and the applause came and it was electric. It took five minutes to get the next words spoken. Lalo came out to applause and waved his cast in the air and collected Julia on his arm and they exited to even greater applause. The baton came up fifteen minutes late and the first chair clarinetist sounded the outrageous cadenza that always announces "Rhapsody In Blue." Gershwin would have been proud. One James Dixon was thrilled. The Youth Symphony players had never done better and the audience was in awe.

Rachmaninoff went just as good. Ed played as if touched by magic as it would later be described. Only the most mean spirited critic could have found fault. Lalo would later say many times he could not have done better. Not even on one of his good days. The audience wanted more but the program was already nearly an hour longer than planned as there were long applause's for the orchestra, conductor, Ed, and for Julia when she was brought back on stage.

Chapter 87

There was a brief meeting after the crowds of well wishers passed by the stage calling out compliments and bravos to the organizers and principals. Most of the musicians had left as the buses arrived to pick them up. The ground crews were noisily stacking chairs starting in the rear of the tent. Lalo and James Dixon were the most in demand but much attention was also on Ed and Julia. Eventually it dwindled down to just the four them on the stage along with Lalo's and James's wives.

The piano had been closed up and covered and as they stood by it Lalo and James gave Ed and Julia the thanks they deserved. Lalo mentioned he was just about Ed's age when he came from Argentina to America to be the pianist and arranger for Dizzy Gillespie in 1958 and his life and career had skyrocketed in every direction since then. He was here as a friend and colleague of James and hadn't meant to be a clumsy city boy not paying attention where he was walking.

Lalo took Ed aside for a moment, away from the others as several more people had come up on the stage, and spoke quietly. "Ed, you and Julia have a special chemistry that is rare in this business. If you want to pursue it professionally I have a contact that can help you both in business and in life. I have a meeting with her in

Newport Beach this coming Wednesday. We are having lunch at the Rusty Pelican and you and Julia may join us for one hour, twelve to one. It will be worth your while."

Ed was caught by surprise by this. He knew he was dealing with someone that was one of the doors of opportunity Ben had advised him, with Julia, to walk through.

"We will be there at 12:00 noon. My father knew Pete Siracusa, who founded the cafe in 1972. They surfed together occasionally before I was born. Every chance we had we would have lunch there. It's a small world," Ed saying this with a bit of sadness in his voice.

"They are in a little financial distress at the moment but the Newport restaurant is still doing fine. We will see you Wednesday. And thanks for being who you are and being here this weekend with a remarkable talent named Julia." Lalo was just able to finish before being hustled off by his wife and James Dixon.

"What was that all about? You two guys of in the corner," Julia asked still on a high from the evening.

"We have been invited to lunch at the Rusty Pelican on Wednesday to discus our life and future with a friend of Lalo's that knows how to handle it. I told him we will be there," Ed said with a smile and putting his arm around her. They said their goodbyes, accepted the thanks and compliments again and left the stage.

They took a courtesy car to the Villa. On the ride back Ed commented "Under the spot light, when you were by the piano, you looked spectacular. I will bet you a quarter you will be on the front page of tomorrow's local paper with a caption something like 'Julia Renquest shines at the Quad Cities Symphony Concert.'"

Julia punched him in the ribs then snuggled closer.

"I felt like a star. I like it. But if you want to know the truth, I'd rather be your caddie."

The flight to Palm Springs was easy. Steve and Jerry were driving to Orlando, Florida for the Walt Disney World/ Oldsmobile Classic and Nicki flew to Milwaukee being picked up by her parents.

Willy picked up Ed and Julia and in less than an hour they were home. It seemed a bit lonely without Ben and Jennifer being there. Julia found something in the refrigerator to put together for dinner and before it got dark they took a walk up and down El Paseo. The high season was just getting underway and they had to wait in line to get their ice cream cone. This time pecan on top, coffee on the bottom, one sugar cone.

As they lay in bed the weeks activities took their toll. Julia mentioned it first by asking Ed why she felt depressed after such a remarkable week. How so much had happened that had been so good. Ed knew the feeling and wanted to be careful on how he answered.

"Julia, in any creative effort you go through stages. First is the thought of what it is you are going to try to do. Once you have what you want to accomplish defined you set about the planning of how to do it. Then comes the process of doing it. When it is done you are left with the good feelings of what you have done but suddenly you realize you are finished. It is then time to plan what to do next. It is in that period between finishing one project and finding the next that one becomes depressed. That only lasts until the next thing you want to do comes to mind. If you are a creative person that will quickly show up. I am thinking between 12 noon and 1:00 pm on Wednesday any depression you still have will completely disappear."

Chapter 88

At ten minutes to twelve Ed drove into the parking lot of the Rusty Pelican. It was Wednesday, October 5th, 1994 and seated next to him was Julia. The next car to enter the lot was a red 1994 Porsche Carrera 911. Ed circled the middle parking area and parked in the first vacant space. The 911 followed and parked in the one next to him. Ed and Julia got out of their car and stretched a little after the two hour drive from Palm Desert. The occupant of the red 911 got out and walked immediately up to them. She was a tall, attractive woman dressed in a well fitting tan business suit.

"You must be Ed Adams," first looking at Ed, "and you, without a doubt, are Julia Renquest. I am Laura, Laura McKinney, Lalo's friend." Her handshake was firm and her smile sincere. Next was, "What a nice 59. Don't see many in that condition except in car shows."

Both Ed and Julia liked her right off and they walked into the restaurant together. They were escorted to a window table overlooking a number of fine yachts at the docks and a view of the harbor. Lalo was at the table and stood, greeting Laura first with a handshake, hug and kiss on her cheek. Next a handshake with Ed and then turning to Julia a handshake and smile that indicated he would like to give her a hug and kiss but would not.

They arranged the seating, each having nice views. The table had been set and water glasses filled, wine glasses available. Lalo started with offering that he had ordered a family style lunch menu with enough variety that all should be satisfied. He then turned to Laura and asked that she make her presentation to Ed and Julia in 30 minutes as that was when lunch would be served. She did not hesitate or indicate that this was in any way an unusual way to do business. Placing her thin leather attache case on the table she opened it and handed Ed a VHS cartridge.

"Ed and Julia, this is the last ten minutes of your performance at the concert. Actually your entire time on the stage together. What occurred was the cameraman was using you to practice for his recording the symphony orchestra and as soon as he realized what was happening he made it a priority. So the first five minutes is a little mixed but the rest is good. Lalo got me the copy and I liked what I saw. You are both photogenic, have presence and talent. Julia is beautiful. Dynamite." She stopped for a sip of water. Then took out two leather covered notebooks.

"I have put together a number of ways you might pursue a professional career in the entertainment world. As a couple, individually, recording, touring and concert performances. I try to include both the good and the bad of each. How it may affect your relationship. How income is to be allocated. And a host of other pros and cons. This sometimes can be a tough business. Some can handle it and others can't. You have to decide which course you would like to pursue and I will be happy to help in any way I can. I would like to be your agent. I wouldn't be here if Lalo didn't think I would be not only good for you both but also be fair."

She handed the notebooks to Ed but in a way that he knew she thought Julia was his equal. She validated that with, "I consider you as individuals of equal importance. Please understand that I mean what I am saying."

There was another pause then she added, "The second notebook has documents having to do with Ed playing as a concert pianist. It has similar information but is different enough to be handled in a separate way. You can take these with you. Read them over, discuss what you think and we can set up another appointment if you wish to proceed. I would like you both to be my clients as I think I can do great things for you, including financially."

Lalo looked at his watch and smiled. Then turned to Ed and Julia and asked "Any questions?"

Ed asked Laura "What is your golf handicap? I predict a seven."

There was laughter and Laura looked Ed directly in the eyes and replied "You are a smart one. Yes, it's a seven."

Lunch was served and was excellent. Only Lalo had a glass of wine and they finished eating at exactly 1:00. Lalo directed his comment to Ed but it was to both of them. "Read what Laura has prepared for you. If you want to pursue a career in music you can't do better than having her for your agent."

He then pulled a small stack of newspapers out he had hidden and handed them to Julia. On the top front page was a photograph of Julia singing with Ed in the background at the piano. The lighting was such that Julia looked stunning. The bold 48 point headline was "Julia Renquest Shines at the Quad Cities Symphony Concert".

Ed Adams Chases a Dream

As they walked to the car both were lost in their own thoughts. Ed unlocked the passenger side door and opened it for Julia. She was carrying the notebooks, newspapers and VHS cassette but slid into the front seat gracefully, tossing her head back with a swirl of blonde hair. Ed could only think that it had been 4 months since he had met her and she had taken a seat in his car as she had done just now. He remembered how good she looked. His next thought he didn't want to do anything that would change what they had together.

He was still harboring that thought when he started the engine. When he put his hand on the gear shift knob Julia covered it with hers. "I'm not sure I want to go there Ed. Too many bad things happen to people in that industry. Relationships go wrong and I can't let that happen to us." Julia spoke with a sadness in her voice.

Ed switched off the engine. "Let's take a short walk. See if we can find some ice cream and a spot with a view where we can talk this over. I am thinking the same thing. Maybe Laura has the answer written down for us but we will take our time and make sure we do it right. I like my life now and don't see how it could be any better."

They had walked a few blocks, holding hands, when a large colorful photograph of a sailboat under sail with a handsome couple at the helm caught Julia's eye. She he pulled Ed over to take a closer look.

"That looks nice. No place for a Parlor Grand."

"An electronic keyboard would work just fine," Ed answered, but wasn't being serious. Then looking at the image a little closer he had a second thought and it had nothing to do with a keyboard. He decided not to share it.

Chapter 89

On the drive back they decided that they would carefully read over what Laura McKinney had prepared for them. Ben and Jennifer would be back on Saturday and they could ask for their advice and support. Sometime a second opinion is better than the first one was Ed's thinking.

"The Texas Open is next week and the Las Vegas Invitational is the following week. The last tournament of the year is The Tour Championship the week after that. It is at Olympic in San Francisco but is limited to the top thirty money winners," Ed said providing a change in the conversation.

"San Francisco sounds fun and Olympic is really a nice course." Julia brightened up. "Have you played it?"

"A couple of times. Once on a beautiful day and the other in a constant drizzle and fog. Guess which day I played the best?"

It didn't require an answer, as she could guess what it was, so Julia didn't give one.

They weren't hungry that evening so breakfast cereal and fruit was taken out to the poolside table and they ate in silence. It all had caught up to them and they were in bed early. Julia fell asleep almost when her head hit the pillow. Ed lay awake for two hours. This was going to be a turning point in their lives. They could play the PGA tour and entertain in a semi-professional way. It would be a fun way to live right now but the golf would become less fun and he, and they, would never find out how good they could be in the music world. He wasn't sure if Julia was bothered by this but he was. To find out might cost him everything and he wasn't willing to go there. It would be Jennifer who could help him. He didn't understand why he thought that but there was something about her that made him think she would have the answer.

They spent most of the next morning carefully reading Laura McKinney's proposals. They were as Ed expected and pretty much in line with Julia's thinking. The simplest was to hire a recording studio and make a professional recording. She would then promote it to the appropriate radio stations and as soon as some interest was shown by sales and inquiries she would set up radio and TV interviews. Ed and Julia would have to front the money for the first disc, including the initial royalty fees, and if she thought it worth the effort she would take over. If successful they would easily get all their money back and do quite well. Then produce a second album and repeat the process.

The next proposal was a combination of the first and an immediate effort on her part to gain access to concerts. First as warm up acts and if they were well received to secure starring positions. This is an order of magnitude more difficult and would be taxing on them both. It was where the really big money was but the competition was fierce. She would only go there with them if their first CD hit the top ten or higher on the Billboard music charts.

For Ed alone it would be different. He would have to start in the lesser concert venues and work his way up. Once one or two performances are made with the major symphonies the rest would come in fits and starts. It could take years but if one wants to be the best, or at least thought to be, that was how it goes.

Laura gave a number of examples and a few had been her clients. She had handled some really big time entertainers. Her work with Lalo Schifrin had come later in his career and was an easier task. Her reimbursement was much less but it placed her in a good position to get new clients. She would never had made their acquaintance if it hadn't been through him.

"Let's go hit some golf balls," posed Ed.

"I think that would be a good idea," Julia agreed.

Practicing was therapeutic. A simple task very difficult to do right. They had lunch at the club and Gary Martin joined them. He was more enthusiastic than ever about trying to play on the Senior PGA and was already putting out feelers on how to get qualified. His game was improving as was, more importantly, his confidence. Julia was beginning to like him and they had an enjoyable lunch. When Ed asked for the check he was informed it had been taken care of.

After lunch they spent another two hours putting and chipping. To Ed's sorrow the Wilson Winsum was replaced by the Cornith. He estimated two strokes a round which would make the difference. He knew better than to think that and it would turn out he was right.

Returning home they found in the mail box a post card from Paris addressed to Julia. Written on the back was "The baguette at Du Pain et Vons bakery was delicious. Corner of Rue du Champs de Mars and Ave Bosquet. No tables outside this time but Ben had a sack with cheese and a bottle of wine. He is positive it was here he met your grandmother. Love, Jennifer "

Ben and Jennifer would be home day after tomorrow almost beating the post card sent three weeks earlier.

Chapter 90

Ed woke first. He didn't need as much sleep as Julia but last night he was able to fall asleep as quickly as she did. They had had a relaxing afternoon after practicing golf yesterday. Julia had brought out several music sheets of popular Broadway shows and movie scores. Ed stacked them up on the music rack and sight reading played what he saw. Another surprise for Julia as most pianist can't do that, or at least not as good as Ed could.

Julia, looking over his shoulder, would sing a few words and they would decide whether they wanted to include it on their learn to do list. They added twelve more to the six they had ready and would concentrate on having at least eighteen that would work together for recording.

Ed had about made up his mind that the route to take should be the slow road. He didn't have the details of how their finances stacked up but thought they had to be pretty good and they didn't have much to worry about for now.

He turned on his side to face Julia and she was facing him. She was just about to wake up and he laid as still as possible and enjoyed the view. Her eyes finally opened and she gave him a smile. It was what he wanted most in this world was to see that smile the first thing he would see each day. Music and the piano was far down the list of what was important.

At breakfast they discussed the songs they had selected and what to do with them. Ed posed first taking the CD route to test the water. Julia asked about his desires as far as becoming a concert pianist and he told her that he would wait on that and see where they could go together. Then he surprised her.

"How about I play in the Las Vegas Invitational. It should be pretty easy to get an invite as the tour is winding down and I haven't won enough money to be in the Tour Championship the following week. That will be the last tournament of the season."

"Sounds good to me. We can drive. Just five hours, about three hundred miles." Julia was quick with her positive response.

"We can rent a car here. Or ship the clubs and drive the Porsche. Or even fly and rent a car there." As Ed ran through the options he remembered the most direct way driving would have them going over Cajon Pass and passing where his parents had been killed. He had avoided that location ever since. He would suggest flying later.

They worked through the scores they had selected. Picked out six and started a more serious effort to learn them. Julia had a remarkable memory. Twice through and she had almost every line and could start working on styling. Ed was the same on the accompanying. By early afternoon they were ready to do some finishing touches and then they could be added to their play list.

It was time to make a grocery store run and it was to Whole Foods to stock up the pantry. Ed did his job as the pusher of the cart, didn't try to help in the decision making and paid the bill with his credit card. There was just enough room in the Porsche to hold the twelve bags and all was unloaded quickly. The two pints of ice cream made it to the freezer with time to spare.

Julia fixed a Waldorf salad and with a muffin and the best parts of a rotisserie chicken they had dinner out by the pool. It had been a good day and they were confident that they had a plan for their future. At least for the next two weeks. They would pick up Ben and Jennifer at the Palm Springs Airport at 4:20 tomorrow afternoon.

Saturday morning they practiced their new songs. The play list had reached eighteen and it was expected to be added to, and subtracted from, but they wanted to have eighteen ready to record when the time came. It was also becoming apparent that Ed could work in some solo works between song tracks that could be done in an interesting manner. Taking well known classical themes to introduce Julia's songs became a game and occasionally they would hit on a winner.

Ed and Julia picked up Ben and Jennifer on schedule and they were home by 6:00 pm. They had spent the previous night in New York City to break up the long plane trip from Rome. After a lite dinner and they begged to be off to their bedroom, try for some sleep and get their biological clocks back on track. Julia showed them the postcard that took three weeks to get to her. The smile Jennifer gave Ben was worth a thousand words and she would tell them what an evil man Ben was in the morning.

328

Chapter 91

The traveler's were weary, glad to be home but had had a wonderful time both in where they had gone and who they were with. Paris, Venice, Florence and Rome. Memories for a life time and Ben said he hadn't felt as good in years. Given a few weeks rest he would be ready to do it again.

Jennifer then smiled and started the highlight story. "Ben chose the hotel on Rue Champs de Mars which was, I was to find out on our first day, one block from the infamous bakery. He knew where it was before we left! From the hotel we went over to Rue Cler, just around the corner, and he bought a wedge of cheese and a small bottle of wine. We then went down one block, over two and then walked up the Avenue Bosquet. Beautiful streets, especially Bosquet. And there across the next street, on the corner, was the bakery of his past. He almost pulled it off but as he pointed out the bakery the street sign just above the window was Champs de Mars and I could see our hotel down the street. We bought the baguette, but with no tables outside, we walked the few blocks to the park. We found a bench with a good view of the Eiffel Tower, had our picnic and talked for the rest of the afternoon."

"You didn't get married two days later, did you?"

Julia questioned and they all had a good laugh.

Jennifer then reached over to Ben and took his hand. There was no doubt things had worked out to the point that nothing more needed to be said about their relationship.

Ed thought of the popular song "The Second Time Around". Maybe he and Julia should add it to their play list and then he thought the better of it.

They talked most of the morning about Ben and Jennifer's trip and then the conversation turned to Julia and Ed's four weeks. All was told in enough detail to keep the listener's interest, especially Jennifer. "Why don't Ben and I look over the agent's proposals? If you would like us to, that is?"

"We were about to ask you to do just that." Ed excused himself, went into the house and brought back the leather bound notebooks. Handing them to Jennifer first he mentioned that he and Julia were thinking to go slow and pursue the recording of the CD option first.

Julia told them of the VHS cassette they had and how well their appearances had gone. How they liked Laura McKinney and how both she and Lalo Schifrin seemed confident they had the talent to succeed with their music. Lalo especially by Ed being able to step in at the last minute and play at the level he did with no rehearsals.

That evening they assembled for dinner and afterwards set up the VHS player and TV in the now named music room. It was a quality cassette, after the first few minutes, showing Julia to have a stage presence and voice that demanded attention. The remaining part of the VHS was of Ed and the orchestra playing "Rhapsody in Blue." Ben smiled at this but Jennifer could barely grasp that

Julia could project such an image under the stage lights and of Ed's performance on the piano. "You two are really good together, and Julia how you can sing like that. Ed, you can play anywhere. With anyone. What gifts you both have."

Ben finally spoke up and was all business. "I would start with doing the recording. It will be simple to do, not really that expensive and teach you a lot about the business. As for the concert tours, both together and at the symphony level, that is a totally different world. You will have to decide if you can handle the personnel aspects of such a life style. If you get to the big time your own life will become dictated by others and your choices will be much more limited than you have now. You will have to give up almost every thing else in your personnel life and try to grasp private time when ever it becomes available. Ed, I think you will have to make the most difficult decision as your time will become subservient to others. It is a big mountain to climb but it is quite a view if you make it to the top."

He stood and nodded to Jennifer "I have to go to bed. Don't wake me when you come in, but if you do I will tell you how glad I am that you are there."

Jennifer started to follow Ben, then turned and sat back down facing Ed.

"Ed, you have something about you that few have. You probably don't realize it but just to give you a hint it is that you have a special gift, if that is the right way to phrase it, that makes the lives of others around you better than they would otherwise be. My husband had some, Ben and Hank do, but not like what you have. I shouldn't even speak to you about it this way. Don't change the way you do things. Just be yourself and please stay close to Ben and I, and even closer to Julia." Jennifer rose quickly and headed back into the house.

Ed sat still and had a puzzled look on his face. Julia hesitated a moment before getting up and coming over to sit on his lap. With her arms around him she kissed him soundly and said "You stay with me. I mean right here this close. If my life can really get any better I will need somebody to blame it on."

Chapter 92

The doorbell rang and Julia answered. It was Andy Letho and he was right on time. Laura had recommended him and his recording studio to do their first CD. He was local, good, fair and she liked his work and him as a person. He was Finnish and had come to the United States as a young boy with his parents. Now a young man, about Ed's age, he had started out with a Rock and Roll band as a musician, then as sound man and now had his own recording business. The last was where he was meant to be as Laura put it.

Ed was at the piano working on one of his interests as Julia brought Andy down the hallway and into the music room. He was shouldering a heavy bag, set it down and looked around. "This is nice. We can do some of the work here, I'll bet."

He and Ed exchanged handshakes and Andy took a closer look at the piano. "Oh man! A older Model C." Andy reached into his bag and pulled out a clip board that had a contract on top and several pages underneath.

"We can get to this in a minute. If you don't mind I would like to just talk about what is involved in producing a CD. It's not brain surgery but if not done right it won't have much value. Twelve to eighteen songs, at two and half to four minutes each. A theme with a good mix. You want to be able to put it in your player and be comfortable listening for at least a half hour. You don't want one song everyone wants to listen to and then a bunch of junk. They will feel cheated and soon you won't hear it played again. It is all common sense but it needs to be said up front. Laura played me some of the tracks from the concert at Callaway Gardens over the phone. Could you do a few of them for me so I can see if we can do some of the recording here?"

Ed and Julia went through the six they had down to memory and Andy just sat and listened without saying anything. He then smiled. "Laura knows when she has a keeper. I think I would like to set up here and I will tell you why and how. That piano cannot be matched in my studio. If we need to I will set up a portable booth for Julia to be isolated but that might not be necessary. I am going to set up several mics and my portable recorder and we will work on one song right now. 'The Way We Were.' I will work it up and bring the CD back here tomorrow. You can listen to it and then we will get down to doing the paper work."

As he set up the electronics they kept up the chatter. Julia read off the play list she and Ed had made up and told him where they were on having them ready to perform. He was getting more excited as the conversation continued. They went though "The Way We Were" twice and then once with Ed alone on the piano and once with Julia singing a cappella. As Andy picked up his equipment and prepared to leave Ed offered him a down payment but he brushed that aside. "I want to get back to my studio and put this together. I already know how it will come out. You two have something special and I want to be part of it. See you tomorrow."

They had a little over a week before heading to Las Vegas. Ed had a spot and they were also booked as part of the entertainment Saturday night for the players, sponsors, friends and volunteers party. It was going to be in one of the casino theaters and they were expecting a full house.

The next five days were non stop. The CD Andy produced of "The Way We Were" was fantastic and they would do the recording in the music room. He and his helper set up the equipment and when they had finished you could hardly make it through to the pool. Ben and Jennifer were hiding in their bedroom and in Ben's office, with occasional hours spent outside by the pool. They took it in good humor and actually enjoyed much of the activities. There was also some very good music to be listened to. The first six songs went quickly, the second six that Julia and Ed had part way readied were done with the help of the scores on paper. The last six were more difficult as mistakes were made and changes needed. They completed the eighteen in three days and Andy was ready to put the collection together in his studio using his special equipment to polish the finished product.

When Ed and Julia got back from Las Vegas they would be able to hear the master tape and make any suggestions they thought were needed. Laura McKinney would make the visit for this and would be the guest of Ben and Jennifer. It had all happened so fast and took so much effort that Ed and Julia were looking forward to the Las Vegas Invitational as a vacation and not as a grueling competitive venture. Making the cut would be the only objective as far as golf was concerned. Their very first formal appearance on stage was another matter.

Chapter 93

The Invitational was a tough five rounds of golf played on three different courses, none of which Ed had ever played. Gary Martin secured the yardage books for each and they were of some help to study, but each course had a number of special holes that made custom selection of Cornith clubs impossible. Ed, with some help from Willy, put together his bag for each course as best they could. Not having ever seen or walked the courses there was a lot of guess work in making the selections.

Ed decided to rent a car in Palm Desert and they drove to Las Vegas on Tuesday afternoon. The traffic was heavy and the long Cajon Pass uphill grade had Ed concentrating so hard on driving he passed by the site of his parents accident without taking notice. As they crested the Pass he took a quick look at Julia and she gave him a smile that said she understood what he was thinking. Ed thought that one more thing that had been haunting him for years was being put to rest.

Wednesday morning Ed teed up on the Las Vegas Country Club course with his first look at the opening hole. He, and Julia, were still worn out from the last two weeks activities but he shot a respectable 2 under 70 and carried this on to the second round on the TPC at Summerlin. It was the home course for the tournament and with a 3 under 69 placed him 5 under but was now already 6 shots behind the current leader going into the third round. The third round at the Las Vegas National was another 69 but he fell another shot out of the lead. Saturday, having made the cut, he shot 2 under at TPC at Summerlin but was even farther behind the leaders and out of the big money.

Both he and Julia were nearing exhaustion after the round and headed to the hotel to shower, rest and have dinner. They were to perform first, as openers for the entertainment at the big players and sponsor's party. They had chosen to do six songs from their CD playlist. The first three being "Show Me", "I'm Gonna Wash That Man Right Outta My Hair' and "Raindrops Drops Keep Falling On My Head." Then to follow with "Take My Breath Away", "Don't Rain On My Parade" and finish with "No Body Does It Better" with Julia's antics mussing Ed's hair as it ends.

They dressed in the same outfits they had worn at Callaway Gardens three weeks earlier, Ed looking good and Julia spectacular. Ed played his accompaniment flawlessly and Julia sang even better than that. They had the audience spellbound and as they finished, with her teasing Ed's hair, had the crowd standing with applause and calling for more. The demanded encore was "On A Clear Day" and "The Way We Were". They left the stage with an ovation and chants for more being repeated.

One photographer was especially attentive during the performance and he caught the photograph he was hired to get that would grace the front cover of their first CD.

That night as they lay in bed the adrenaline had

them wide awake. Julia couldn't stop smiling and Ed just enjoyed watching the enjoyment she was exhibiting.

"That was so much fun. We did it. We really did it Ed. I wasn't scared or even nervous," she said as she rubbed his shoulder.

"You were fantastic. Never once off note or cue. Even better than on our recordings. No one could do it better. I feel sorry for the rest," Ed responded singing the last two sentences.

Julia was suddenly quiet and a serious look came over her face. "You know what it is, don't you. It's what Jennifer said about you making the lives of others around you better than they otherwise would be. The way you play for me is so good I can sing better than what should be possible. It gives me the confidence to do it like I do."

Ed put his arms around her and whispered, "We are a team. Perfectly matched to perform at this level and that is where we should go so let's see how far this can take us. What we feel right now makes life so worth living I want to see what will come our way next."

Sleep finally came and it was sound. The next morning they prepared for the last round of the tournament slowly, very tired but relaxed.

Sunday was a survival round for Ed and it turned out he would have his best day. Having now played TPC at Summerlin twice before helped. Carding a 4 under 68 left him 14 strokes behind Bruce Lietzke, the winner.

He wasn't last by a long ways and earned enough to pay the expenses. His caddie's ten percent was accepted but not thought of as a just payment for her efforts. He told her he would somehow try to make up for that when they got home on Monday. He was too tired, or frightened, to go over Cajon Pass after dark so they stayed the extra night. It was a good decision as that evening while at dinner at the hotel several of the dinners approached them with compliments on Saturday nights performance and expressed hope to see them on stage again.

Art Myers

Chapter 94

On Tuesday morning Andy Letho arrived early and set up the music room with special high fidelity speakers and his big half inch tape player. He did a quick test and the sound was excellent. Laura McKinney had arrived while this was going on and Ben and Jennifer had her settled in Julia's old bedroom which had now become the house guest room.

By ten o'clock all were settled in the music room, in comfortable chairs facing the big speakers placed near the piano. Andy bustled around excitedly readying for the demonstration of the results of his efforts. He finally sat down and touched the play button on the tape recorder. For the next 62 minutes no one uttered a sound. Andy had arranged the songs so they flowed together in a way that as soon as one finished you wanted to hear the next. The only initial comment was Laura saying "Oh my!"

Then she repeated the "Oh my!" with, "That is really, really good. I think you have a winner. Good to go as is. This is going to be fun to watch what happens when it goes public." Then the talking got underway as each had their own thoughts and opinions, none of which had anything that wasn't positive.

They formed a partnership of sorts and the contracts were discussed openly. Once explained by both

340

Ed Adams Chases a Dream

Laura and Andy, Ed and Julia, with Ben and Jennifer nodding heads in agreement, signed in the numerous places and all were satisfied that things had been done right. Ed paid Andy's initial billing which was thought to be fair and he and Laura agreed on how many CDs should be made in the first run. She would assist in the cover design and showed off the photograph taken in Las Vegas that she was given yesterday morning.

Laura would also, with Ed and Julia, write up the biography and have a small print shop she used to layout the case insert. Her office staff would take care of the royalty agreements and use a collection and payment service she liked to take care of those.

Laura McKinney knew she had a winner and was not going to let anything get in her way. She was thinking it was good enough to rival Barbra Streisand in quality and appeal. She could hardly disguise her excitement. It had taken only three hours to put together the contracts, instead of days, or weeks, or months and sometimes never. Besides that, she liked the people she was dealing with.

A late lunch was served at poolside and Andy and his helper were included. Tuesday afternoon October 25, 1994 would be remembered by all there as the day the ball started to roll. It took only four weeks to put the package together and have the first boxes of CDs distributed into the "stream" where the money flows in the music industry. Laura's group went on a full court press to radio stations, retail outlets, newspapers and magazines. The production costs of the first run were born by Ed and Julia and were about what his best paycheck was for a third place finish on a PGA tournament. For what was coming it made little difference.

Laura had a box of one hundred CDs sent to Ed and Julia. They could hand them out to friends and relatives or to anyone they thought could be a possible asset. More important to them, however, was a beautifully framed enlargement of the CD cover photograph. Ben immediately insisted it have a special place in his, and now their, home.

On the afternoon of Monday, the 28th day of November, 1994 Ed and Julia were in the 1959 Porsche Coupe driving up Highway One to Carmel. The plans were to spend a few days relaxing and play Pebble Beach and Spy Glass Hill golf courses. They were just approaching where the view of the Pacific Ocean comes up again as you enter Carmel Valley. It was a gorgeous day, the windows were open and the old Blaupunkt radio had just picked up the local FM radio station when a familiar and extraordinarily beautiful voice came in singing "The First Time Ever I Saw Your Face."

As the vista of Monastery Beach came fully into view Julia reached over and lightly placed her hand on Ed's arm. Her tears had begun falling and Ed quickly found a pull out before his own eyes filled. They sat together with the sound of the surf seeming to blend in with their wonderful recording of the song. The poetry of the words being sung was in a manner that was mesmerizing to them both. As it ended, with Julia's interpretation of the last line "The first time ever I saw your face, your face, your face, your face," Ed turned to look at her. He knew at that moment the chase of his dream was over and that he was with the one person who would make his future so much more than he could ever have dreamed possible.

PLAY LIST

JULIA RENQUEST with EDWARD ADAMS

1   *Show Me*
2   *I'm Gonna Wash That Man Right Outa My Hair*
3   *Rain Drops Keep Falling On My Head*
4   *You've Lost That Loving Feeling*
5   *Woman In Love*
6   *The Way We Were*
7   *Take My Breath Away*
8   *Don't Cry For Me Argentina*
9   *The Man I Love*
10   *The First Time Ever I Saw Your Face*
11   *The Shadow Of Your Smile*
12   *Send In The Clowns*
14   *Don't Rain On My Parade*
15   *On A Clear Day*
16   *The Wind Beneath My Wings*
17   *The Windmills Of Your Mind*
18   *Nobody Does It Better*

About The Author

Art Myers was born in 1935 and grew up in the small southern California town of La Mesa. He graduated from San Diego State College in 1958 with a BS Degree in Engineering. Several employments in the Military Industrial Complex lasted until end of 1969. His first layoff was in 1961 and he spent the fall months working as construction labor in Mammoth Lakes, CA and the winter of 1962 skiing in Aspen, CO. Another stint in engineering and a second layoff occurred which found him with a wife, daughter, house payments and just beginning what became a 30 year career as a professional sculptor. Interspersed in that 30 years were a variety of residences and occupations for both he and his wife. Retiring in 2002 they bought a sail boat and spent 10 years living aboard and cruising both US coasts. They have lived in a variety of places including Saratoga, CA, Aspen and Loveland, CO, Lake Forest, IL and currently in Vero Beach, FL. His first book was an autobiography written for family and friends in 2015. His fourth work of fiction is "Ed Adams Chases a Dream."